HOGGS II

PRISON JOURNALS

Terol McCullar (T-MAC)

ISBN 978-1-77839-086-9 (paperback)
ISBN 978-1-77839-090-6 (hardcover)
ISBN 978-1-77839-092-0 (eBook)

Printed in the United States of America

For those who survived and who didn't survive
"The Toughest Beat in the State"

TABLE OF CONTENTS

PROLOGUE AND MISSED RECOGNITIONS

These journals of plagiarized truths are delivered with a literary license to safeguard legal ramifications. While the events have actually occurred, locations and personnel may have been altered to achieve dramatic effect.

While I was an instructor at the academy, I was asked by cadets to recount "war stories." My reply was that anyone could make up their own story and it is likely that is has already happened or it will happen; such is the nature of the prison environment.

I have hundreds of situations available for delivery, and yet each staff member has hundreds of their own stories and live a new one each day.

I was remiss in my first offering, *HOGGS: Prison Journals*, by my lack of recognition of those who offered their specific stories.

This is my correction of that omission.

The episode of "I'm Not Who You Think I Am" was offered by Anthony "Tony" Kane.

The episode of "With One You Get Eggroll" was offered by my grandson, Brent Johnson.

The collection of episodes in this work contains some instances of unflattering aspects of the prison regimen. For those who view the world with rose-colored glasses, best refrain from further indulgence.

LOCKER BOB AND FRIENDS

Julie shoved Frank against the doorjamb and bolted past him into the living room and slung open the front door into the midnight.

The streetlight lit up her nakedness as she ran across the street and up the steps to Jason's house. She pounded relentlessly on the door, pleading, "Help me, help me! Open the door, please!"

Jason was awakened by the banging on his door. He heard the screams and rolled out of bed and grabbed his .45 S&W off the top of a dresser and scrambled toward the door. The banging on the door had ceased. He made his way through the living room and to the front door. As he got to the door, he peered out a sidelight. He saw that the woman had run back down the steps and north on the sidewalk. He unlocked the door, opened it, and stepped outside.

He yelled to her, "Hey, hey. Stop!"

She either didn't hear Jason's shouts or her fear consumed her thoughts. She continued running up the street. Jason turned and went back inside. He hurried to the bedroom and put on some pants and slipped into a pair of shoes. He rushed back outside, but there was no sign of the woman. He sprinted down the steps and headed toward the corner. He turned the corner, but she was nowhere in sight. There were several apartment complexes along the street, and Jason stopped and listened for any commotion. He heard a dog barking and followed the source to a complex on the left side of the street. He walked toward a short cyclone fence, and a dog inside the fence barked at him. He turned and went back into the middle of the street and scanned the streets while he listened for any other noises. Trying to think like an escapee, he surmised that he would head toward a commercial area.

With that as a guide, he walked quickly toward the nearest business, two blocks away, a Quick Stop market. As he neared the market, he put his .45 in his waistband and covered it with his T-shirt. He scanned the inside of the store from the parking lot. He saw no sign of any unusual activity that a naked woman might attract. The traffic was somewhat busy for 0030 hours on a Tuesday. He squinted his gaze farther up the street in search for a likely destination of a scared victim. He saw a Manteca PD unit pull into a Shell gas station on the next block. The officer activated the flashing lights on the unit and opened the door of the car. Jason followed his instinct and headed for the Shell station. The officer was sitting in the driver's seat on his radio. Jason made a wide swing to the left of the patrol unit so that the officer could plainly see him. The officer noticed him, and Jason raised his empty hands to the height of his shoulders.

"Evening, officer. I'm an off-duty correctional officer, Jason Miller."

"Yes, sir, can I help you?" the officer asked as he stepped out of the car.

Jason asked, "I was wondering if you are here in response to a woman in distress."

The officer covered his weapon with his hand and shined his flashlight in Jason's face.

"Why do you ask?"

"A naked woman frantically banged on my door several blocks away on Second Street yelling for help. By the time I got to the door, she was running away. I gave chase." Jason realized those words were suspicious and added, "Or rather, I tried to follow her but I lost sight of her."

The officer seemed to relax his posture and asked, "Do you know who she is?"

"I don't think so. I didn't get a look at her face."

The officer asked, "Could you step over to the front of my car?" Jason thought, "This could go south quick," and quickly added,

"Yes, sir, I will comply."

Jason walked slowly to the front of the vehicle with his hands still raised. "But I need you to know that I do have a concealed weapon in my waistband. As I said, I am an off-duty CO and have a CCW permit, but I didn't have time to dress properly and bring my badge wallet."

The officer became more cautious and followed Jason's movement intently.

"Okay, when you get to the front of my unit, put both hands on the hood, and don't move."

Jason had played the reverse roll several times in his career.

He put his hands on the hood and advised the officer, "It's on my left side front."

The officer slowly walked up behind Jason and secured the weapon from Jason. He removed the magazine and ejected a round and opened the chamber. He put the weapon and the magazine in his pocket.

"Do you have any other weapons on you?"

"No, sir," Jason replied.

The officer said, "Okay, stay still. I'm gonna pat you down."

"Of course, I know the drill," Jason replied.

The officer made quick work of his search and said, "Okay, Jason was it?"

"Yes, sir."

"You can relax and turn around."

Jason noticed the name tag on the officer. "Officer Chan, is it?" Chan replied, "Yes."

Another patrol unit rolled up to the scene. Chan said, "Stand here for a moment, Jason."

Jason nodded.

Chan walked up to the other officer, and they spoke to each other. The other officer walked off toward the gas station.

Chan came back over to Jason and took out his notebook and wrote as he spoke. "Okay, it's Jason Miller, CDL number and address?"

Jason supplied the appropriate information.

Chan said, "Stay here and I'll check your info out."

"Okay," Jason said.

Chan went to his unit and got on his computer. After a few moments, he leaned out the car door and asked Jason, "Mr. Miller, can you face me?"

Jason complied.

Chan shined his flashlight into Jason's face and looked back at the screen on his computer. Satisfied, he stepped out of his unit and closed the door and walked back up to Jason.

He retrieved Jason's .45 and his magazine from his pocket and handed it back to Jason.

"Sorry, Mr. Miller, but you know how this looked, your story needed to be checked out." Chan looked down toward the ground and visually searched it.

"Your cartridge should be somewhere around here."

Jason joined in the search and mentally followed the possible trajectory of the ejected round. He walked to his left and found the round. He loaded the round into his magazine and inserted the magazine into his weapon and put it back in his waistband.

Chan began his questioning. "So you said the female knocked on your door, let's start from there."

Jason fell into report-writing mode.

"At about 0030 hours, I was awakened by loud banging on my door. I responded to the door with my S&W .45 and saw a naked female running down my steps away from my house. I opened the door and shouted for her to stop, but she continued running north on the street. I returned to my bedroom and got partially dressed and went out my door and gave chase. I didn't see where she went. I followed my instincts and saw your patrol unit."

Jason asked, "Now, did anyone find her? Is she safe?"

Chan said, "Jason, I understand and appreciate your concern, but as you well know, this is now an ongoing investigation and I can't give you any information. But, as professional courtesy, I can say that she is safe and she alerted the station employee that she had been assaulted. Other than that, I have no more information as you know I've been here with you."

Jason smiled "Sorry for the diversion, Officer Chan, but I couldn't just do nothing."

Chan took out his business card and wrote on the back of it. "Here's my card and my cell number. Someone may call and ask some follow-up questions. Can I reach you at SCC?"

Jason replied, "Sure, I'm in Ad Seg [Administrative Segregation] second watch with Tuesday/Wednesday off."

Chan smiled. "Well, have a good couple of days off."

Jason shook his head. "Yeah, right. Now I've got a Law Enforcement Contact report to file."

Chan nodded. "Such is the life of a concerned citizen. I thank you personally."

Chan held out his hand, and Jason shook it. "Be safe, Chan."

Chan replied, "It's David, David Chan. Thanks, Jason."

*****

Officer Karl Starke stood along the inside of the track across from the Northern weight pile (weight lifting areas). The end of a beautiful spring day at Deuel Vocational Institution (DVI) and a thousand inmates were taking advantage of their evening yard program. Starke maintained his vigilant awareness of his area of supervision. As some inmates ran on the track, he pictured an inmate having a running start at the fence that sat only some twenty feet from the arc of the track. Surely such an attempt would fail, as the gunners in the perimeter Tower 6 and Tower 13, in the center of the yard, would quell any such attempt. And then there was the razor wire atop two fences the inmate would have to contend with. It was just a thought. Starke walked across the track onto the weight pile and stood along the fence line bordering the weight pile and watched about one hundred inmates lifting weights. He saw Rec (Recreational Officer) 4 Officer Betty Potter walking from the Southern weight pile to the inside of the track. Potter had returned last year from a call-up for Desert Storm. He walked through his section of inmates and across the track and met Potter on the inside of the track.

"Hey, Babs, what's cookin'?" Starke asked.

"Nothin' but my arms and legs from waterskiing got a little burned," she replied.

"Hot time on the lake or river?"

"Spent the weekend at Lake Comanche with my peeps, had fun though, despite getting toasted," she said.

Starke grinned and scanned the inmates on his weight pile. "Was that sun toasting or booze toasting?"

She laughed and turned to stand back-to-back with Starke. "Mostly the sun, but I did suck down a few beers."

"Really?" he said with an incredulous chuckle. "Whatcha putting on your sunburn?"

"Aloe vera gel."

"Does it help?" he said, turning toward her.

"It keeps it from crusting over, that helps." She looked over toward her weight pile.

"I try not to be a sun worshipper," he offered.

"Guess I should have made a few less trips around the lake."

"You think?" He laughed and faked a slap on her back. "Does it hurt here?"

She winced a little from an anticipated slap on her back and shoulder.

She smiled and said, "You ass, that hurt, just thinking about getting hit hurts."

Starke chuckled.

Quietly they scanned their assigned areas of responsibilities.

Starke broke the silence. "Hey, you live in Manteca, don't you?" She replied, "Yep."

"My buddy Miller, who works at Sierra, lives there on Second Street, and he said there was an incident involving a female assault there. You hear anything about it?"

She shook her head. "When was that?" she asked.

"Late last Monday night," he said.

The PA blurted out its message. "Yard recall, yard recall."

Starke cocked his head and tossed his hands slightly. "We'll talk again in a few."

Potter nodded and headed toward her work area.

Starke scanned the track and crossed over it to the Northern weight pile. He directed the inmates running on the track and lifting weights, with hand motions and voice.

"Okay, guys, let's take it inside. Yard recall."

There were always a few inmates that continued working out, putting in a few extra reps. Starke casually walked toward those stragglers.

His radio crackled. "Rec 5, get your inmates off the yard."

Starke knew the voice of the messenger and looked across the yard at Officer Grey and smiled to himself and shook his head. He ignored the message. He meandered farther into the weight pit, nodding to inmates as they gathered their clothing and others that finished their last pumps on the weights.

The radio remessaged.

"Rec 5, this is Rec 1, do you copy?"

Again Starke ignored the radio call. He walked behind the last of his charges, following them across the two hundred yards of the main yard. He joined Potter as she followed her group.

She mocked the radio call, "Rec 5, get those inmates off the yard."

Starke chuckled. "Grey's a little intense as usual."

Potter laughed and they slowly walked toward the yard exit gate. The last of the inmates went into the building, and the yard crew moseyed after them. Officer Grey was talking to some other Rec officers (Yard Officers) and saw Starke walk in and spoke.

"Starke, you need to get those inmates off the weight pile quicker."

Starke smirked and rumpled his cheek to one side.

"So, Grey, whose inmate was the last one off the yard and into the building?"

Grey wrinkled his brow and asked, "What? What's that matter?" Starke shrugged his shoulders and said, "Exactly."

Grey countered, "Those inmates are gaming you."

Starke pursed his lips, then said, "Officer Grey, are you Rec 1 or Rec 5?"

Grey responded, "Rec 1."

Starke authored, "You do your job and I'll do mine, thank you."

Grey shook his head and left abruptly down the hallway.

The recreational officer crew flowed toward Center Corridor. They each looked at the assignment sheet on a small table.

Starke saw his assignment was Y-Dorm. He turned in his Rec 5 equipment into Control and started to exchange it for Y-Dorm equipment, when an alarm sounded. They looked toward the alarm sound and saw by the flashing blue light above the Z-Dorm door that it was coming from Z-Dorm.

The radio announced, "We have an alarm in Z-Dorm."

The full complement of the Rec crew ran toward Z-Dorm. As they arrived at the door, Z-Dorm staff opened it from inside. The officer held up his hands in a "stop" position.

"Sorry, guys, false alarm," the officer announced. Starke and Potter took a few steps into the unit, and the sergeant was standing near the door. He keyed his mic.

"Control, this is Z-Dorm Sergeant Hall. I have a false alarm in Z-Dorm. I repeat, a false alarm in Z-Dorm."

The radio reported, "Control to all units, there is a false alarm in Z-Dorm, no further response is needed. Watch Commander, you copy?"

"Watch 1 copies," was the answer.

Starke and Potter turned and left the unit. They walked back toward Center Corridor and Control. Starke finished his equipment exchange for Y-Dorm equipment.

Potter had a Z-Dorm assignment and picked up her equipment. She and Starke headed toward the break room to pick up their stashed lunch boxes. They were heading the same direction and talked as they walked.

Starke said, "As I was saying about the female assault, my buddy talked to the officer involved in the case and found out some juicy stuff."

Potter asked, "What's that?"

"It seems that the woman was at her boyfriend's house, and he held her down as his brother raped her. She broke away and ran naked across the street to Miller's house and banged on his door to get help. He heard the banging, but she ran away before he could get to the door. He put some pants and shoes on and went to find her. Eventually, he came across the officer that responded to the gas station she ran to for help."

Potter added, "That boyfriend needs his ass handed to him."

Starke continued, "That's only the beginning. The PD he talked to told him the boyfriend works here at DVI and he and a couple of other staff that work here are being looked at."

Potter stated, "No shit?"

"Yeah. It seems that they workout and smoke pot in the boyfriend's garage with the garage door open."

Potter asked, "You have those guys' names?"

Starke shook his head. "No, but I could probably find out."

They arrived at Potter's Z-Dorm assignment, and she knocked on the door.

"I'll catch you later, Babs," Starke said and continued toward Y-Dorm.

Z-Dorm and Y-Dorm were under the same roof but were separated by a twelve-foot cyclone fence. They had separate entrances and shared a gun-walk with a gunner thirty feet above the floor.

Starke retrieved a key group from his duty belt and opened the door to Y-Dorm.

He stepped inside and locked the door. He started down the three steps in to the unit and saw Officer Darrell Marcum searching an inmate who he had pressed against the wall. That alerted Starke, as putting an inmate on the wall was a signal of a high-risk search. Starke noticed there was an inmate in a holding cell.

Starke immediately sat his lunch box down and hurried over to Marcum.

Starke asked urgently, "What you got, Darrell?"

He replied, "These two guys were fighting and I notified the gunner and he sounded the alarm."

Starke stepped over to hold the inmate against the wall for Marcum while he put cuffs on him.

Starke keyed his radio.

"Control, this is Officer Starke in Y-Dorm. The Z-Dorm alarm was for Y-Dorm. Officer Marcum had an inmate-on-inmate assault, and they are now under control. I need a supervisor and a couple of S&Es [Search and Escort]."

The radio responded.

"This is Control. There is an emergency in Y-Dorm. Watch Commander, you copy?"

"Watch 1 copies."

Less than a minute passed, and the door to Y-Dorm opened up and Sergeant Hall and several officers came in. The two inmates were eventually secured and taken away. Starke and Marcum got busy writing their incident reports. When they finished, they caught up on each other's lives while they polished off their lunch boxes.

Starke and Marcum settled into a quieter evening seated at the officer's podium with a view eight feet above the ninety-eight inmates in the open dorm setting. There were normal inmate activities to supervise: TV watching, playing dominos, drawing, writing letters, and preparing various snacks. As they watched over their group from the podium, Paul Quiroz walked the gun-walk above both Y-Dorm and Z-Dorm, more notably called the Zoo. Splitting his time perusing the 98 or so inmates on one side and the 250-plus inmates on the Z-Dorm side was actually a better job than manning a perimeter tower with owls and raccoons to watch.

Paul became curious as he watched various inmates walk up to the same four-foot-locker, number 73, open the door, and stand in front of the locker drinking something, reading, or stirring the same cup. From his vantage point, he could only see the back of the locker. He toured back to the Z-Dorm side and then back to the Y-Dorm side.

Paul's curiosity got the best of him. He picked up his phone at the end of the gun-walk and dialed Marcum on the podium.

"Marcum, Y-Dorm," Marcum said.

Quiroz spoke softly, "Darrell, this is Paul on the gun-walk, don't talk too loud, I'm trying to be sneaky."

"Okay, what's up?"

"I've been watching some strange activity at locker 73. I've seen several dudes walk up to the same locker, open the door, and stand there for maybe four to five minutes, drink something, write on something, or just stare at the fence. It's really weird."

Marcum replied, "Okay, we'll check it out. Thanks."

He turned to Starke and spoke softly, "That was Paul on the gun. He said there is something strange going on at locker 73. Inmates are going over to the locker and standing for a few minutes then leaving."

Starke nodded, and they sat watching the locker on the sly. Sure enough, a couple of inmates took turns at the locker.

Marcum looked at the bed roster and noted the name in bed 73, Robert Powell. He looked at the file ID and showed it to Starke.

"You see Powell anywhere?" Marcum queried. Starke scanned the area. "Nope. You see him?"

Marcum said, "Okay, why don't you take a walk toward the bathroom and I'll watch to see if there's a lookout?"

Starke stood up and walked down the three steps to the floor and turned toward the bathroom. Marcum noticed an inmate on the bunk behind 73 watching Starke's movement. Starke came back after only a minute and sat down.

Marcum said, "The inmate in bed 23 was watching you." Starke said, "Okay, it's your unit, how you want to handle it?" Marcum thought. He dialed the gun-walk phone.

Paul walked over and picked up the phone. "Quiroz, Y-Gun."

Marcum spoke quietly. "We got a plan. Keep an eye out, we're moving in about a minute."

"Copy that," Paul said and hung up.

Marcum said, "You step down and fade to the right and circle back around left. I'll wait for bit and rush the locker."

"Sounds good to me," Starke said.

After a few seconds, Starke stood and faked a stretch and walked down the steps and walked to the right.

Marcum waited until Starke got a short distance away and slowly walked down the steps. As he reached the floor, he hurried toward the target, locker 73. The lookout saw Marcum coming and called out.

"Bob, shut it down."

The inmate standing at the locker reached his hands down toward the inside of the locker and started to close it. Starke stepped out from between the bunks and told the inmate to stop and put his hands on top of the locker. Marcum arrived a split second later. Starke told the inmate to step aside. Marcum opened the locker door the rest of the way and looked inside. He saw an inmate tucked inside. Starke noticed that his inmate had his pants unbuttoned and partially unzipped. Marcum told his inmate to come out of the locker. He stepped out of the locker.

"I guess you are Powell, right?" Marcum asked. The inmate nodded.

Starke pointed to his inmate's pants in its unbuttoned state. Marcum shook his head and said incredulously, "You shitting me?"

Starke had his inmate button his pants and got the inmate's ID. Marcum said, "You want to stay here and secure the locker and

I'll escort Powell to a holding cell and come back and get the other guy?"

"Sure," Starke said, nodding.

Marcum took Powell to the holding cell, searched him, and locked him inside. On the way back to the locker he retrieved a combination lock from his desk and went back and put it on the locker. Starke and the other inmate followed Marcum back to the other holding cell. Starke searched the inmate and locked him in the other holding cell. Marcum went back to his desk and called Sergeant Hall and told him what they found. While waiting for Sergeant Hall to arrive, Marcum called Paul on the gun-walk and gave him the 411.

Starke said, "How about I take a tour of the unit for you since you're busy?"

Marcum nodded. "Thanks, Karl, I'd appreciate that."

Starke took a security tour of the floor of the dorm. As he walked by the locker, an inmate said, "They call him Locker Bob."

Starke looked at the inmate and repeated, "You said Locker Bob?"

The inmate nodded. Starke made it back to the podium and sat down. He waited for Marcum to get off the phone.

"I guess you busted the notorious Locker Bob."

Marcum smiled. "Is that what they called him? Wow! Full service by Locker Bob."

Starke chuckled. "You're bad."

*****

Starke stood at the base of Tower 6 talking to the Tower 6 gunner, Jerry Rousan. He was standing in the shadow of the tower so he could see Jerry when they spoke.

"When are you coming back, Jerry?" Starke asked.

"The cruise gets back into San Diego June twentieth," Jerry said.

Starke added, "I'll have to take a cruise like that sometime."

"This will be my third trip to the Islands. We always enjoy it."

"Okay, Jerry, I'll catch you when you get back. Be safe, Jerry."

"Thanks, Karl, you too."

Starke walked along the fence, skirting the inmates working out. Certainly to the layman, letting inmates have access to metal weights and bars is a scary situation, but pumping iron is a great release for the doldrums of prison life. Surely, they can be used to bash someone to death, but the stats for those occurrences are lower than one would think. The movement for taking weights away rested mainly with the inmates getting bulked up and presenting a danger to the public when they get released. And most all of the inmates eventually get released.

Starke saw Potter talking to transportation officer Phil Cherry near the Southern weight pile. Starke scanned the inmates working out in his area. He walked through the center of the weight area nodding to various inmates and interacting with some others.

He crossed the track and stood inside the track area on the grass. A group of inmates had just finished kicking a soccer ball around. He walked toward the north end of the track to avoid looking into the sun as much as possible. He saw Officer Cherry coming toward him and waited for him.

"Hey, Phil, no transportation or med runs today?" Starke asked.

Cherry replied, "Had some earlier, but the med transports are back, and they sent us out to the yard for extra coverage."

Starke said, "I'm surprised they didn't send you guys inside to help with dayroom coverage."

"Some of us did go inside, but I'd rather be out here in the fresh air," Cherry related.

Starke quietly questioned Cherry's reasoning as most redirected staff preferred to be inside, out of the sun.

Starke responded, "Well, there's plenty of fresh air out here if you don't count the heat."

Cherry smiled. And they watched the yard activities together for a moment.

Starke was aware that Cherry was one of the staff members who were being watched by the Manteca PD, along with Bob Grey and Frank Arthur, the boyfriend of the female assault victim.

Cherry tried to pry some information from Starke.

"Hey, I was talking with Potter, and she said you mentioned something about Manteca PD watching some guys. Did you hear any more about that?"

"No, haven't heard anything more. Didn't seem like there was too much to it. It was no big deal to me," Starke lied.

Cherry added, "Just curious, I wanna keep my kids safe."

"I hear that."

Cherry changed the subject. "Well, I guess I'll go say hi to my buddy in Tower 13."

"Okay, Phil. Good seeing you again. Be safe, guy." Cherry walked away toward Tower 13.

*****

The next day, Starke saw Gene Jones, the Investigative Services captain, in the hallway.

Starke nodded to him to get his attention. Jones stopped and nodded. Starke spoke quickly. "The subject I told you about last week is feeling the heat. I hope they get the attention they deserve."

Jones nodded again. "The PD is working on their end, and we are working on our end, and we are going to put the squeeze on them soon."

Starke nodded and said, "Later, Gene."

*****

Starke eased back in his recliner, talking to Jason on the phone.

"So what did the inmate say when you guys rolled up on them at the locker?" Jason asked.

"Really, neither one said nothin'. Just stood there, literally with his pants down. And Darrell had his guy come out of the locker. He asked him if his name was Powell, and Powell just nodded."

"What did the other inmates say about the bust?"

Karl explained, "I didn't hear much from them until I took a security run and one guy said Powell was called Locker Bob."

"That's funny. What a moniker to be stuck with." Jason added, "It's a good catch for the gunner though. What was his name?" Jason asked.

"Paul Quiroz."

Jason questioned, "I wonder how long that had been going on." Starke chuckled and said, "Don't know, but for most...probably just a few minutes."

Jason said with a sneer and laughed. "No...you really didn't go there."

They laughed for a bit about the incident.

Starke changed the subject. "Captain Jones said the time is getting short for those guys across the street."

"Yeah? Haven't seen them working out lately. Guess they are laying low," Jason said.

"The captain did imply that they were doing more than pot in the garage," Starke related.

"That might explain some of what my contact at the PD said. It seems that the DA has enough to charge Frank and his brother with 261s," Jason added.

"Good, those dudes need to burn. But won't you need to testify to support the case?" Starke asked.

"Yeah, and glad to do it," Jason replied.

Starke thought for a moment and suggested, "Hey, maybe those two and Locker Bob could wind up being cellmates."

Jason chuckled and tagged on, "Just imagine that moniker, Locker Bob and friends.

IT'S ABOUT CHOICES: BAD, GOOD, AND ALARMING

Officer Janell Nichols stood at the control panel, even with the second tier. She picked up the Reception Center (RC) inmate listing clipboard and chose a cell number. She pressed button 203, and the cell door on the second tier, number 203, clicked and slid open. She called out to the opened door.

"Salgado!"

Momentarily, an inmate stepped partway out of the cell. "I'm Salgado, CO," he said.

She motioned to Salgado. "Could you step over here and talk to me?"

Salgado walked over to the bars separating the control panel area and the tier.

Nichols asked, "Salgado, you want to do a little janitorial work for me?"

He inched his neck and said, "Sure, CO."

"Okay, get dressed and come on down to the officer's station," she said.

He turned and went back into his cell. After a couple of minutes, he stepped out wearing his orange jumpsuit and made his way to the stairwell and started down the steps. Janell pressed another button, and the cell door closed, and the light on the button went from red to green.

She turned a key on the panel, and the panel turned off. She turned and walked down the stairs to the area below that had bars on two sides and a bathroom and back wall on the other two sides. She unlocked a gate leading into a sally port. She stepped into the sally port, locked the gate behind her, and stepped across the six-foot space to the officer's station, unlocked that gate, and went inside.

Salgado approached the officer's station and stood looking through the bars at Nichols. She wrote some notes in the Daily Activity Report (DAR) log. She stepped out into the sally port, closed and locked the officer's station gate, and turned and unlocked the unit entrance gate, went through, and locked it.

"Okay, Salgado. Follow me and we'll get you started."

Salgado nodded and followed Nichols. She unlocked a janitorial door and said, "Could you take the push broom, broom, and dustpan and sweep the first tier and put the trash and debris in the trash can by the officer's station?"

"Yes, ma'am, er, CO," he replied. "Thank you, Salgado," she said.

Nichols turned and walked back to the officer's station, locking all the gates, and busied herself with paperwork and watched Salgado sweep the tier.

Officer Dave Parker came out of the RC sergeant's office and turned the corner to the right. He walked past East Hall and the canteen area and went into G-Wing. Janell saw him come in.

He unlocked the officer's station door and stood at the desk. He had two 154s, "inmate bed move" papers, and put them on the desk. "Hey, Janell, Sarge gave me a couple of 154s for after chow is done."

"Coming in, out or in-house?" she asked.

"Two, in-house moves, to make room for two incoming," he replied.

Parker noticed Salgado on the tier sweeping up. "Who you got out sweeping?" he asked. "Youngster Salgado from 203," she replied. "You had him out before?" Parker asked.

"No, just trying him out," she said.

"Hmm, that's cool. Hope he's a good worker," he stated. She looked out on the tier and said, "He's keeping busy." Parker nodded his head and sat down at the desk.

Twenty minutes later, Salgado came up to Nichols and said, "CO, there is some sticky stuff by one of the tables, would you like me to mop it up?"

Somewhat surprised at his request, she smiled and replied, "Thank you, I'd appreciate your doing that for me."

"No problem, CO." He turned and went back to the janitorial storage closet.

Parker smiled. "That doesn't happen often, asking for more work."

Nichols watched Salgado and noted his work ethic and politeness. She knew from his intake file that he was a Youth Authority (YA) reject, meaning he was deemed unsuitable for continued presence in a YA institution. She was curious about his story.

Eventually, Salgado finished and put the supplies away and asked, "CO, you want me to close the janitorial door?"

Nichols stood up and said, "Thanks, Salgado. I'll come and lock it up."

She unlocked and locked the needed gates and went over to Salgado and locked the janitorial door. They walked back over and stopped in front of the officer's station.

"Is there anything else you need, CO?"

Nichols looked at the floor on the tier and replied, "No. Thank you for doing a good job."

"You're welcome. It's good to get out of the cell for a while."

She replied, "Most of the inmates do appreciate the time out of the cell, but I appreciate you not milking the job. I try to spread the work around, but since I know your work, I may use you more while you're here." She paused. "You mind me asking how old you are and what brought you to prison and, now, to the adult side?"

He thought for a moment and began, "I just turned eighteen. I caught a murder beef two years ago. The dudes in YA wanted to punk me out, and I wound up cutting a couple of them. So they bumped me up to here."

Nichols questioned, "What about the 187?"

"My woman and I went to the mall that was out of my hood, and some red-rag dude pulled a gun on me."

Nichols added, "So you shot him?"

"No, I didn't have my piece with me," he explained. "So what happened?" she queried.

"I went back home and I found out who the *puta* was and went to his crib and knocked on his door. When he opened it, I shot him and the dude standing behind to him."

Nichols shook her head and asked, "Why didn't you just let it go?"

He replied, "I couldn't let him disrespect my woman by pulling a gun on us."

Nichols shook her head sadly. "Do you regret what you did? Salgado shrugged his shoulders.

"So...you killed two people and will probably spend the rest of your life locked up, to protect your reputation and to protect your woman?"

"Yeah." Salgado nodded slowly.

Nichols asked, "So...Salgado, who's protecting your woman now?"

*****

Matt Solis stood between the lines in North Corridor, covering the mainline chow releases. He watched the inmates come around the corner past Center Corridor. He scanned each inmate for any unusual appearance: improper state-issued clothing; bulges in clothing; shirt not tucked in; cuts, bruises, or abrasions; sometimes just a suspicious look. On those occasions or just randomly, Solis would initiate a clothed body search.

A rather large inmate rounded the corner, and Solis selected him for a random pat-down. He caught the eyes of the inmate and pointed his hand at the inmate. Solis pointed down to the floor at his feet. The inmate understood the universal hand signal and walked over to Solis and stopped. He handed Solis his plastic cup and ID. The inmate turned and faced away from Solis and stood with his arms stretched out to either side. Solis inspected the cup and put it back in the inmate's outstretched hand.

He checked the ID and said, "Morgan, stand still and don't move, okay?"

Morgan nodded.

Solis straightened out his plastic gloves and reached up to the inmate's hair—nice-looking dreadlocks. He began to squeeze the top of the braids. The inmate ducked his head and looked over his shoulder at Solis and stated, "You can't touch my hair."

Solis stopped the search and brought his hand to his chest, in a somewhat defensive stance. He wrinkled his brows.

"What?" Solis asked.

"You can't touch my hair, it's a religious right," he replied.

Solis said, "Well, Morgan, I have to search for contraband or weapons."

"But my hair is a religious right," Morgan insisted.

Solis looked up at the dreadlocks and explained, "Sir, you certainly have the right to wear the dreads, but I have the right and obligation to search for contraband and weapons, and your hair could conceal either. Now I can put on fresh gloves and search your hair or I will wait right here while you take the dreadlocks out and run your hands and fingers through your hair to show there is no contraband or weapons in it."

Morgan scowled. "You know how long it takes to put the dreads in?"

Solis replied, "No, sir. I don't know how long it takes to put them in or take them out, but you can show me."

Morgan thought and sighed. "Okay. Put on some new gloves." Solis took the used gloves off and put on a fresh pair.

He continued his search of Morgan's hair, squeezing and bending it when necessary. He finished searching his body through his clothing, ending at his ankles. Solis gave Morgan back his ID and said, "Thank you."

Morgan turned, and as he walked away, he said, "Fuckin' pig." Solis continued his security duties.

*****

Officer Rachael Nava stood watch from inside the front door of Dining Hall 2. As the inmates filtered in from the far door along the left wall, a waist-high, two-inch pipe railing guided them along to a stainless steel wall hiding the serving line.

Officer Lethea Dickerson stood at the rear of chow hall, keeping watch on the inmates dishing out the food onto trays behind the "blind" steam line. It was called blind due to the seven-foot sheet metal wall extending from the wall to almost half of the width of the dining hall. The wall extended down to about one foot off the floor. That prevented the inmates on the steam line (serving line) dishing out the food behind the wall from seeing who they were serving so they don't double up the food portion on the tray for their *homies*. Each server was assigned to put their specific scoop, portion, or slice of a food item on the tray in front of them and slide it down the line to the next server. The tray that wound up at the end of the serving line was the one that the next inmate in line received. Occasionally, an inmate would take issue with the size of the allotted items on their tray. The steam line officer would either correct or deny the dispute. Normally, the request was denied, with the officer saying, "That's your *issue*," but occasionally, the officer would agree the size of a cake or a portion was deficient and correct the error.

However, on this specific occasion, Dickerson noticed that a server stepped around the other servers and placed an extra portion of meat on the tray. Dickerson stepped over to the end of the line before the inmate picked up the tray and took it off the line. The inmate took issue with the removal of the tray.

"Hey, CO, that's my tray," he protested.

She replied, "The veggies on the tray were light, so I'll get some more, take the next tray."

"But, that's okay, I'll take that one," he pleaded.

She shook her head and said, "I don't want you to get shorted on getting your issue. Take the next tray." She took the tray back down the line and put it at the beginning of the serving line.

The inmate saw that his request was rejected and took the next tray.

Dickerson walked over to the meat server.

"Miller, you trade with Yee and serve vegetables."

She gave Miller a scowl and went back to the head of the line. The tray in question made its way back to the end of the line,

and the receiving inmate was very pleased with his issue.

Dickerson smiled and slightly nodded.

The steam line officer also kept watch or, rather, an ear out for another scheme. A server, behind the steam line, would have a plastic serving glove prepared with a *boneroo* (extra) portion of the preferred entrée stuffed in it. When he got a whistle, call, or special knock from an inmate on the other side of the partition, he would slide or drop and kick the package under the partition to the other side. The inmates have 24-7 to find ways to beat the system.

Out in the dining hall, Nava was mindful of the inmates' choices of seating at the four-man tables. While there were exceptions, the flow of inmates generally settled according to ethnicity and gang affiliation.

As the tables began to fill, the officer at the entrance door estimated the number of inmates in line and surveyed the empty tables. He used his discretion and closed the door. The inmates in the corridor were waved to the next chow hall.

The flow of inmates in the corridor dwindled, and doors to the dining halls all closed. Culinary Sergeant Hunter saw that the doors were closed, looked at her watch, and walked over to Chow Hall 1 and looked into the small window in the door. She struck up a conversation with a few of the officers in the corridor.

Dickerson watched as the last of the inmates picked up his tray and sat down. Behind her was a grill gate that opened to a rear corridor leading behind the dining halls. Each dining hall had a grill gate that opened into the rear corridor. An officer was assigned to each grill gate to open and close when food or carts needed replenishing. Their main security issue was to watch their officers and the inmates in the chow hall for any disturbance.

Nava walked toward the rear of the chow hall and stood next to Dickerson. They spoke for a while and watched the inmates eat and socialize. About fifteen minutes had passed and most of the inmates were finished eating and sat talking.

Sergeant Hunter looked at her watch and keyed her radio.

"Program 1, Culinary Sergeant. They're coming back."

"Program 1. Send 'em," was the response.

The officers in the corridor outside each of the dining hall doors opened them up.

Nava and Dickerson heard the radio transmission, and Nava walked toward the front of the chow hall and pointed to the tables nearest the door, signaling it was time to leave. As their table was released, the inmates stood up and walked toward the door and dumped the contents of their tray in a garbage can, put their trays on a table, and left the dining hall. An inmate worker organized the empty trays on the table. Nava and Dickerson watched as the inmates stood and left the dining hall.

Suddenly, a crash was heard, and Nava and Dickerson turned and saw several trays bouncing on the tables and floor. Two inmates were fighting and wrestling near the rear of the chow hall by the steam line. Dickerson pressed her PAD (personal alarm device), and the blue light above the door on the outside of Dining Hall 2 flashed, and a loud buzzer was heard.

Dickerson and Nava yelled, "Get down!" And they both ran toward the fighting inmates.

The other inmates in the dining hall, either got out of the way, sat down at their table with their feet under the table, or pressed their backs against a wall.

The officer at the rear grill gate closed and locked the grill gate. He looked through the bars in the gate into the dining hall. The officers at the doors to the other dining halls closed and locked their doors. The officer at the door of Dining Hall 2 stood fast and held the door open for responding staff to go in. The staff in the corridor ordered, "On the wall!"

The inmates in the corridor immediately went against the walls of the corridor.

Sergeant Hunter announced on the radio, "Control, we have an alarm in chow hall two."

The radio crackled and echoed the emergency.

"Control to all units, we have an alarm in chow hall two."

Dickerson and Nava skirted around several tables of inmates. They both shouted, "Get down!" several times as they made their way to the incident. Dickerson had arrived an instant before Nava.

A shaved-headed inmate was holding a dark-haired inmate with his left arm wrapped around his waist from behind and hitting him in the right side of the face. The dark-haired inmate locked his right arm over the right arm of the inmate attacking him and spun him to the left against a table. Dickerson pulled her baton and hit the darkhaired inmate with a strike to his right thigh and another strike to his right shoulder. As she did so, she shouted, "Stop! Down!"

The inmate winced in pain.

Nava charged into the other inmate's left side with her right forearm and knocked him off balance to the floor. Responding Officer Ben Curry used his momentum to push the shaved-headed inmate off a table against the seat of the next table.

Officer Jan Carter jumped over the nearby pipe rail and planted his knee in the back of the shaved-headed inmate that Nava had knocked to the floor. Nava promptly put both of her knees on the legs of the shaved-headed inmate, and they both held him down.

The other inmate started to gain his balance, but Dickerson use a two-handed strike to drive him against the pipe rail, and Officer Curry used his left leg to sweep the inmate's legs from under him. He fell to the floor, and Dickerson used her baton to lace it through the inmate's arm and twisted him onto his stomach. She and Officer Curry put their hands, elbows, and body weight on him to keep him down.

Several other staff members joined in subduing and handcuffing the combatants.

The inmates were eventually removed to Ad Seg, and the alarm status was cleared. The institution continued feeding chow.

Nava and Dickerson fed two more waves of inmates without any further incidents.

When the feeding was done, Dickerson and Nava stopped off in the break room to pick up their lunch boxes and finish out their shifts in the housing units. In their own after-action review, they recounted their parts of the story.

"You know, every time I get involved in an incident, I don't remember thinking about what to do, I just react as though I had been in that situation before," Nava said.

Dickerson thought and replied, "Yeah, that's scary. You're probably like me. I put myself in a hypothetical situation and try to think, 'What would I do *if?*'"

Nava agreed, "The more you think about what could happen, the better the choices you make."

AD SEG: THE JAIL WITHIN THE PRISON

Sergeant Nick Lopez stood at the solid entrance door of Building 6, Ad Seg, waiting for it to finish sliding open. He stepped inside the sally port, and as it started to close, the unit entrance door with bars at the other end of the sally port began to slide open. As he made his way through the sally port, he looked up through the heavy glass viewing ports in the ceiling. From the control room above, Officer Sara Harrigan watched Lopez through the viewing ports in the floor. When the sergeant cleared the door, she pressed a button to close it. Lopez took a few steps into the unit and stood for a moment. He scanned the 270-degree unit from left to right, noting the three sections of the two tiers of fifty double occupancy cells. Each section had a lockable grilled shower area, and directly ahead on the first tier, there was a barred gate that led to the exercise yard. Interspersed on the floor of the unit, the dayroom, were several four-man metal tables with seats affixed to them.

This Ad Seg sergeant position was a temporary assignment for Lopez, working as detached duty from the Academy.

Lopez turned and looked up at Harrigan through the glass-wire windows and bars of the fifty-by-fifty-foot control booth and nodded to her. Below the control booth on either side were two offices. Lopez saw two officers in the office to his left and surmised that the other was the sergeant's office. He noted an inmate locked in a holding cell around the corner of the sergeant's office. He went over to the door and sat his lunch box and briefcase on the floor. He removed a set of keys from his belt and tested his key group knowledge. He fingered through the various keys and decided on one key and successfully unlocked the door. He picked up his briefcase and lunch box and went into the office. He sat his lunch box on the floor and sat his brief case on a desk. He scanned the office and was pleased. He went back out the door and looked around the tier and saw an officer on the first tier talking to an inmate at a cell door. One of the officers in the officer's station stepped out of the office and came up to Lopez. He extended his hand, and Lopez shook it.

"Hey, Sarge, I'm Vejar."

"Good to meet you. I'm Lopez, Nick," he replied and added, "Are you a five-day or a relief cop?"

Vejar replied, "It so happens that today we're all regulars. Harrigan in the booth is working her RDO [regular day off] on a swap."

Lopez nodded. "You like this unit?"

"Yeah, we all like it here. We all are on our second bid for our jobs except for Kerry Reyes there," he said, nodding at the office. "She's an admin choice."

Lopez smiled. "That's good to hear."

Lopez walked over toward the officer's office and went in. He nodded to the other officer and extended his hand.

"I'm Nick Lopez."

Reyes said, "Good to meet you. I'm Reyes."

Lopez smiled and looked down at the DAR [daily activity report] logbook she was reading.

"Anything in the log worth mentioning?" he asked.

"No, didn't see anything, and shift change said all was good."

Lopez looked around the office, noticing the inmate picture board, then looked out onto the unit.

"What we got going on right now?"

Vejar said, "Just settled in. We have one intake and waiting for the 154 on inmate Barker in the holding cell. Then we're gonna go over the inmate logs."

Lopez said, "How about we step outside and have a meeting?"

"Sure," Vejar replied.

Lopez stepped out the door and stood and looked up at Harrigan and motioned her to the front of the booth. She slid open a window.

"What's up, Sarge?" she asked.

Lopez smiled and said, "I heard you're Harrigan. I'm Lopez, Nick."

Harrigan smiled. "Hey, Nick. What's up?"

Lopez said, "If you can listen in, I'd like to have a powwow." Harrigan shrugged and smiled. "Okay, Sarge."

Lopez turned to Reyes and asked, "Who's the cop on the tier?"

"Perry," Reyes said.

Lopez called out, "Perry," and motioned for him to come over. Perry nodded and joined the group.

As Perry got to Lopez, Lopez held out his hand, and Perry shook it.

"I'm Nick Lopez."

Perry replied, "I'm Perry King."

Lopez smiled and spoke loud enough for Harrigan to hear, but not so loud to broadcast it to the inmates, although they are adept at listening in on every conversation.

"You're a fine-looking crew."

His audience mostly smiled and nodded.

"You probably have some 411 on me already, but just in case, I'll summarize it."

Lopez began, "I've got twelve years in DVI, Coalinga, CMF, and the academy, and now here. I've worked almost every position at DVI and a bunch at Pleasant Valley and CMF. I'm on loan from the Academy due to low staffing needs. At some point, I may have trained you or someone you know. I try to learn a little about everything, mostly because I listen, watch, and try to learn. That's what I want to do here. I'm a hands-on sergeant. I don't want to change your program. I'm happy to let you do your job. If you need help, I'm here. I slop trays, escort inmates, cover yard activities, and deal with inmates on an easygoing level. I don't think you'd call me weak for giving an inmate what they have coming. I want to observe the unit and, if necessary, make suggestions on a better and safer way to do things. My goal is to keep you safe and for all of us to go home to our real lives. Don't let this job consume you. When you get home, leave the job here. If you worry about the job while you're at home, then you need to change something. The state doesn't pay you to bring work home in your head. Conversely, I understand it's difficult, but don't let your home life distract you from doing this job. A lock not locked or an inmate overly trusted can get you or your partner hurt. Your mindset is important. It's not your job to punish the inmates. Their punishment is being separated from society. You all know what respect means to inmates. Give respect to get respect. And you've all heard that an inmate is an inmate is an inmate. And you've probably learned that ninety-five percent of the inmates will do what you tell them to do, but staff is more likely to give you the blues." Lopez took a breath. "So…that's my soliloquy, the floor is yours."

Vejar smiled and looked at Lopez. "Could you repeat that, Sarge?"

Lopez chuckled as did the others.

Reyes nodded slowly. "I think that was part of the 'supervision of inmates' academy class."

Lopez nodded. "I guess once an instructor, always an instructor." King added, "But, Sarge, it's good to hear what your expectations are. We got some scoop on you but didn't know what to expect." Lopez smiled. "I've been in your shoes before, having a new sergeant come into the unit and change the whole program. I want to work with you rather than have you work against me."

Vejar spoke, "Well, I appreciate your setting the tone. I look forward to having you in the unit."

Harrigan chimed in from the control booth, "Yes, Sarge. Welcome."

The crew appeared receptive, but prior experiences with a new sergeant made them guarded.

Lopez took a breath and asked, "Okay, what we got going next? Showers, yard, laundry?"

"We have to bring in the walk-alone yard in, and then we'll send the Southerns out," King stated.

"Who's on the gun?" Lopez asked. "Campbell," came King's reply.

Lopez asked, "What's the phone number for the yard gun?"

"6414," King replied.

Lopez went into the office and picked up the phone and dialed. "Campbell, Seg gun," was the answer.

Lopez said, "Campbell, this is Seg Sergeant Nick Lopez."

"Hey, Sarge," she replied.

"Just wanted to say hi and let you know we're coming out for the walk-alones."

"10-4, Sarge," Campbell said.

Lopez hung up the phone and went back out and joined the group.

"Okay, how can I help?" Lopez asked.

Vejar said, "We pretty much have it handled, but you can watch."

"Okay, whenever you're ready," Lopez replied.

Vejar nodded and went into the office and retrieved the wand (handheld metal detector). Lopez followed his crew toward the exercise yard gate. Several bunches of handcuffs were cuffed together and hanging from the fence. Lopez took one pair of cuffs off the fence and put them on his duty belt. Lopez continued out into the cyclone-fenced sally port. He searched around the building walls for the yard gun enclosure.

He saw Campbell in the window and waved to her. She waved back.

Lopez stepped back under the building overhang. The inmates took turns walking over to the yard exit gate at one side of the yard. One at a time, each inmate put his hands into a narrow opening (cuff port), and Reyes removed a pair of cuffs from one of the strings of cuffs hanging on the fence and cuffed him and then did the same for each of the inmates. When they were all cuffed, Reyes signaled Campbell to open the gate. The gate slid open, and one inmate would step into the sally port, and the gate would slide closed. Reyes would open the exit gate and send an inmate toward a waiting officer.

Vejar passed the wand over the clothed areas of the inmate. He handed the wand to King, and Vejar took control of the inmate and walked him into the unit. Vejar asked the inmate his cell number.

"113," was the answer.

Vejar escorted the inmate over to his cell. Harrigan waited in the control booth for Vejar to signal that he was ready, and she pressed a button that slid open the cell door. The inmate stepped in, and Harrigan closed the door. Vejar unlocked the food tray access port, and the inmate put his hands out of the port. Vejar removed the cuffs and closed the port door. Vejar went back to escort another inmate and replaced the handcuffs on one of the strings of handcuffs.

Each officer would wand their inmate and then escort him to his cell in the same manner.

When the inmates on that side of the yard were removed, King started the process on the other side.

There were a total of eight inmates that were at some risk of being assaulted that placed them in the *walk-alone* status. Often, similar concerns, such as being a child molester or a snitch, would allow some inmates to exercise together in a *walk-alone* yard.

Lopez followed each part of the process, mentally noting the seamless flow.

When the yard was cleared, the group went back to the tables by the office. King stayed behind and went into each exercise area and inspected the fence and toilet areas for security and to search for contraband. Being satisfied, he joined the others.

The officers had retrieved rolling file carts from along the wall and began filling in information in each inmate's 114-A, which logged any daily activity such as yard program, chow, shower, etc.

Lopez went into the officer's office and perused the inmate picture board. He noted the random placement of ethnicities and gang affiliation and was pleased. He counted eighteen inmates with a designation of Southern gang affiliation.

He went back out and walked around the unit floor, starting on the left side. He walked over to the inmate in the holding cell dressed in boxers and slippers. He noticed a cut on his cheek and an abrasion on his forehead.

"Afternoon, what's your name, guy?"

"Barker," was the reply.

"I'm Sergeant Lopez. Tough day?" he added.

"You might say that," Barker said with a frown.

"Well, you should be safe while you're here," Lopez said.

Lopez continued his trek around the unit. He looked into several offices, one that probably served as an Institutional Classification Committee (ICC) meeting room. Among other determinations, the ICC assesses the need for placement or continued placement of an inmate in an Administrative Segregation unit, essentially putting an inmate in a jail inside the prison.

He noticed other offices that might serve as a medical assessment area or a conference room.

Lopez walked around the cells on the first tier, looking in some of the cells. He went up the stairs to the second tier and walked along the cells. He continued around the tier and walked past the shower area and a storage room. He went down the stairway to the first tier. During his walk, he nodded and chatted with some of the inmates. He felt somewhat at ease in the environment, although his awareness was appropriately heightened. He wandered back to the tables to his staff as they were preparing to collect the Southern inmates for yard release.

Each officer had a list of inmates that could go to yard.

Lopez walked over and unlocked the yard gate and opened it.

He took the wand that was hanging on the fence.

Reyes checked her list and walked up the stairs to cell 206. She looked in the cell and asked, "Morgan, you going to yard?"

He replied, "Yeah."

He draped a towel around his neck and backed up to the door. Reyes unlocked the cuff port, and Morgan put his hands through, and Reyes cuffed him. He pulled his hands back, and she closed the cuff port. She raised her hand above the door, which signaled Harrigan that she was ready for the door to open. The door opened, and Morgan stepped out, and the door closed. Reyes firmly grasped his elbow and escorted him down the stairs to the yard gate. She saw that Lopez had opened the gate and had the wand.

Lopez said, "I'll be your gatekeeper."

Reyes raised her brows approvingly and handed control of Morgan to Lopez. Lopez ran the wand over Morgan's body and put him in the fenced sally port and closed the gate. Morgan backed up to the gate and put his hands through the cuff port. Lopez uncuffed Morgan and motioned to Campbell. The exercise door slid open, and Morgan stepped onto the yard, and the door slid closed.

Lopez added the handcuffs on to the cuffs on the fence. Lopez opened the sally port gate and continued the process.

Vejar looked at the list and said to King, "Let's get two out of cell 220."

King nodded, and they proceeded up the stairs to cell 220. "Ruiz, Maldonado, you going to yard?"

"Yes, CO," was the reply.

Staff always asked if the inmate wanted to go to the yard as it was optional. However, it was mostly superfluous to ask a Southern if they were going to yard, chow, etc., since it was a gang mandate. The shot caller for the institution set the rules.

The inmates each backed up to the cuff port and were placed in cuffs and also escorted to the yard gate.

The last of the inmates were put on the yard, and Lopez counted seventeen. He recalled that there were eighteen Southerns.

He asked, "Aren't we missing one Southern? I counted eighteen." Vejar said, "There are eighteen, but Zepeda was on the *walk-alone* yard."

Lopez winced somewhat. "Oh, must be persona non grata." Vejar nodded. "He's gonna debrief and then on his way to protective custody somewhere."

Lopez added, "Probably PC [protective custody] up in Corcoran." Vejar nodded.

The crew went back to the tables and the rolling file carts. They busied themselves with paperwork. Lopez took the opportunity to check out his office. He stepped in and picked up his lunch box and pulled out a banana and put it on the desk. He took a mug and a container of tea out of the lunch box and set the mug on the desk. He opened the container and poured half a mug of tea and put the container back in his lunch box. He decided to try out his chair. He rolled it back and sat down. It was surprisingly comfortable. He swiveled it back and forth a couple of times. He picked up his mug and sipped as he spun easily in the chair. He peeled his banana, took a bite, and chewed slowly. He looked over against the wall and reached over and retrieved a clipboard off the wall. He thumbed through several pages of memos that offered the standard fare of state-generated memos. He put the clipboard back on the wall. He opened several drawers, searching for the Ad Seg sergeant's post orders. He was successful in his second choice of drawers. He retrieved the orders and scanned through the usual boiler plate and settled on the meat and potatoes specific to his assignment. As he read through the pages, it became apparent that there was little change in the expectations of the job over the last eight years. He dutifully signed and dated the acknowledgment that he had read the post orders.

He put the folder back in the drawer and took another drink of tea. He stood up and looked out into the unit. He eyed Officer King cuff an inmate, Shaw, in cell 228 and escort the inmate carrying a towel in his cuffed hands to the shower. When they got to the shower, King took the towel from the inmate and laid it in between the bars, and the inmate stepped into the shower. King locked the grill gate, and the inmate backed up to the cuff opening, and King removed the cuffs.

Lopez drank the rest of his tea and put the mug back in his lunch box. He went back out into the unit and made his way to the tables next to the officer's station.

From the control booth, Harrigan called down to Lopez. "Hey, Sarge, here's the 154 for Barker." She was holding up a slip of paper.

Lopez nodded and went into the officer's station and looked up at Harrigan through the glass port. She opened the port and handed the form 154 down to Lopez.

"Thanks, Harrigan," Lopez said. Harrigan nodded and closed the port.

Lopez looked at the 154 and saw that Barker was going into cell 228 with inmate Shaw.

Lopez went back out to the tables and handed the 154 to Reyes. She said, "Thanks, Sarge."

She looked at the 154 and got up and walked over to a storage room door and went in. Momentarily, she emerged with a netted laundry bag with sheets and bedding in it. She went over to a bin and pulled out a "fish" kit, a paper sack containing toiletry items. From a bookcase against the wall, she put three pairs of boxers and three pairs of socks in the laundry bag.

Lopez knew the routine and saw a food cart against the wall. He started toward the cart and asked, "Are the sack lunches in the cart?" Reyes saw Lopez moving toward the cart. She smiled and said,

"Yep, that's right."

Lopez took a sack lunch out of the cart and walked back over to Reyes and put the lunch on the table.

Lopez asked, "You want me to get Barker out of the holding cell?"

"No, I can do it, Sarge."

Lopez said, "That's okay, Reyes. You can take his bedding and stuff, and I'll bring him up to you in 228."

She raised her brows and said, "Okay, Sarge, if you want to."

Lopez reached over and picked up the sack lunch off the table and headed over to the holding cell.

"Barker, your accommodations are ready, sir."

"Okay, Sarge," Barker said.

Lopez put the sack lunch on a nearby table. He took out a pair of plastic gloves from a pouch on his duty belt and put them on. He asked, "I know you've been stripped out a couple of times already, but since I didn't see it, can you do the 'dance' for me one more time?"

Barker half-smiled and nodded. He took off his T-shirt, boxers, and slippers and handed them to Lopez. Lopez twisted and folded the clothing and bent the slippers. Barker faced Lopez and opened his mouth wide and stuck out his tongue, put his fingers in his cheeks, and pulled them side to side. Lopez observed each sequence of the process, looking for any hidden contraband: drugs, metal, or cuff key. Barker ran his fingers briskly through his hair. He held out his hands and spread his fingers apart. He reached down to his scrotum and lifted his testicles. He raised his arms above his head and turned slowly around. He picked up his feet one at a time and showed the bottom of his feet, wiggling his toes. He did three deep knee bends and bent over and spread apart his butt cheeks and coughed.

Lopez handed the T-shirt, boxers, and shoes back to Barker.

Barker got dressed and backed up to the cuff port, and Lopez unlocked it. Barker put his hands through the opened port. Lopez took a pair of handcuffs from his duty belt and cuffed Barker. He unlocked the holding cell and guided Barker out. He locked the holding cell and picked up the sack lunch and put it in Barker's cuffed hands. He escorted Barker up the stairs to cell 228. Reyes was waiting at the cell and had placed the laundry bag and fish kit on the top bunk. Barker's cellmate, Shaw, was still in the shower.

Lopez led Barker into the cell, and Reyes signaled Harrigan to close the door. Barker backed up to the cuff port and Reyes unlocked it. Reyes took the cuffs off and closed the port.

Kerry and Lopez went back down to the tables by the officer's station.

Vejar and King finished putting two inmates in the shower on the lower tier and came back to the tables. They picked up their drinking containers off a table and took some swallows of their beverages. Reyes looked up at the second-tier shower and saw Shaw drying off.

She asked Vejar, "Vejar, you want to go with me to get Shaw and put him back?"

King asked, "Do we need two officers to pick him up?"

She explained, "The Sarge and I just put in his new cellie, Barker."

"Oh, okay, guess we do need two. I'll go with Jerry and put him in," King replied.

Reyes added, "You might want to tell him he has a cellie, I don't know if second watch told him he's getting company."

King nodded.

Vejar held his drink up and toasted King, "Let's do this," and took another swallow of his drink.

They sat their drinks on the table and proceeded to the second-tier shower to collect Shaw.

Lopez looked at Reyes and offered, "I know it's more efficient for only one officer to escort an Ad Seg inmate, but I always erred on the side of safety and preferred to have two on an escort. However, there was a time when I, alone, would escort an inmate to an occupied two-man cell and have the other inmate kneel down at the rear of the cell and face away from the door. Then I would key open the door and have my inmate step in and turn and face against the near wall while I slid the door closed. Then I would take the cuffs off." He paused and added, "I'm glad we are using two staff to escort to a two-man cell."

Reyes nodded. "We try to be as safe as possible. Some RDO staff are a little lax, but we don't let them slide on safety."

Shaw draped his towel over his neck and put his hands through the port. Vejar cuffed Shaw, and King unlocked and opened the grill. Shaw stepped out of the shower, and they started walking him toward his cell.

King said, "Shaw, just letting you know, you just got a new cellie."

Shaw stopped walking. Vejar had Shaw by his left elbow, and King grabbed the other elbow. They both felt Shaw's resistance.

"What's up, Shaw? Let's go," Vejar said.

"Why did I get a cellie? This is a setup," Shaw said. "What do you mean a setup?" King asked.

Shaw struggled to get free from Vejar and King. "You're gonna kill me. Help! They're gonna kill me!" Shaw yelled.

They locked both of their hands around Shaw's arms and braced their stances. Shaw leaned back against their holds and lifted his feet off the ground, bouncing up and down in their grasps.

"Help! They're gonna kill me," he yelled again.

Certainly, Lopez and Reyes heard Shaw's shouts. They jumped up and ran toward the stairway, and Lopez arrived as Shaw jumped again. Reyes stood behind Lopez.

Lopez held out his hands in a "stop" gesture and said, "Shaw, Shaw. Hold on, hold on," to get Shaw's attention.

Shaw calmed down a little.

"Okay, Shaw, take it easy. I'm Sergeant Lopez, no one wants to hurt you," Lopez said.

"You put a dude in my cell to kill me," Shaw said. "Why would he want to harm you?" Lopez asked. "That's what you do in here," Shaw said.

"Shaw, Shaw," Lopez said to get Shaw's focus on him. "Have you seen or heard anyone get hurt while you've been here?"

Shaw took a breath. "No."

"How about this, Shaw. Let's go over to your cell and you can see and talk to the guy in your cell. His name is Barker. How about that?"

Shaw took another deep breath and relaxed a little. "Shaw, hey, can we do that? Go talk to him?"

Shaw relented, "Okay." He began to walk toward his cell with the help of his two supporters.

When they got to cell 228, Lopez unlocked the food/cuff port so he could talk and hear better. He looked in the six-by-ten-inch plated window and called to Barker inside the cell. "Barker."

Barker looked at the window and walked toward the cell door. He stood at the door and looked at Lopez.

"Yeah, Sarge."

"I have your cellie out here, and he thinks you were sent to hurt him," Lopez said.

"He what?"

"His name is Shaw. He thinks you were sent here to hurt him." Barker shook his head. "I don't know anyone named Shaw.

What's he look like?"

Lopez touched Shaw's shoulder, and Shaw slowly walked to the window. Shaw looked in the window.

Barker shook his head. "Hey, man, why would I want to hurt you?"

Shaw said, "That's what the others said they would do, send someone to finish the job."

Barker asked, "Did the guys beat you up because of what you did on the street?"

Shaw nodded his head. "Well, buddy, they did the same to me," Barker said, pointing to his face. "I got no beef with you."

"So what do you think?" Lopez asked Shaw. "You ready to go in?"

Shaw nodded.

"Okay, Barker, cuff up so we can open the door."

Barker turned around and put his hands out of the port, and Lopez cuffed him.

"Step to the back of the cell and face away." Barker complied.

Lopez raised his hand above the door and shouted, "Open 228." The door slid open.

While Vejar and King finished putting Shaw in the cell, Lopez and Reyes strolled down the stairs back to the tables. King and Vejar finally returned and settled in at the tables. Lopez started to sit down but changed his mind. He looked up at Harrigan and motioned her to the window.

"Harrigan, thanks for covering the situation. I just thought of something."

"What's that, Sarge?" she asked.

"You need to change your first name." She was puzzled as were the others.

"I've got a crew named Jerry, Perry, and Kerry, so you gotta have a rhyming name, something like Sherry or something."

Reyes laughed and said, "How about Scary?"

Harrigan smiled, chuckled, and slid the window closed. Lopez shook his head and said, "Now that was scary." Vejar and King softly laughed.

Vejar looked at his watch and said, "Okay, Sergeant Harry, time to bring in the yard."

The crew laughed together. They gathered their composure and forged ahead to the yard gate.

The yard complement of inmates was successfully removed and escorted to their assigned cells. The crew was taking a short break. Lopez was in the officer's office noting the Shaw situation on the Daily Activity Report log.

The phone rang, and Lopez answered. "Ad Seg Sergeant Lopez."

"Hey, Sarge, Lieutenant Villanueva. I got a 154 for an inmate Yeager going into cell 237. I checked the compatibility with second watch. I snuck him in on ya before count, just a heads-up."

Lopez wrote a couple of notes on a piece of paper. "Okay, Lieu, we got it covered."

Lopez put the note in his vest. He walked out to the tables and announced, "We have an inmate Yeager coming in before count, going in to 237."

A familiar ruckus in the sally port engaged Lopez's attention. He stood up and walked out of the office. He looked in the sally port and saw rolling culinary food carts lined up in the sally port. The door slid open, and Lopez watched the crew as they went to work pushing carts into preplanned locations on the unit floor.

Lopez asked, "You guys announce chow, or do they just know it's chow time?"

Perry said, "They usually know, but we usually announce it.

You can do the honors."

Lopez used his loud correctional voice. "Chow in the unit! Chow time! Get ready!"

The sally port door slid open, and an officer came through carrying her lunch bag. She sat the bag on the table. She looked somewhat familiar. She walked up to Lopez and held out her hand, and Lopez shook it.

"Hey, Sarge, I'm Connie Campbell."

Lopez nodded. "Hi, you're the yard gun. I'm Nick Lopez."

"Right-o, Sarge," she replied.

"This your after-gun assignment?"

She shrugged her shoulders. "Actually, I'm usually supposed to help out with chow on the yard, but Sergeant Stancil lets me choose. I'd rather be in here helping out than on the yard. I like this unit."

Lopez nodded. "Okay. Welcome."

She went straightaway to help with chow.

The culinary carts contained premade meals on covered trays.

Depending on the institution, the trays were partitioned plastic on trays with polyurethane molded tops and bottoms, sometimes called slammer trays. Lopez recalled using metal trays that the staff would manually dish out portions from kitchen food carts. Regardless, the objective was to feed chow.

One of the staff would go by each cell and unlock the food port, and another staff would follow behind with food trays and put one or two trays one at a time in the port and the inmate would take it.

Lopez went over to Vejar and asked, "Are there any special diet trays to hand out?"

He pointed over to a shorter solitary cart.

"They should be in the short cart and have a name and cell number tag on them, but we'll get them, Sarge."

Lopez said, "I don't mind helping out."

"Actually, Sarge, if you want, you can pour the drinks, it's probably Kool-Aid or OJ."

Lopez nodded. "Okay."

Lopez walked over to a large ten-gallon galvanized liquid container and picked up one of the two large pouring pitchers on the table beside it. He dispensed some of the liquid into the pitcher and decided it was Kool-Aid. He filled both containers three-quarters full. He looked around the tier to determine where the chow was being served first. He assessed his starting point, and as he went over to cell 101, he called out, "Cups out, Jim Jones."

As he approached the cell, the inmate would put his cup out of the port. Lopez would pour the liquid in the cup, or cups, and close the port after the cup was pulled back. Occasionally, there would be no cup visible, and Lopez would ask, "Jim Jones, cups out."

Usually, the inmate would bring their cup to the port or wave or shake their head in decline.

Campbell walked up to Lopez and smiled and said, "Sarge, you took one of my jobs." She pointed to the pitchers in his hands.

Lopez laughed and said, "Oh, *pardonnez-moi*, madam?" and handed the pitchers to Campbell.

Lopez feigned rejection. "Guess I know when I'm not needed."

Lopez saw the operation was going smoothly and decided to do his job: supervise.

He went back to the tables by the officer's station and sat on the edge of a table and watched the feeding process unfold.

After the meals were dispensed, the crew sat at the tables, talking for a few minutes.

Shortly, King stood up and asked, "Are you guys ready to do this?"

The others collectively sighed and stood up and began the next phase of chow: picking up trays and trash.

Once again, the process was to open the ports and retrieve all the trays, tops and bottoms, as a tray could be modified into a weapon or escape implement in short order. Also, someone would follow behind with a trash bag to receive any trash from the cell and subsequently close the food port. The next hour or so was time for staff to eat and document the individual inmate's activity on each 114-A log: yard release, shower, or chow. Lopez chose to eat with his crew instead of in his office.

The conversations ranged from polite to tossing digs at one or more of the participants, normal trash-talk among COs.

The familiar sound of the outside sally port door opening was heard by the staff. Reyes and King eased over to look into the sally port. The inside grill gate slid open, and two officers were holding an inmate against the wall. Reyes and King took control of Yeager from the other officers. One of the officers handed a 154 to Reyes.

"Okay, we got 'em guys," Reyes said. The officers said, "Thanks," and left.

Lopez pulled a note from his vest and read it. "This must be Yeager. He's going into 237."

Reyes held her hand on Yeager's back, holding him against the wall, while King removed Yeager's shoes and socks. He searched Yeager through his clothing, and they escorted Yeager to the holding cell and locked him in it. They retrieved his ID and proceeded to have Yeager strip out, checking for contraband and note any injuries.

Reyes handed the ID to Lopez and escorted Yeager over to a table and had him sit down.

Soon, King returned with a laundry bag of bedding, underwear, socks, and a pair of state-issued slippers.

They proceeded to the stairway to drop off Yeager in cell 237. Lopez went into the officer's station and punched a hole in the

ID and hung it on a hook on the inmate picture board with inmate Parsons's ID in cell 237.

Lopez went out of the office and picked up his lunch box and walked around the tables and went into his office. He sat his box down and sat in his chair. He opened his briefcase and took out some papers. He began to read when Reyes came to his door.

"Hey, Sarge. Parsons in 237 says he doesn't want a cellie and won't cuff up so we can put Yeager in."

Lopez lowered his brows. "He what? Doesn't want a cellie?" Reyes nodded. "He's as much as threatened Yeager."

Lopez stood up and took a breath. "Okay, let's see what's up with Parsons."

Lopez followed Reyes up the stairs to cell 237. King was holding Yeager on the tier near cell 237.

Lopez looked into the cell. He saw that Parsons had removed the mattress from the upper bunk and had the entire bunk covered with papers and folders. On the floor was a carton file box with folders in it.

"Parsons, I'm Sergeant Lopez. What's going on, guy?"

Parsons seemed agitated and looked at Lopez. "I don't want a cellie. I don't have room for one. I have a court case."

Lopez asked, "You have a pending case to prepare for?"

"Yeah, Sarge, I can't deal with someone in the cell disrupting my system."

Lopez looked around the cell and said, "Parsons, hold on for a few minutes, will you?"

Parsons nodded.

Lopez said, "You guys hang tight for a little bit. I'll be back." Lopez went down the stairs and went into the officer's office.

Vejar was sitting at the desk. Lopez looked up at the inmate picture board and scanned for a solution. He noticed several "white" cells with only one inmate. He wrote down the cell numbers and went back out to the tables.

Vejar followed him out.

"What you looking for, Sarge?"

Lopez said, "I need to check these inmate files to see what their lockup status is. I want to find a compatible white cell for Yeager."

Vejar said, "Arthur in 140 should be a match."

Lopez pulled the file on Arthur and read a few selected lines. He said, "Yep, he should do."

Lopez went back into the office and took Yeager's picture off the board and went over to cell 140.

He knocked on the door to get Arthur's attention. "Arthur, Sergeant Lopez. Can we talk?" Arthur came to the door. Lopez held up Yeager's picture.

"Do you know this inmate?" Arthur shook his head.

"Okay, I need a cell to put him in, and I'd like to put him in with you. He's not a molester."

Arthur shrugged his shoulders and said, "No problem, Sarge."

"Thanks, Arthur."

Lopez went up the stairs to cell 237 and spoke to Parsons. "Parsons, I'm under the guns here. I need you to take Yeager as your cellie, just until count clears, and I'll move him right out." Parsons said, "Sarge, I know what's up, you put him in and he'll stay."

Lopez took a breath.

"Parsons, you know I'm new to the unit and all I have right now to give you is my word. If I don't keep it, what good will I be working here?"

Parson thought for a moment and said, "No dice, I don't trust you."

Lopez paused. "Okay, Parsons, but can you do me a favor?"

"What?" Parsons said with a sneer.

"I need you to neatly pick up your papers and files off the top buck and put them in your file box or someplace safe out of the way where they won't get damaged."

"What for?"

"I don't want them damaged when we come in to extract you out of the cell for refusal to comply with a lawful order. I'm not sure how gentle the extraction will be. You know how that goes."

Parsons looked at his papers and folders and sighed. "You'll take him out after count?" he asked.

"All I have is my word, Parsons, and you're the first one to get it."

Parsons relented. "Okay, Sarge, I'll trust you."

"Okay, back up and cuff up, please."

Parsons complied, and Reyes and King completed the transaction.

Lopez went back to the office and replaced Yeager's picture on the board. Vejar had followed him into the office.

"Vejar, cut a 154 for Yeager to move to 140."

"You got it, Sarge."

Lopez went back to his office and continued his reading. The Ad Seg count was completed without discrepancies.

Inmate Yeager's visit with Parsons in cell 237 was short as promised.

Lopez was still reading in his office when his phone rang. Lopez answered it. "Ad Seg Sergeant Lopez."

"Hey, Sarge, Villanueva. I have an inmate's family death notice for you to deliver."

Lopez sighed. "Okay, Lieu, let's have it."

Lopez wrote the information down and ended the call.

He stood up and walked over to the officer's station. King was sitting at the desk. Lopez searched the inmate picture board for inmate Brown's picture in cell 102.

King asked, "What's up, Sarge?"

"Got to give a family member death notice to Brown in 102. His father passed away."

King shook his head. "It's bad enough to be in prison, but to have family die while you're in here is really sad."

Lopez asked, "Could you get someone to go with you to tell Brown I'd like to see him, and bring him to my office? So I can give him the news."

"Sure, Sarge."

King stood up and went out to Reyes to have her go with him to get Brown.

Lopez went back to his office. He moved a chair across the desk from him. He turned the back of the chair facing the desk.

Shortly, King arrived with Brown. Lopez stood as he came in.

"Mr. Brown, could you have a seat?"

Lopez led Brown to the chair and had him straddle the chair. "Mr. Brown, I'm Sergeant Lopez. How you doing?"

"I'm good, Sarge. What's this about?"

Lopez's face twisted. "You're not in trouble, but I just got a call from my lieutenant. I'm sorry to say that he received a call from your aunt, Jan Weeks. She told him that your father passed away today at two thirty from congestive heart failure."

Lopez watched for Brown's reaction. Surprisingly, his reaction was subdued.

"Is there anything we can do for you right now? I know it's late tonight, but if you would like to make a call, we can do it now, or I can authorize one tomorrow morning."

Brown thought for a moment. "Dad was almost ninety. He wasn't in good health anyway. I expected it to happen."

"Would you like to talk to a clergy or church member?" Lopez offered.

"No, I'm all right. It's too late tonight, but I'd like to make a call tomorrow morning though."

Lopez said, "Okay, I'll set it up. You need anything?"

"No, thanks, Sarge," he said.

"You want to just sit here or talk?" Lopez asked. "It's okay. I'll go back to my cell," he said.

"Okay, if you're sure." Lopez added, "Officer King, how about you give him a sack lunch to take back to his cell...oh, and another for his cellie."

King nodded.

Brown stood up, and King escorted him out of the office. Lopez sat for a moment and rolled his chair over to the computer and opened up a file for a 128-B to document the death notice. He called the lieutenant and set up a phone call for Brown the following morning. He had Reyes note the death notice on the DAR and in Brown's file.

Shift change in Ad Seg from third to first watch was usually seamless. The control booth officer and only one officer replaced the entire floor staff in the unit.

This shift change was a little different tonight and possibly for a few more shift changes. The unit staff waited for Harrigan to get relieved, and they all left quickly.

Lopez greeted the remaining first watch officers and wished them well. He picked up his briefcase and lunch box and stepped into the sally port. The inside door closed and the outside door opened. Lopez stepped out and saw the crew waiting outside.

Vejar said, "Nick, you mind if we escort you out?" Lopez smiled and nodded.

ACADEMY POTPOURRI

Sergeants Mora and Flores walked past several cadets in the parking lot. When they reached their cars, they took their uniform shirts off and put them in their vehicles. Having been relieved, their shift was done. They wished each other a good night and got in their vehicles.

Several cadets hurried past the memorial and went in the double doors of the academy entrance. They were greeted by Sergeant Ron Fox at the front desk in the Watch Office.

They continued to the left and went into the hallway connecting the North Corridor and a large room called Glass Hall.

It was named such due to its prior use as a church structure replete with stained glass windows when it was a Catholic seminary. The ornate glass had been removed when the state acquired the site. The use was now as a training and exercise venue for cadets.

The cadets signed in on an electronic ID reader and exited into the North Corridor. They veered into the courtyard and continued to the South Corridor just as Outside Patrol (OP) Sergeant Darlene Gordon was approaching from the classroom hallway of the North Corridor. She turned to the left and stepped into the foyer and over to the Watch

Office. Sergeant Fox rolled his chair over to the door and turned the doorknob to let her into the office.

"Everything is secure. The doors at the west end of the South Corridor are still unlocked until the canteen closes," Gordon announced.

"You do great work, partner," Fox stated.

She nodded. "That's why I get the big bucks."

She went over to her lunch box and took out a soda and opened it. She took a drink and looked up at the TV monitors on the upper wall. Nothing of interest on the monitors caught her gaze. She went over to the left corner and sat in a chair.

The clock on the wall showed 2150 hours.

"I think that group of cadets was the last ones coming in.

Cutting it close, ten minutes to spare," she stated.

Fox scanned the monitors and added, "Yeah, hope all the kids are in, don't need any reports to write."

Gordon stood up and went over to a radio and tuned it to a country station, keeping the volume low. She went back and adjusted her holster to a more comfortable position and sat down.

Fox was on the computer typing in information on a DAR file.

The phone rang.

"Watch Sergeant, Fox," he stated.

He listened for a bit and said, "Thanks, Pat. Good night." Gordon asked, "That Pat from the canteen?"

"Yep, they're closed and headed home," Fox replied.

Gordon stretched out her shoulders. "Well, I guess I'll go lock the doors."

She stood up and opened the office door. As she started out, she saw a young woman coming from the North Corridor into the foyer. She wore a wrinkled brown blouse and shorts, obviously not a cadet.

Gordon stepped out of the office. "Can I help you, ma'am?" The woman seemed distraught.

"I...was raped," she whimpered.

Gordon went over to her. Gordon touched her arm and put her other hand on her back. She guided her over to a sofa chair.

"Here, sit down, miss." She eased her down. "When did this happen?" Gordon asked.

The girl sighed. "A little while ago."

"Where did it happen?" Gordon asked.

"A guy put me in a van and took me. He raped me and I got out of the van somehow."

"Where is the van?"

"It was on the road across the field." She pointed toward the field across from the academy, Christiansen Road.

"You were on the road and crossed the field?"

She nodded. "I came through the doors back there."

She motioned again toward the west side of the academy. Fox was standing in the office doorway.

"Is the guy still there?" Fox asked.

She shook her head and shrugged her shoulders. "I don't know."

"What's your name?" he asked.

"Julie Parks."

"Okay, Julie, are you injured or bleeding?" She shook her head, looking at the ground.

Gordon asked Fox, "Can you get Julie a blanket from the clothing room and I'll call Galt PD."

Fox nodded and left.

"Can you sit here for a moment?" Julie nodded.

Gordon went into the office and decided to call the PD on the phone, although she had a radio with a police channel.

Gordon related the assault and was advised that a unit was on the way.

Fox came back with two blankets and a pillow. Since Gordon was a female, he didn't want to startle Ms. Parks, so he gave Gordon the blankets to hand to Ms. Parks and put the pillow on the chair arm. Gordon wrapped the blankets around Parks and sat next to her, holding her hands.

Knowing investigation procedure and the concern about trauma and victim statements, Gordon refrained from asking more questions.

Fox turned the radio channel to the police channel and heard the dispatcher call a unit and listened until the unit arrived.

Gordon and Fox allowed the local police to take over the situation. The PD spent about forty-five minutes interviewing the girl until EMS arrived and evaluated her medically. EMS personnel found her suitable to transport, and the entourage left.

Fox called the Administrator of the Day (AOD) and related the incident, and Fox documented the incident. He and Gordon sat talking about the encounter for a while. The night fell into dawn with no further incident.

The next morning, Fox and Gordon were replaced by the morning crew: Sergeants Kaihe and Maloney.

Sergeant Rudolph came to the counter and gave Maloney a brass tag (chit), and Maloney promptly walked back to the key board and took a set of keys off a hook on the board and replaced it with the chit with Rudolph's name on it. He walked back to the counter and handed the keys to Rudolph. Rudolph turned and went back out to his car and drove around to the sergeant's modular. He retrieved his briefcase from his vehicle and walked into a modular and went to his desk and sat down.

Soon, Sergeant Weaver came into the modular. He saw Rudolph and went over to him. "You and me, Rudy, Tactical Simulator, huh?"

Rudolph nodded. "Yep, Uniform Company, you want A-Squad or B-Squad?"

Weaver said, "I'll take B-Squad."

"Okay. The schedule says lunch break is at 1130," Rudolph said. "All right, we got the plan." Weaver gave Rudolph a fist bump and left.

*****

Sergeant Jay walked up the three steps of the modular and unlocked the door. He went in and nodded to Sergeant Bettencourt sitting at a computer and walked around to the left. Jay continued to the corner of the unit and scanned the row of lesson plans on a shelf. He quickly found his target and snapped it out of line. He glanced around the modular and saw no one else. He walked back toward the exit and patted Bettencourt on the shoulder and said, "Hey, Bubba."

"Hey, T-Jay," Bettencourt replied without looking up.

Jay went out the door and down the steps. He made his way to the academy canteen and went over to the cold-tea dispenser and refilled his forever-present sixteen-ounce plastic container. He walked over to the clerk and placed a dollar on the counter. She smiled and took the dollar. Jay nodded and went out the door and walked down the ramp toward the academy building. He went through the double doors and into the hallway. He strolled past several classrooms and went into Echo Classroom. He walked around to the left to the front of the classroom and put his Use of Force (UOF) lesson plan on the podium and sat on a table in the corner by the windows. As he was forever early to class, he sipped some on his beverage and waited patiently for the cadets to filter in.

Cadets were supposed to be in their seats five minutes before the start of the class, which was usually impossible since they often didn't get released by the previous instructor on time. Jay was never a stickler on time constraints, but did appreciate his class starting at the top of the hour.

Jay nodded and responded to each cadet that noticed or spoke to him as they took their seats. Eventually, the class seemed ready to begin. The JCC (Junior Company commander), Cadet Singleton, looked around and said to Jay, "We're up, Sergeant."

Hearing the JCC, the cadets all stood to attention at their seats.

Jay stood at attention also.

THE JCC ANNOUNCED, "ECHO COMPANY ATTENTION, SOUND OFF."

The cadets delivered their motto, loudly.

"ECHO COMPANY! EXEMPLIFY! COMMAND! HONOR! OVERCOME! ECHO! HOOAH!"

Jay responded, "As you were!" The cadets sat down.

Jay took a long look around the room. There were five rows of four tables across and a separation between the four tables. Two cadets sat at each table.

"Welcome to Use of Force," Jay announced.

He casually walked down the center of the room, looking side to side. He made a point to engage eye contact with each cadet and studying each cadet. When he reached the back row, he paused and scanned the class and walked casually back to the front of the room. He strolled back over to the table by the windows and sat on the table. "I'm Sergeant Jay. You may call me Sergeant T-Jay during class and in our personal conversations."

He took a deliberate breath.

"During this class I hope to get to know more about each of you, your life experience and your decision-making process."

He paused. "But for now, I'm going to assume that you know nothing about the CDC Use of Force policy. So...I will give you a short version of the policy."

He looked around the room.

"You may use force that is reasonable and necessary to control, overcome, or stop a threat to you or another person from injury or prevent escape. There are various types of actions or force that the CDC identifies: verbal persuasion and orders, physical strength and holds, handheld batons, chemical agents, launched rubber rounds, and projectiles from a weapon, such as a Mini-14. Don't confuse 'types' of force with 'levels' of force. That implies steps from one level to the next. Depending on the situation, you may select and use any available action or force to stop the threat."

Jay paused and walked to the back of the classroom. The cadets followed his movement.

He continued, "Although it is preferred, when feasible, it is not necessary to give a warning before using force. The force you use need not be equal to that used by the perpetrator, but should be sufficient to stop the threat."

He walked back to the center of the classroom.

"Be advised, when you use force, you will be judged by the standard of what a trained competent officer would do given the same circumstances. The key legal term you need to remember is 'reasonable.' We'll cover that later."

He walked back to the front of the classroom and went back to the table in the corner and sat on it.

"For now, I want to put each of you in a yard-gun position, a six-by-ten structure attached to the side of a building, thirty feet off the ground. On the floor of the structure are two narrow heavy glass ports that can be opened to allow you access to the area below you, in case you want to throw something or shoot at someone. There are several windows that give you full view of the area below you, a yard exercise area of about sixty yards wide and one hundred fifty yards long."

He paused again.

"You have available to you various equipment that you may use to notify someone or to stop some inappropriate or violent act."

He eased off the table and went to the front of the class.

"Let's see…how about I give you a public address mic, a handheld radio with a mic attached. Let's give you a 40 mm launcher that discharges three hard rubber inch-and-a-half projectiles to an effective distance of about forty feet. Or as an option, you can put a chemical agent round in the 40 mm launcher that discharges three small chemical agent canisters to about, oh, maybe eighty feet. Also, I will give you several handheld chemical agent canisters to throw." Jay paused. "And lastly, I will give you a Mini-14 with three .223 thirty-round magazines."

He looked around the room.

"Oh, and some of you will need a toilet and sink and maybe a pair of handcuffs. Don't know why you need the cuffs, but you may want to get kinky." Some cadets laughed.

Jay smiled, took a few steps forward, and began his soliloquy. "Okay, you're in the tower. There are three yard officers at the far end of the yard. There are ten inmates on the yard about sixty-feet in front of you. Each of the inmates pulls out a ten-inch knife and begins stabbing each other."

He tossed his hands urgently back and forth and looked around the room asking the class, "Whatcha gonna do?"

He approached several cadets at different tables, enticing an answer from someone.

A few cadets said, "Shoot!"

Jay said in urgency, "Shoot? No warning?"

A cadet replied, "You said you didn't need to give a warning." Jay turned to him and said, "You're right."

Jay took a breath and walked to the front of the class and turned around to face the class.

"How about you yell out, 'Stop, get down,' or get on the radio and notify the officers on the yard, or get on the PA and announce there is an emergency. How about firing the rubber rounds at them or shooting the chemical agents at them or toss some handheld chemical agent canisters down at them."

Jay paused and took a couple of steps toward the center of the classroom.

"But, you're right, you don't have to give a warning, but you could do any of the things I mentioned and one of them may stop the incident."

Jay shook his head and wrinkled his face.

"How about a warning shot? Anybody want to fire a warning shot?"

He looked around, and a few cadets raised their hands.

"You can fire a warning shot if the circumstances warrant the use of deadly force, but you need to shoot in a place that would not hit or ricochet and injure anyone else."

Jay walked back to the front of the classroom.

"Now let's talk about your obligation as a correctional officer. You are sworn to prevent escapes and protect life, that includes inmates."

Jay paused in thought.

"Let's get back to the inmates stabbing each other. Let's fire a warning shot into the soft dirt off to one side. They don't stop. Another warning shot, they don't stop…enough with the warning shots. Now, you have to fire for effect. You *are* going to shoot, but which one you going to shoot?"

Options offered by the cadets ranged from the closest one, the one stabbing the most, to keep shooting inmates until they stop.

Jay listened to the choices, paused, and looked around the classroom, shaking his head slowly.

Finally, a few cadets asked, "Which one do *you* shoot, Sergeant?"

Jay took a breath. "It doesn't matter which one you shoot. *You* took the shot, and you probably took a life. *You* chose who to kill."

Jay wrinkled his face and brows and said earnestly, "I don't envy that responsibility you will have. But if that is a position you are put in and you don't think you can take the shot...this job is not for you."

Jay spoke deliberately in a metered pattern, "You have to be able to take the shot."

Jay walked back over to the corner table by the windows, picked up his beverage, and sat on the table. He took a drink.

"Ten-minute break."

Sergeant Jay waited for most of the cadets to leave the room. He blended in with the last few cadets out the door. He walked down the North Corridor toward the west doors and exited toward the academy canteen.

He met Sergeant Rudolph coming out of the canteen door. "Hey, Rudy, what's up?"

Rudolph gave him a fist bump and a quick bro hug. "Just heading over to Tac-Sim with Uniform Company." Jay smiled. "Yeah? I had them for Use of Force Tuesday."

"We'll see how much they absorbed," Rudolph stated.

Jay took a fist bump, and Rudolph headed for the tactical simulator classroom.

The tactical simulator is a canned video with interactive scenarios. The sergeant operator selects the scenario and has a cadet make decisions based on an inmate's actions. During the scenario, the sergeant chooses the branch or reaction the inmate takes depending on the words and actions the cadet uses.

The choices available to the cadet are explained before each scenario. The choices are always a Use of Force option: verbal persuasion and orders, physical strength and holds, baton, chemical agents, or deadly force shoot or don't shoot.

Sergeant Rudolph sat in the darkened room, operating the computer-controlled tactical simulator named Milo. He chose the next cadet to participate.

"Cadet Lindsey. Front and center."

There were whoops and encouraging chants from the group.

Lindsey was given options of the types of force available in the scenario and a brief statement about the scenario.

The video started, and it showed two inmates standing by a table arguing. One inmate, Berry, threatened to cut the other inmate. Lindsey verbally intervened and got inmate Berry's focus on him.

The other inmate left the scene, and Berry was agitated and displayed a knife at his side. Cadet Lindsey pressed his alarm button and told the inmate to put the knife down. Lindsey put his hand on his baton but didn't draw it. He calmly engaged Berry in conversation. Sergeant Rudolph watched and listened to the interaction. Lindsay used words that seemed to deescalate the tension, and Rudolph selected the inmate's reaction to comply. The inmate dropped the weapon and followed Lindsey's orders and submitted to restraints. Rudolph stopped the scenario and discussed it with Lindsey. He noted Lindsey's calming interaction and that he didn't immediately use physical force or chemical agents.

Applause was delivered by his classmates.

Rudolph looked over his list and selected the next cadet. "Cadet Frazier, your turn."

Again, there was encouragement offered from the group.

As usual, Rudolph went over the force options and stated that the scenario was set as an inmate transport to an outside hospital.

Rudolph advised Frazier that he had options of using a baton, spraying chemical agents, or using his firearm.

Rudolph began the video showing an inmate had two doctors cornered in a room, shouting at them. Frazier asked the inmate to calm down. The inmate turned toward Frazier and displayed a knife and pointed it at Frazier. Frazier drew his firearm, pointed it at the inmate, and told the inmate to drop the weapon. The inmate didn't comply. Frazier again told the inmate to drop the knife.

Rudolph noted that Frazier's choice of force was an acceptable option and the doctors were not in the line of fire.

Rudolph observed intently, Frazier's words, body language, and tone of voice. Rudolph decided not to escalate the inmate's actions and waited for more of Frazier's verbal interaction.

Frazier again told the inmate to drop the knife and shouted the order two more times immediately after the first order.

Rudolph felt that there were no calming words or discussion coming from Frazier, so Rudolph selected the option for the inmate to turn toward the doctors and raise the knife and move toward the doctors with the knife.

Frazier fired his weapon, twice, and the screen reacted to the shot placements, and the inmate fell to the floor.

As Rudolph prepared to stop the scenario, Frazier paused for about two seconds and shot two more times at the inmate on the floor in the video.

"There, stay down, asshole," Frazier said in a stern tone of voice. Rudolph froze the video. Some gasps and soft chuckles were heard from the class. Rudolph took a breath and thought for a moment.

"Okay, why don't we take a break? Frazier, you can stay, please." The cadets stood and filtered out of the classroom.

Frazier quickly removed the equipment he had donned for the scenario.

The video was yet frozen. Rudolph stood and went over to Frazier.

"Cadet Frazier, I want to go over the scenario with you."

"Okay, Sergeant," Frazier said quickly as he stood at attention. "At the end of the scenario, you seemed to stop talking to the inmate, why was that?" Rudolph asked.

"He wouldn't drop the knife, so I had to shoot," he said quickly.

Rudolph noted the anxiety in Frazier's voice and his rapid breathing, almost hyperventilating.

Rudolph sighed and said, "After he was down, why did you shoot him two more times?"

Frazier said quickly, "I had to make sure he didn't get up." Rudolph looked at Frazier and nodded slowly. "Thank you, Frazier. You can go now."

"Thank you, Sergeant," he said and quickly left the room.

Rudolph sat down and took a deep breath. He went over to the phone on the wall and dialed.

"LT, I need to talk to you. Are you available at 1130?" He paused.

"It's about a cadet." Again there was a pause. "Okay, I'll see you then."

Sergeant Rudolph sighed deeply and left the room.

*****

Rudolph knocked on the Program II lieutenant's door.

Lieutenant Porter called out, "Come in." Rudolph went in. "Morning, LT."

Porter answered, "Good morning, Sarge, what's up with your cadet?"

Rudolph sat down and handed Porter a sheet of paper.

Porter read the report and then asked Rudolph to tell him what happened.

Rudolph began, "I was instructing Uniform Company in Tac-Sim, and Cadet Frazier was given a scenario for assessment. I wrote down some of the details of the scenario. I don't necessarily have any issue with his handling of the scenario. It was an inmate threatening medical staff with a knife at an outside hospital. It had several options of Use of Force, including deadly force. As the scene developed, Frazier's actions led to a need to stop a possible deadly assault. Frazier chose to shoot the inmate twice. At that point, I felt his choice was justified, but other options could have been addressed. However, after he shot the inmate, he paused for a second or two, and shot the inmate two more times, saying, 'There, stay down, asshole.' I had the class take a break. I asked Frazier why he shot the inmate after he was down, and he said something like, 'I wanted to make sure he didn't get up.' I have to also say that Frazier seemed anxious and hyper after the scenario. I don't know his background, but his actions cause me concern for his suitability as a correctional officer."

Lieutenant Porter listened carefully and reread the report

Rudolph had given him. Porter said, "I see your concern. I'll talk this over with the disciplinary lieutenant and the captain. We'll see where this goes. Thank you for bringing this to me. I'll get back to you."

Rudolph stood up and said, "Okay, LT, thanks for listening."

*****

Sergeant Jay returned to his classroom and methodically impressed the Use of Force lesson plan into each of his cadets. Eight hours of intense questions and answers revealed Jay's passion for instruction. At the end of the course, Jay administered the thirty-question exam and gave the cadets a fifteen-minute break. When they returned, Jay went over each question on the test and explained the correct answers.

*****

A few days later, Jay was called into the lieutenant's office. He knocked on the door, and a voice from within said, "Yes, come in."

Jay went in, and Lieutenant Sherry said, "Good morning, T-Jay, have a seat."

Jay did as asked. "What's up, Lieu?"

Sherry picked up a paper and said, "I have a report here that brought a concern about a Use of Force class you taught the other day."

Jay asked, "Which one?"

"Echo Company."

"Yes, I taught that company."

"The report says that you gave them the test, and then at the end of the class, you went over the questions and gave them the answers."

Jay nodded. "Yes, Lieu, that's right. I've always gone over the answers to the Use of Force test with the cadets."

Sherry asked, "Who told you to do that?"

Jay replied, "I don't know if any specific person said to do it. When I was certified some years ago in Use of Force, it was something that was done to ensure the cadets knew the right answers."

Sherry said, "You know that if a cadet fails the test, they have to take a retest, don't you?"

"Yes, sir, I know that," Jay replied.

"That sort of defeats the integrity of the testing process, doesn't it?" Sherry asked.

Jay raised his brows. "I don't really see it that way, Lieu."

"Why do you say that?" Sherry asked.

Jay explained, "How important is Use of Force training? I believe it is the most important training at the academy. If a cadet gets the wrong information, then they can be held liable as can the department by extension."

Sherry questioned, "And that's why we train them, isn't it?" Jay seemed confused. He thought for a moment.

"Okay, Lieu, let's go down a hypothetical-thought rabbit hole." Jay settled in his seat.

"I instructed a Use of Force class to Echo Company. I go over all of the material perfectly and give the test at the end of the class. One cadet fails the course because he missed four questions. Does testing tell that cadet which questions he missed?"

Sherry replied, "I don't think they do." Jay affirmed, "No, they don't."

Sherry said, "So?"

Jay continued, "The cadet studies for the retest and passes the retest. Does testing tell the cadet his score?"

Sherry said, "I don't think so, it just says he passed."

"You're right, Lieu, it only shows he passed," Jay reaffirmed.

Sherry asserted, "Okay, the cadet passed, the process worked without impugning the integrity of the testing process."

"Really, Lieu?"

Jay took a breath and forged ahead.

"The cadet graduates and is assigned to a perimeter gun position. He sees four minimum inmates working near the state vehicle parking area. One inmate decides to take a hammer and starts to break the windows in a vacant transportation bus. Two of the other inmates start fist-fighting with no weapons visible. The other inmate begins to run toward the minimum unit and begins to climb the fence that goes into the minimum unit compound."

Jay stopped and asked, "Do any of these actions warrant the use of deadly force?"

Sherry replied, "No."

Jay was relieved at his response. "Good, Lieu, you passed. But the new officer shoots the inmate breaking windows in the bus for excessive property damage. The officer also shoots one of the inmates fist-fighting to stop the fight. And finally, the officer shoots the inmate trying to escape by climbing the fence into the minimum unit."

Jay paused. "Was he wrong? Should he be held liable?" Sherry said, "Certainly."

Jay replied with a slow, "Okay," and continued.

"So the officer gets fired and the state gets sued, and the officer decides to include me in the suit, for insufficient training. I am called to testify, since I trained the cadet on Use of Force. His lawyer cites 'insufficient training' as the reason for the shooting. Seems that the officer passed the course, although the three questions the officer got wrong were not to use deadly force to stop property damage, unless it presents a likelihood of death or escape; stop altercations that do not present a threat of death or GBI; and climbing a fence that is not a risk of escape. The officer never was told what questions the officer got wrong and the reason the answers were wrong."

Jay summarized, "If the cadet had been given the correct answers or, better yet, explained the reasoning behind the answers, then there might not have been such an incident or, at least, the state and I would have a defense."

Jay looked at the lieutenant. "I, LT, have a defense." Jay paused.

"If we want to avoid such a bizarre scenario, then we have to rethink our testing process, at least for the most critical training aspect, Use of Force. If I am to stop giving the answers after the test, I will do so, but I will apprise *all* cadets that after all testing is done, I will take *my* time to give them the correct answers and explain the reasoning."

Jay finished, "So, LT, I await your decision." Lieutenant Sherry sat for a moment.

"Okay, T-Jay. You've made your case. I'll have to get with testing and the administrator and get back to you."

Jay smiled and nodded to Sherry. "Thanks, LT."

Jay stood up, turned, and left.

*****

The selection process while a cadet attends the academy is ongoing. Any conduct, good or bad, is subject to documentation by all staff at the academy, uniformed or not. On-site activities and off-site personal activities are always subject to scrutiny. After several weeks of investigation and interviews, Cadet Frazier was deemed unacceptable as a correctional officer candidate. In the end, Cadet Frazier was rejected on probation.

FROM TOWER 9 TO PITCHIN' 'N' CATCHIN' AND CAUGHT

Central Control Sergeant Gonzales finished correcting numbers on the institutional count board. Officer Ken Sosa nodded to Sergeant Gonzales that he was ready.

"Be right there, Ken," Gonzales said.

Gonzales went into the armory room of Central Control. He prepared and logged out the equipment for Officer Ken Sosa. Sosa collected his weapons and munitions and put the weapons in one canvas bag and the munitions in a separate bag.

Gonzales went to a panel and pushed a button, and a grill door popped open.

"Don't use up all the ammo while you're up there, I'll charge you extra if I have to send someone up to resupply."

"I thought I was getting credit for the ammo I brought back," Ken quipped.

Gonzales replied, "You do, but I have to pay overtime for the extra delivery."

Ken chuffed. "I'll pay you two soups for your trouble."

"Not top ramen again," Gonzalez whined.

Ken slung his canvas bag of weapons onto his shoulder, leaving the munitions bag, and stepped into the stairway. Gonzales closed the grill door behind him. Ken walked up the steps, and Gonzales pushed another button, and the lock on the door at the top of the stairs buzzed, and Ken pushed it open. He stepped outside onto the roof and closed the door. He turned left, walked on a walkway past several windows in the top edges of buildings, and made a right turn up a slight incline toward his assigned post, Yard Observation

Tower 9. He unlocked and opened the door of the small six-by-eight wooden structure and stepped in and closed the door. He sat his bag against a wall and took out a Mini-14 and sat it in rack on a shelf facing the three windows overlooking the main yard. He took out a 37 mm launcher and sat it in a holder near the Mini-14. He unsnapped his holster and drew his .38 S&W and rechecked that it was loaded. He rechecked his two speed-loaders on his duty belt that they were also loaded. The handgun was carried for self-protection from an unplanned attack while en route to and in the tower. He looked out the windows onto the yard. He turned around and looked out a port in the door and saw Officer Cruz coming toward him with the canvass bag of munitions.

Cruz handed the bag through the door port. "Here ya go, Sosa."

"Thanks, Cruz," Sosa replied.

"Be safe," Cruz said.

"Will do," Sosa replied as Cruz turned and left.

The normal manning of gun positions has the weapons brought first to the gun position and then the munitions, keeping the two separate and unusable without the other.

Sosa sat the bag on the table and took out the three thirty-round .223 magazines. He placed two magazines in a holder on the shelf. He inserted the other magazine into the Mini-14 and sat it back on the shelf. He took out six 37 mm rounds and sat five in a holder on the shelf. He placed the remaining rubber bullet round into the 37 mm launcher and sat the launcher on the shelf with the breach yet open.

He placed the last of the munitions, four chemical agent CS (orthochlorobenzalmalononitrile) canisters on the shelf in their holder. He surveyed the room and equipment one last time. He keyed his radio.

"Yard Sergeant, Tower 9 is up."

In the yard shack below Tower 9 off to the left, Yard Sergeant Rawlinson keyed his radio and replied, "Copy, Tower 9."

The recreation officers disseminated to their assigned areas on the two-hundred-by-three-hundred-yard-wide exercise yard.

Rawlinson keyed his radio.

"Program 1, Program 2, mainline yard is open."

The program sergeants both replied, "Program 1 copies," "Program 2 copies."

The housing units systematically released their inmates in an orderly manner. They filtered into the hallways and eventually out to the yard. Tower 9 was placed on the edge of a building, thirty feet above the yard, directly overlooking the entrance gate into the mainline yard. Across from Tower 9 was a wall of a building that contained an inmate canteen and a large inmate dormitory, Z-Dorm.

The inmates emerged onto the yard through a gate into a paved area between Tower 9 and Z-Dorm and then out to the yard.

Ken watched the yard movement and the staff interacting with the inmates. Occasionally, he decided to step out of the tower and onto the roof that had a waist-high fence at its edge, and he would continue his observations. About ninety minutes into his shift, Sosa scanned the yard, and some quick movement caught his attention. A black inmate quickly ran toward a white inmate, directly below Sosa's position, Tower 9. The black inmate approached the left side of the white inmate and hit him in the left neck area with his right fist. The white inmate fell down to the ground.

Sosa unslung his Mini-14 and racked a round into the chamber as he yelled out, "Yard down!"

The black inmate retreated away from Tower 9 toward the opposing wall. Sosa raised his weapon and held it up at a forty-five-degree angle and, with his left hand, pointed above the inmates head. "Get down! Get down!"

The inmate, wearing blue jeans and a medium gray sweatshirt, looked up at Sosa and slid along the wall toward the yard. Sosa continued to point and yell, "Get down! Get down."

The entire yard was following the instructions from Sosa and other staff to get on the ground. The inmate continued looking at Sosa as he went over to the end of the building to a cyclone fence, reached up to the top of the fence, then turned and sat down between two other black inmates, also wearing similar gray sweatshirts. Sosa kept constant eye contact with the inmate and pointed at him, yelling, "That's him, that's him."

He heard staff getting closer and asking, "Where? Is this him?"

Officer Sosa kept pointing and yelling, "Over there, that inmate."

Eventually, Sergeant Rawlinson came to the correct inmate, and Sosa said, "That's him."

The staff cuffed and took control of the inmate. Sosa kept watch over his immediate area and looked down at the inmate that had been attacked. Sosa saw blood on the ground next to the victim. He kept watch until medical staff removed the downed inmate.

The yard was eventually cleared, and Sosa returned to the tower building. He removed the magazine from the Mini-14 and unloaded the live round from the chamber. He loaded the round back into the magazine. Officer Patton came up to relieve him from his post. He went back down the walkways and back to the door entering Central Control. He pushed a button near the door, and soon the door lock popped, and he pulled it open and went down to Control. He made his way back into the institution and into the Watch Office. Watch Commander Lieutenant Logan saw Sosa come in.

"Sosa, good job out there."

"Thanks, LT," Sosa said. "Guess I'll get a form and write my report."

The lieutenant pulled open a drawer and pulled out a couple of papers and handed them to Sosa.

"You want to write it here?" Logan asked.

"That's okay. I'll go out to the admin lunchroom," Sosa replied. Logan nodded. "Okay."

Sosa went out of the Watch Office and made his way past Central Control and exited through the North Gate and south door entrance into the administration building. He turned right then left into the lunchroom. He got a soda out of a machine and sat down. He began to write his recollection of the incident.

When he finished, he reread the report and was satisfied with his account. He took the report back to the Watch Office and gave it to Lieutenant Logan. Logan read it over and said, "Looks good, Sosa. Again, good job."

Sosa said, "Thanks, LT."

He left the Watch Office and headed down the North Corridor toward D-Wing. He walked past a few inmates, and one of them said to Sosa, "Hey, eagle eye."

He thought to himself for that to mean the inmates knew he identified the right inmate involved in the assault. Sosa was pleased with himself.

Sosa stepped into the D-Wing sally port, and Officer Mimilis was up above on the unit panel, opening and closing cell doors and watching Officer Farner, who was on the tier with several inmates, locking them back into their cells from returning from the mainline yard. Sosa let himself into the officer's station to the right and set down his lunch container. He quickly went out onto the first tier, opening and closing grill gates as he went. He went up to an inmate standing in front of cell 106.

"This your house?" Sosa asked. The inmate nodded.

"Show me your ID."

The inmate gave him his ID. "What's your cellie's name?"

"Jackson," he said.

Sosa took out his keys and unlocked and slid open the cell door. Another inmate was in the cell.

He asked the inmate, "What's your name?"

"Jackson," he said.

"What's your cellie's name?"

"Harper," was his answer.

Sosa looked at the ID, and it matched the name the inmate gave him. He let Harper in the cell and closed it.

Sosa continued a similar process, putting inmates back into their cells. If he recognized the inmate at the cell door as being the one that lived, there he would signal Mimilis to open the cell door and let them in, and Sosa would close it. Sosa noticed several inmates in the sally port waiting to come into the unit. He went over to the grill gate and opened it.

"You guys come in and step over to the left for a moment," Sosa said.

The inmates did as directed. Sosa closed the gate. "Okay, go stand in front of your cell door," he ordered.

The inmates strolled down the tier, some going up the stairs to the second or third tier.

Finally, the crew finished locking up the returning inmates. Farner came down from the third tier and met Sosa on the first tier.

"That was a cluster fuck. Yard recall in the middle of showers and laundry exchange," Farner exclaimed.

Sosa smiled, and they both went back to the officer's station and joined Mimilis as he came down the internal stairs from the control panel. They each settled down into one of the chairs and took a collective breath.

"What the hell happened on the yard?" Mimilis asked. "Someone got stuck," Farner said.

Mimilis happened to think. He looked at Sosa and asked, "Hey, Sosa, what you doing back from Tower 9 so early?"

Sosa smirked. "I had to write my Part B report."

"What for? You see something?" Farner asked.

Sosa slowly nodded. "Yeah, a guy got stuck right below my tower."

"It's your fault they closed the yard down." Farner chuckled. "Didn't hear any gunshots," Mimilis said.

"Nope, no need. Didn't see the weapon," Sosa added.

Sosa recounted his part in the incident and took ribbing from his partners. They sat for a while, digesting the incident.

Inmate Barnes stepped into the sally port. Sosa said, "Barnes, where you coming from?" Farner interceded, "He was on a visit."

Sosa said, "Okay, since it was my fault the yard came back, you lazy asses just sit and relax. I'll let Barnes into his house."

Sosa stood up and opened the necessary grill gates and followed Barnes over to his cell. He unlocked the door and slid it open. He looked into the cell. He held his hand up to stop Barnes from entering.

"Barnes, have a seat at the table over there," Sosa said, pointing to a far table.

Sosa called out to his partners. "Hey, guys, you gotta see this." Mimilis said, "Can't you put him in by yourself?"

Sosa stretched his face out in consternation. "I'll probably need your help to sort this out."

Farner asked, "What now?"

"Just come see for yourselves," Sosa said.

Curiosity pulled the two out of their chairs and over to the cell door. They stopped at the door and looked into the cell.

Two inmates sat sheepishly on the lower bunk and yet another stood next to them.

Farner exclaimed, "Sosa, you're fuckin' bad luck today." Mimilis put his hand on Sosa's back and said, "Yep, I agree."

Farner called into the cell, "Okay, guys, step out and have a seat at this table." He pointed to an empty table.

They complied and sat down. "IDs please," Farner said.

Mimilis collected the IDs.

Farner said, "I know Taylor is assigned to this cell, but why are you two—" Farner stopped his thought.

Mimilis looked at the inmates' IDs and said, "Burris, you live in 222, and, Kelso, you're supposed to be in 302."

Sosa asked, "I don't guess anyone wants to explain why you are all in a two-man cell when only one of you is assigned to it."

No one said a word, as expected.

Farner chuckled. "Sosa, you found them, you get to do the write-ups."

Sosa nodded. "Just what I need, more report writing practice."
Sosa said, "Okay, guys, unless anyone was assaulted, I guess
Kelso and Burris are out of bounds."

Mimilis said, "Taylor, Barnes, back in your house. Barnes, you
might wanna get some clean sheets."

The two stepped into the cell, and Mimilis closed it. Mimilis said,
"Kelso, Burris, go stand at your doors."

Sosa and Mimilis followed the two to their cells and put them in,
checking to make sure there would be no more than two in their cell.

They came back down the stairs and joined Farner. The trio
walked back toward the officer's station.

Farner began rambling, "Aren't you gonna ask who was pitchin'
and who was catchin'? It probably was a three-way...yeah, all three at
once. Mimilis, how's that work?"

Mimilis said, "Don't ask me, you're the expert." Sosa shook his
head and continued walking.

Farner continued to expand his imagined physical positions of
an all-male three-way encounter. Mimilis and Sosa tried to ignore the
onslaught, until Mimilis remembered that he yet had a few laundry
bags to hand out and some to deliver to laundry.

He went over to a storage closet and opened the door. He pulled
out several netted bags of laundry and sorted the incoming from the
outgoing.

"Hey, Sosa, I've got some laundry to hand out and some to take to
laundry. You wanna hand these out or take those to laundry?

Sosa answered, "I'll hand out the incoming."

"Okay, I'll take these to laundry. I need a break from Farner's
'three-way' diatribe."

Mimilis laughed. He picked up the three bags and went out the
sally port into the West Corridor. He ambled past C-wing and the
infirmary and continued to Center Corridor. He stopped to talk to
Center Corridor Officer Paul for a moment and then turned left down
North Corridor. He stopped at the laundry entrance door and knocked
on it loudly, as there was normally a lot of noise in the laundry complex.
Soon, a staff member slid open a viewing port and opened the door.

Mimilis stepped in and headed over to the supervisor's office. He set the bags on a counter and spoke to the laundry supervisor, Blake.

"Hey, Blake, here are some leftover bags from D-Wing."

"Thanks, I'll put them in the bin in the corner." Mimilis picked them up and said, "I'll put them in it."

As he swung the bags to toss, he saw a letter in one of the bags. He stopped his swing and set the bags down. He opened up the bag and pulled out a letter addressed but with no return address on it. The letter was sealed.

Prison mail has to be unsealed with both addresses to and from. It is to be sent to the mail room to be read then sealed and mailed by the institutional mail system. This letter was circumventing the process. He showed it to Blake.

"This is not good," Blake said. "Where'd this come from?"

"D-Wing, outgoing laundry," Mimilis said.

"Seems like someone is trying to send mail out through someone here in laundry," Blake said.

"Yeah, seems like it. I'll check the other bags," Mimilis said.

He opened the other bags and found no other letters. He put on some gloves and picked up the letter.

Mimilis noted the cell number on the bag, D-225u.

"I don't recall who lives in 225, but I'm sure ISU [Investigative Services Unit] will be interested."

Mimilis sighed. "I guess ISU is my next stop."

Blake nodded. "Okay, I'll check and see who was supposed to pick up the mail in D-Wing and let them know."

Mimilis didn't want to open the letter as that might disturb any prints or evidence. He nodded to Blake and left.

He made his way out to the administration building and went down some stairs into the ISU office.

He gave the letter to ISU Sergeant Reyes and apprised him of the situation. Reyes said he would handle it from there.

Mimilis smiled and left.

When he got back to D-Wing, he went over to Sosa and grinned. Sosa noticed the grin and lack of words.

"What?" he asked.

"Shoulda let you go to laundry."

"Why?"

"When I took the laundry bags back, I found a letter in one of the bags. It was sealed and had no return address," Mimilis explained.

Sosa squinted. "Whose bag was it?"

"225 upper."

Mimilis and Sosa looked up on the ID board and found the name of the inmate assigned to cell 225 upper.

They both nodded. Sosa said, "Castillo."

"Blake, the laundry super said he would check his roster and find out who was scheduled to pick up the laundry," Mimilis relayed. "But I saw Foster drop off laundry today, but he didn't finish picking up all of the outgoing laundry because we had to shut the unit down when *you* caused the problem on the yard," Mimilis said with a chuckle.

Sosa smiled. "So it's all my fault?"

Mimilis shrugged his shoulders. "I'm just sayin'."

Mimilis chuckled and picked up the institutional phone directory. He thumbed through it. He picked up the phone and dialed the laundry.

Blake answered the phone. "Laundry, Blake."

"Hey, Blake, Mimilis here. Did you check to see who was supposed to pick up laundry for D-Wing?"

Blake replied, "Allison was supposed to do it, but Foster said he would make the run instead."

"Is that normal for someone to choose a specific run?" Mimilis asked.

Blake replied, "Now that you ask, I remember Foster wanting to make a lot of the laundry runs."

"Sounds suspicious now, after finding that letter," Mimilis added.

"Sure does," Blake replied.

"Well, I think ISU will want us to bug out of the investigation, but this info will put them on the right track," Mimilis said.

"Yeah, I think you're right. I'll just let them handle it," Blake replied.

"Okay, talk to you later," Mimilis said and hung up the phone. Sosa said, "Sounds like something suspicious going on."

"Yeah, he said Foster tries to get most of the laundry pickups in the units," Mimilis related.

Sosa added, "I heard you suggest that we do nothing and let ISU handle their business so we don't screw it up."

Mimilis nodded. "We think that's the best way to handle it, but we can still keep a close watch on both of them."

Sosa said, "Copy that."

*****

A couple of months later, Sosa received notification that he was to attend a pretrial conference with the DA.

He dutifully showed up at the appointed time and place wearing his Class A uniform. He was asked to recount his observations and actions while working in Tower 9 during the incident on the yard.

During the discourse, he was asked, "When you were pointing at the inmate and shouting at him, what were the other staff members doing?"

Sosa replied, "I don't know what they were doing, but I could hear several voices asking if they were near the inmate or if the one they were next to was the perpetrator."

"Did you look at the officers asking the questions?" one questioner asked.

"No, I didn't want to take my eyes off *my* inmate. He was knelt down between two other black inmates wearing similar gray sweatshirts. I didn't want to lose sight of him in case he ran around the corner of the fence to the yard."

"When did you take your eyes off the inmate?" he was asked.

Sosa replied, "When I saw Sergeant Rawlinson touch the inmate's shoulder and I confirmed that he had the right inmate and he put him in restraints."

"Did you know the inmate before the incident?" he was asked.

"I may have had contact with him, but I don't recall where or when," Sosa said. "I didn't know his name or the name of the inmate he assaulted until the next day." Sosa paused. "I heard that his name was Harris, and the inmate he assaulted, Garrett, was jabbed in the neck with a sharpened piece of angle iron that nicked his carotid artery. I understand inmate Garrett recovered."

"Why didn't you shoot at or shoot Mr. Harris when he attacked inmate Garrett?"

Sosa replied, "I didn't see a weapon. I understand now that Harris had dropped it over the fence behind him and that it was discovered during a search of the area."

The fact finders seemed satisfied and relented with no further questions asked.

Sosa left the room and went home.

A few days later, Sosa was called into the Watch Office and given a letter of recognition for his actions that day and for making the identification of the perpetrator.

Subsequently, the attorneys for Harris accepted a plea for "assault with a deadly weapon on a prisoner."

*****

The investigation of the letter in the laundry bag revealed several inmates were giving the noncustody laundry worker, Foster, letters and having him mail them out in exchange for pay from the inmate's families. Foster and other inmates were found guilty of circumventing institutional mail policy. Foster was fired, and the inmates received increased sentences.

The stabbing incident at Tower 9 led to the discovery of two other illegal acts. Surely, one thing often leads to another.

EL PÁJARO CANTOR

Sergeant Dave Willey approached the unique main entrance to the institution. Two large sliding cyclone gates and two smaller pedestrian (ped) gates served as a sally port entrance. The large gates were wide enough to accommodate a fire truck, and the entire sally port fence structure was fifteen feet high.

They were controlled by an officer in Tower 1 adjacent to the sally port.

Willey waited at the west-side ped-gate (pedestrian gate) for the Big East vehicle sally port gate to finish sliding closed. The staff went to work checking out the van that had just come through it. One officer was inspecting the inside of the vehicle and under the hood for contraband and unauthorized inmates. Another officer made her way down some stairs into a pit the van had straddled over, also checking the underside for contraband and inmates. Officer Casey waited in the booth in the sally port for an all-clear from the other officers. When the security check was completed, he called up to Tower 1 above, "Open Big West and West ped-gate."

Willey heard the lock snap on the gate and pulled it open and closed it behind him. He went over to an opening in the booth.

He sat his lunch box on the counter and handed Casey his ID. Casey looked at it and handed it back to Willey. Willey opened his lunch box, and Casey glanced into it.

"Thanks, Willey." Casey called up to Tower 1, "East ped-gate."

"Have a good day, Casey," Willey said as he closed his lunch box and turned and walked toward the ped-gate. He saw Officer Woodard coming away from the stairs out of the pit.

"Hey, Woodard," he said.

She nodded and replied, "Hey, Sarge."

Willey continued to the ped-gate and timed his exit with the opening of the gate. He turned to the left and scanned the expanse of a building to his right that contained the warehouse and other plant operations facilities. He walked past a large opened gate and made his way to B-Yard entrance. He looked through a window in the door, into the control room, and saw several staff waiting for the other sally port door to open. Momentarily, the waiting staff exited into B-Complex. The door in front of Willey slid open, and he walked through up to the control booth and handed his ID to the officer through an open port. The officer looked at it and handed it back. The B-Complex door slid open, and Willey stepped out onto B-Yard.

The yard was rather large, maybe two hundred yards wide and two hundred yards long. There were perhaps two hundred inmates on the yard taking advantage of a fine spring afternoon. The center of the yard offered a grass-covered field, with room for baseball and soccer, surrounded by a running track. On the far sides were two paved areas for basketball and tennis. The complex was enclosed on all sides by walls and buildings. Two of the buildings at the far end contained two housing units in each building. The buildings on the left side contained indoor recreational facilities and several offices and religious offerings.

Willey turned to the left and went around a fence and into the complex offices. Officer Nevis was standing at a counter.

"Afternoon, Sergeant," Nevis said cheerfully.

Willey nodded and smiled and returned his cheerfulness.

"And good afternoon to you, Nevis." He veered to the right and went into his office. He sat his lunch box on the floor and went to his desk and checked for any messages on his desk. He saw none and went back out and scanned the office area for Officer Boone, but he didn't see him.

Officer Boone was sitting in the custody office in between the big side and the small side of B-Yard. He was talking to Officer Lebeck when Lieutenant Morris called out to him.

"Boone, I've got a job for you."

Boone broke his conversation and walked around a desk that separated them.

"Yes, LT, at your service," he said, smiling as he swept his right arm to his midsection and partially bowed.

Morris shook his head and smiled.

"Here's a 154. I want you to pick up inmates Rios and Alvarez in B-2 and escort them to R&R [Receiving and Release]. They are leaving."

Boone shook his head and feigned shock.

"Oh no, they don't like it here? You want me to talk them in to staying? What about job security?"

Morris replied, "They probably don't like the food we serve here."

"But everyone likes Burger Thursdays," he mused.

Morris sighed and forced a stern look on his face. "Boone." Boone broke character and said, "Okay, two to R&R."

"They know they're leaving, and the unit probably will send them down in a bit," Morris relayed.

Boone replied, "Okay, let me go see if Willey can spare me." He turned and left the office.

Office inmate clerk Zamora heard the conversation between Boone and Morris, and it piqued his interest. He followed Boone out the door and over to the gate going into the big side. Zamora veered away from Boone and went up to the far-left side of the fence and stood for a moment. He caught the attention of inmate Huerta on the yard. Huerta nefariously made a stroll around to a wall of the building to the edge of the fence and looked out at the yard while listening to Zamora.

"Diga a Borrego, el pájaro cantor esta moviento ahorita." (Tell Borrego the singing bird is leaving right now.)

Huerta got the message and walked away with a purpose.

He scurried toward the Southerns' basketball court and got permission to talk to the shot caller on the yard, inmate Borrego. He told Borrego what Zamora had said.

Borrego summoned two of his *lieutenants* and they exchanged thoughts. Summarily, the group dispersed and splintered in three different directions.

*****

Sergeant Willey was looking over the daily report log when he saw Officer Boone come into the office and walked up to him.

"Afternoon, Boone," Willey said.

"Afternoon, Sarge," Boone returned. "You need me for anything?"

"At the moment, no," Willey said.

"Okay, I've gotta take a couple of inmates from B-2 to R&R."

Willey nodded and smiled. "Okay, I'll survive without you for a minute."

Boone chuckled and turned and left the office. He went out a gate and turned left back toward the office between the big side and small side. It was a large open-air sally port with a roof over it and a twelve-foot cyclone fence on both ends. He went up to the gate and unlocked it. He went through the gate and locked it back. He walked past the offices on the left and went over to the gate at the other end of the sally port. Beyond the gate was what was referred to as the small side, as the yard area was about a third of the size of the main yard. This yard was also enclosed by walls of four housing units on three sides and the back side of the buildings in common with the main yard.

Boone waited at the small-side fence talking to Officer Lebeck.

After about fifteen minutes, Boone saw two inmates walking toward the sally port gate pushing a flatbed cart with both inmates' property on it. When they arrived at the gate, he took out an inmate movement slip from his vest.

"Okay, guys, give me your IDs." The inmates did as instructed.

Boone looked at the IDs and looked back at each of the inmates a couple of times. Their names on the IDs were Rios and Alvarez.

He looked at Zamora and asked, "What's your name and number?"

"Zamora, AA65872."

Boone turned to Alvarez and asked, "What's your name and number?"

"Alvarez, BB20913."

Boone saw the IDs, and information matched the information on the 154 that they were going to R&R.

He nodded to the inmates. "Okay, hang here for a minute."

He turned and scanned the sally port and saw a couple of inmates, one was Zamora.

He asked Officer Lebeck, "Carl, can you put those inmates in the sally port somewhere so I can escort these two through?"

Lebeck walked over to the inmates in the sally port. "You two step inside for a minute."

The inmates went into the office, and Lebeck locked the door and stood by it.

Boone saw the area was clear and opened the gate and let his two inmates in with their cart and relocked the gate.

Boone looked at the cart and saw two TVs and two security-sealed gray containers.

He had the inmates turn and put their hands on the fence and searched them individually.

When he was finished, he turned and called out, "Escort!"

He led his inmates over toward the other gate Officer Lebeck was tending.

Willey stepped out of his office onto the yard. He began walking straight ahead toward Building 5 at the end of the yard, near the Southerns' basketball court. Several Southern inmates saw Willey heading their way. They were also watching for Borrego to give some sort of signal. Inmate Huerta and two other Southerns, Harris and Garza, were strategically placed near the B-Yard exit door.

Yard Gun Officer Rose, thirty feet above the office complex, perused the yard activities.

Officer Boone nodded to Lebeck, and Lebeck opened the gate and said aloud, "Escort!"

The announcement of "escort" gives notice to staff to clear the way of other inmates. Inmates are to follow the direction of the staff.

Office Nevis stepped out of the office and locked a gate near the office. Inmates near the office were directed to step away.

"Let's go, guys," Boone said to his inmates as he stepped through the gate. Inmates Rios and Alvarez followed Boone with their cart of property.

After they cleared the gate, Officer Lebeck locked the gate and went back to the office complex and unlocked the office door and went across to the other side and unlocked another office door. Inmate Zamora made his way out of the office over to the fence by the big-side yard. He intently watched the escort in progress.

Officer Lebeck went back to the big-side gate and also watched the escort.

Officer Nevis walked about fifteen feet ahead of the procession, clearing the way. As the detail neared the B-Yard entrance/exit door, the Southerns' plan was put into play. Sergeant Willey's timing in the incident that was about to unfold was perfect for Borrego. Just as Willey approached Building 5, Borrego gave a nod, and four Southern inmates grabbed each other and began to shout at each other, feigning punching each other and rolling on the ground. Willey saw the altercation and yelled, "Stop, stop. Get down! Yard down!"

He pulled out his pepper spray. The inmates did not comply. Willey thought it curious that there weren't any serious blows being delivered.

Again, he yelled, "Stop, get down!"

The shouts of "Get down!" had a ripple effect on the yard, and the inmates on the yard began to comply, but the four-man altercation continued.

The beginning of the fight near Building 5 drew the attention of the staff away from the escort in progress. That momentary distraction presented the opportunity the Southern contingent was waiting for.

Inmates Huerta, Harris, and Garza simultaneously darted for their target, inmate Rios. Their attack was to be without care for their safety. Their goal was to take out Rios at any cost.

Although Nevis was watching the Building 5 altercation, he noticed inmate Garza sprinting from the right toward the escort. Nevis yelled, "Stop, get back!" at Garza as he moved to intercept while drawing his baton.

Garza paid no attention to Nevis. Nevis raised his baton, holding both ends and slammed it chest high into Garza, knocking him to the ground.

Boone watched the beginning of the distant fight near Building 5, but the rapid movement of inmate Harris toward his position prompted him to put his left elbow up to defend against an impending blow as he moved to intercept inmate Harris. Boone noted that inmate Harris's angle of attack was not toward him but toward either inmate Rios or Alvarez.

His elbow hit inmate Harris on his left shoulder. Boone tried to grab inmate Harris with his right hand or arm but was unsuccessful. Inmate Harris bounced away from Boone. Inmate Alvarez jumped aside as inmate Harris was deflected toward him by the contact with Officer Boone. Inmate Alvarez scampered a few feet away and got on the ground.

From the far left, inmate Huerta jumped over inmate Alvarez and the cart he had been pushing and grabbed inmate Rios around his left shoulder with his left arm. Inmate Huerta had a sharpened piece of metal in his right hand and jabbed it into inmate Rios's neck several times.

Inmate Harris, having been deflected by Boone's contact, spun away slightly but regained his balance and brandished a long piece of metal and plunged it several times into the midsection of inmate Rios.

Sergeant Willey realized that the inmates he was tending to had stopped fighting. He turned around and saw the engagement happening in front of the office area. He sprinted toward the *real* altercation. An alarm sounded across the yard.

Officer Lebeck, still at the big-side gate, saw the commotion. He turned to the sally port area and shouted to the inmates in the area, "Get down."

He also made eye contact with inmate Zamora, who reluctantly got on the ground. Lebeck opened the gate, drew his baton, and ran toward inmate Huerta and inmate Harris's attack on Rios.

Above in the gun position, Officer Rose had her Mini-14 poised for discharge, but she had no clear shot since Lebeck and now Officer Boone were in close proximity to the attackers.

Boone saw a weapon being used on inmate Rios and hit inmate Harris on the back of his neck and head area twice with his baton.

Officer Lebeck raised his baton and struck inmate Huerta's arm, hand, and shoulder, then jabbed his ribs with the baton. Inmate Huerta had been holding inmate Rios up, but the jab to his ribs delivered by Officer Lebeck caused him to let go of inmate Rios, and both inmates Huerta and Rios fell to the ground.

Inmate Harris, having been struck by Officer Boone, stumbled away from inmate Rios as Rios fell.

Several officers swarmed inmates Huerta and Harris and disarmed inmate Huerta while inmate Harris tossed his weapon away. Sergeant Willey arrived at the scene and tackled inmate Harris, and they both went to the ground. Other staff helped overwhelm the attackers and placed them in restraints and sat them on the ground.

Officer Rose above in the yard gun kept vigil over the yard while staff began controlling and clearing the yard of inmates.

Sergeant Willey gathered his composure and quickly went up to Officers Boone and Nevis, who were standing together near the sergeant's office, to check on their condition.

Willey noticed blood on Boone's shirt. "Hey, Boone, are you okay? Is that your blood?" Willey said, pointing to Boone's shirt.

Boone looked at his shirt and patted his own arms and torso, checking for injuries. Boone responded. "I don't think I have any injuries."

"Nevis, how about you?" Willy asked. Nevis shook his head. "I'm okay, Sarge."

Officer Lebeck was tending to the many wounds suffered by inmate Rios.

Willey went over to Lebeck, who had blood on his shirt and hands, only one hand had a latex glove on it. He was applying pressure on two of the several bleeding wounds.

Willey asked, "Lebeck, are you injured?" Lebeck glanced at Willey and shook his head.

Willey took out a pair of gloves and put them on. His put his hands on two of the several wounds and applied pressure on them.

Medical staff soon arrived and took over taking care of Rios, trying to stop the continuous flow of blood.

Lebeck and Willey watched as inmate Rios was immediately taken toward the infirmary.

Willey and Lebeck looked at each other's bloody hands and sighed.

Willey had a half grimace on his face. "How about we go get cleaned up?"

Lebeck nodded.

Willey led the way to the bathroom in the office complex.

They removed their shirts and began to wash the blood off their hands and arms. Willey was washing the blood off his elbow and discovered a scrape on it.

Lebeck noticed the scrape. "Sarge, did you get stuck?"

Willey thought and said, "You know, I remember falling on my elbow when I blasted inmate Harris away from inmate Rios."

Lebeck chuckled. "I sorta remember the hit you put on him.

That was worthy of a linebacker highlight reel."

Willey smiled. "I'll have to get some five-by-seven prints from the video and autograph them for five bucks each."

Lebeck chuffed. "I'll take one, Sarge."

Inmate Rios was immediately prepared for transport to an outside emergency room. However, it was soon determined that he did not survive the attack. Inmate Alvarez was unscathed as he was not the target.

Inmates Huerta, Harris, and Garza were taken to medical for evaluation, and later they were secured in Ad Seg.

Eventually, the crime scene area was determined to be the lower twenty yards of the yard. The staff found four inmate-modified metal stabbing weapons. One was found on the ground in the open-air, fenced-in sally port in between the big side and the small side near the custody office.

An investigation revealed the obvious conclusion. Inmate Rios had indicated that he would "debrief" (give up information) about certain assaults and murders carried out by the Southern inmate prison gang. Inmates Huerta and Harris, along with inmate Garza, were found guilty of murder of a prisoner.

Certainly, Rios's plans to snitch made him a target for the Southern inmate population that sought to silence "the singing bird," *el pájaro cantor.*

ESCAPE: SEALED UP

Officer William Kauffman sat in the culinary custody office looking over the inmate movement sheet. He noticed a change in his inmate back dock work crew. Inmate Dorn was going on "S" time. That meant he was getting ready to parole. He was being replaced by inmate Seal. He stood up and went over to an eight-foot-wide white board attached to the wall. He took an eraser and erased Dorn's name from the list of back dock workers. He read from the movement sheet and wrote in inmate Seal's name and number, replacing Dorn in his spot. He also changed a name and number on the board for a Dining Hall 2 position. He went back over to the desk and sat down and put the movement sheet down on the desk. Sergeant Janis Miles and Officer Bates came in the office. Miles went to her chair and sat down. Kauffman looked up.

"Morning, Sarge. Morning, Bates."

"Morning, Robert," Miles replied.

Officer Bates said, "Good morning," and walked over to Kauffman and sat on the edge of the desk. She reached down and picked up the movement sheet off the desk and looked it over. Momentarily, she put the sheet back down and said, "No changes on my crew just back dock and Dining Room 2."

Kauffman said, "Yep, I just changed them on the board."

Miles looked up at the board and said, "Not bad, only two changes to deal with."

Kauffman asked, "Julie, can you check what we're serving this morning?"

Bates reached behind her and took a clipboard off the wall.

She read the meal listing aloud.

"Scrambled eggs, toast, two sausage links, fried potatoes, OJ, and coffee."

Kauffman looked at Julie and scoffed, "Sausages, huh? Good luck keeping up with that."

"Yeah, have to watch it close when we run mail line chow. At least we can control the *short line*."

Bates looked at the clock and stood up and stretched her arm out. "Okay, time ta go."

Kauffman and Bates left the office and headed down a corridor toward Dining Hall 2.

Officer Lowery was out in the corridor at the door of Dining Hall 2 checking in inmate workers. As the inmates were checked in, they went in the chow hall and picked up their food tray dished out by staff, called a short line, before they started work. This process gave the officers an opportunity to set up the position of the food item on the serving line and the portions served. They then would use that process for each chow hall.

When the short line was done, the inmates filtered to their assigned areas for the day.

Kauffman went back to the office and walked over to his lunch box and took out a small orange juice bottle and a bag of chips. He put them in his coat pocket. He headed through the kitchen and through two floor-to-ceiling barred gates that went into the scullery area. The last solid door led out to the back dock. He unlocked the door and stepped out onto the back dock area.

The back dock was an eight-by-thirty-foot cement platform about four feet above the paved area that extended to the back of the institution. Several cargo CONEX-type containers lined up close to the dock area. On the left side of the lot were the loading docks of a warehouse complex.

There was a ramp and stairway to the left of the dock platform that led down to paved area.

Several large rolling garbage bins and trash bins were lined up to the right side of the dock. The bins were emptied daily by off-site trash and garbage removal contractors. To the right of the dock on the pavement was a cardboard bailer machine. When a bail of cardboard was complete, it was banded and rolled out of the compactor onto a pallet. It was then taken by forklift and staged in the lot for removal weekly also by an off-site recycling contractor.

Kauffman checked his elevated dock area for hidden contraband as well as the lower lot area: the rolling bins, the CONEX containers, and the areas around the containers. He was totally aware that the inmates were experts at hiding every type of contraband: tools, metal stock, weapons, food, and clothing.

He checked over, under, and in between everything accessible to inmates. He also checked locked areas and switch boxes and panels.

His workers began to arrive and check in with Kauffman. When he had a full complement of workers, he pulled his lead worker and the new inmate, Seal, aside.

He spoke to inmate Seal. "How much time you got left?"

Seal replied, "Eleven months."

Kauffman nodded. "Where did you work before?"

Seal replied, "West Corridor and laundry."

"You worked for Silva in West Corridor?" Kauffman asked.

Seal nodded.

Kauffman began, pointing to inmate Barker, "This is Barker. He's going to give you a rundown on what we do here. I expect you to keep as busy as you can. If you see something that needs to be done and you want to impress me, then do it. I realize this job is not that difficult and it can be boring. While you are picking up trash and garbage, don't give other staff a reason to come to me to complain about you. These jobs are to help you develop a work ethic and self-discipline. I realize that you might want to stop and talk to homies, but keep it short. If you have time to kill, then do it here on the back dock with the other guys. I'm easy to work for, but I do search workers and work areas randomly, so don't get pissed if you think I'm picking on just you. I know there are a lot of opportunities to scoop up food and other things, but if it's not contraband, then let me know about it. If it's contraband, then don't take it. This is usually a fairly fun job to do if you do your job and stay in the work area that Barker will tell you about." He paused. "You have any questions?"

Seal shook his head. "No, CO. I got your message. Thanks."

"Okay," Kauffman said and turned to inmate Barker. "Barker, he's all yours."

Barker nodded and led Seal back through the door into the scullery room.

Kauffman watched his other inmate workers, Ramirez and Durst, as they rolled two empty bins around and up against the back dock. They came up the stairs and went inside. Kauffman followed them inside, and they continued through the opened gates into the kitchen. Kauffman scanned the scullery area and saw no inmates. He went back outside, leaving the door all the way open. He stepped to the right and sat in a well-worn swivel bar stool that sat next to a well-worn desk. There was a two-drawer metal cabinet next to it that had a padlock securing it. He took out his bag of chips, opened it, and ate a couple of chips. He took out his bottle of OJ, opened it, and took a drink.

Inmate Barker was showing Seal the pickup procedure for collecting various trash and garbage from the cans in the dining halls and kitchen areas. A simple process, but it was continuous, especially during morning chow.

Throughout the morning, the inmates would pick up bags from the various trash and garbage cans and bring them to the back dock and toss them into the appropriate rolling bin. They would also pick up soiled trays from the chow halls and bring them back and run them through the dish washing machine.

They picked up the empty serving pans and carried them back to the scullery and wash them out and place them in a rack to dry.

As the morning wore on, Kauffman bounced between the scullery and back dock in his normal routine.

When the chow was finished, the kitchen workers would clean the dining hall tables and counters, mop the floors, clean the dish machine, wash the food prep kettles and tables, and finish washing the pans in the scullery. The workers were then searched by their work supervisor or Officer Lowery as they were released back to their housing units. The staff would go through their work areas, checking for anything out of sorts or inmates lingering around.

Kauffman followed his routine search and inspection of his area. He secured his area and went back to the office and recorded the hours worked for each inmate on their time sheet. He picked up his lunch box and met up with a few other officers, and they left for the day.

*****

Several weeks went by, and Kauffman once again sat at a desk in the office preparing for the day. Dining Hall Officer France was working in Bates's job in Dining Hall 3. The morning went as usual. They served the short line and kept an eye on the *hot* item for the day, polish sausage. Kauffman's workers performed their usual tasks and came to the back dock to pick up their jackets or put their work gloves away.

Officer France came out to the back dock and said, "Hey, Kauffman, the sarge needs you to fill out Bates's monthly inmate work report, since you know her inmate workers and I don't."

Kauffman sighed and nodded. "Okay, I'll trade key groups with you so you can lock this up when my workers get done."

Kauffman unhooked his key group from his duty belt and handed them to Officer France and took France's group and put them on his belt and left for the office.

In the office, he settled into a chair, opened a drawer, and retrieved the folder for Dining Hall 3. He began to fill out the required information for Bates's inmates. He finished her report and started on his inmate monthly report.

Soon, Officer France came into the office. "Here are your keys, Kauffman."

Kauffman stood up and took the key group off his duty belt and traded with France.

"Thanks for doing this, bud," France said.

Kauffman nodded. "No problem, pal. Glad I could help out. Did you kick my inmates out of the back dock and send them home?" France replied, "Yep, all three were chomping at the bit to go."

Kauffman gave France a puzzled look. "I had four inmate workers."

France wrinkled his face. "I only sent three out." He pulled out his notebook and repeated the names.

"Barker, Ramirez, and Durst."

Kauffman said, "Okay, but I wonder what happened to inmate Seal?"

He went over to the inmate picture file and showed inmate Seal's picture to France.

"I didn't see him," France said.

Kauffman sat down and dialed the phone.

Officer Reginald Lowery picked up the phone in the corridor by Dining Hall 2.

"Lowery," he said.

"Reggie, Robert. Did you see inmate Seal come out?" Kauffman asked.

Lowery thought for a moment. "You know, I don't remember him coming out yet."

"Okay. If you see him, call me on the radio." Sergeant Jan Miles was nearby Lowery.

"Hey, Robert, the sarge is right here. You want to talk to her?" Kauffman said, "Yeah, put her on."

Lowery handed Miles the phone. "Miles here."

"Jan, Kauffman. France didn't see inmate Seal when he cleared the back dock. I'm gonna go check it out an' see if he's still here."

Miles said, "Okay. Where's he live, and I'll call his unit."

"J-122 up," was Kaufman's reply.

"Okay, got it," Miles said as she pushed and released the hang-up lever and dialed J-Wing.

"J-Wing, Miller."

"Miller, this is Sergeant Miles. Has inmate Seal made it back to the unit? He lives in 122."

"Hold on, I'll see if he's in the corridor, and then I'll check his cell."

Miller set the phone down and stepped out into the corridor. He saw no inmate in the corridor. He saw his partner, Allison, on the tier and called out, "Allison, check and see if inmate Seal is in 122."

Allison waved his hand and walked over to cell 122 and unlocked the door and looked inside.

He waved his hand and said, "No, Seal is not here."

Miller picked up the phone and said, "Sarge, inmate Seal is not here. Is he MIA?"

Miles said, "I hope not, but if you see him, let me know."

"10-4, Sarge."

Kauffman and France scanned the rooms and corridors on their way to the back dock. They reached the back dock and opened the door. They scanned the upper level and went down the stairs to the lower parking lot. They made their way over to the warehouse loading docks. Since it was Sunday, the bays were closed and the entrance doors were locked. They systematically began to search the area. Sergeant Miles and several other staff joined them in their endeavors. They searched inside the rolling bins, in and on top of the CONEX containers, behind the bales of cardboard, and inside, in between, and on top of the two buildings.

Eventually, the warden made the call to lockdown the institution.

Every nook and cranny was searched and researched. Every vehicle was searched, and no vehicles had left the institution since before inmate Seal was deemed missing. Every inmate was accounted for with a picture ID comparison.

The notice went out that there had been an escaped inmate. A search of the local community also was conducted.

The next day, there was a modified program, and Kauffman continued searching his area for inmate Seal while performing his regular duties at the back dock. He supervised the garbage trucks as they picked up the garbage and the cardboard bails were loaded on a flatbed and chained down. All vehicles were thoroughly searched prior to leaving. Every person entering and exiting the institution was matched with ID and facial verification.

The garbage trucks made their way to the dump site, and the bails of cardboard were transported by the recycling company and stacked in the nearby recycle facility.

A worker, Sara, at the recycle facility was restacking the bails of cardboard next to a wall with her forklift. As she finished moving and restacking the bails, she turned off the engine, jumped off the forklift, and started to walk away. She stopped when she heard muffled moaning coming from behind the first row of the stacked bails of cardboard. She walked closer and listened.

A faint voice said, "Hey, help me."

She got closer and heard the voice again. "Help me. I can't get out."

She got back on the forklift and lifted the top bail of cardboard off and took it to the side and set it down. She removed the second bail and set it aside. She turned off the engine and got off the forklift. She walked over closer and heard the voice again.

"Help, I can't get out."

At first she thought the voice was coming from behind the bails, but the voice was coming from inside the bottom bail.

She now realized that the bails had been picked up at the prison and was aware of the escape alert.

Sara asked the voice, "What's your name?"

"Jerry," was the answer.

"Are you from the prison?" she asked. There was a long pause. "Yes."

Sara asked if he was inside the bail of cardboard. The answer was, "Yes."

Sara dialed 911 and related that she believed that the escapee from the prison was trapped in a bail of cardboard at the recycling facility.

After Sara answered the standard questions, the dispatcher suggested that Sara leave the inmate where he was until the police arrived.

Sara waited until the police arrived to remove the top bail. The police cautiously approached the remaining bail and discovered it had a single cardboard layer on the top and the inside had been gutted to allow the inmate to hide inside and slide a cardboard cover over him. The prison staff arrived at the scene and took inmate Seal into custody. Apparently, he hadn't planned on another bail being stacked on top of his bail. His escape plan had been *Sealed.*

THE HEART WANTS WHAT IT WANTS

Officer Danielle Craft stepped through the sally port gate and headed up the walkway toward the administration complex. She walked past the inmate visiting center on the left and scanned the large grass area on the right. She greeted several staff passing her on their way out of the complex. She arrived at the door to the complex and pulled it open and proceeded down a long hallway. She continued past an intersecting hallway that led to offices in both directions. At the end of the hallway, she stopped, pressed a button on the side of the door, and waited for the Central Control room officer to buzz her in. She could see several staff in the sally port/foyer were waiting their turn to show their IDs to the officer.

When the officer had checked the IDs, she buzzed the internal door to the right, and some of the group exited. The remaining staff waited at the other side of the door Craft was waiting at. The door in front of her buzzed, and she opened it and let the exiting staff out first, and then she entered the sally port. The door closed behind her.

She took a few steps forward and stopped at a ported opening in the wire-plated glass window in the control room. She sat her lunch box down and gave the officer her ID. The officer checked it and handed it back to Craft.

"Tool room, Danielle?" he asked.

Craft nodded and handed several key tags to the officer. The officer swiftly made his rounds in the room and returned with a key group, OC pepper spray, baton, handcuffs, and an alarm pad device. She placed the equipment on various parts of her duty belt and continued toward the yard door. She picked up her lunch bag and stepped to the exit door. When she heard the buzz of the door, she opened it and turned left and exited through another door into the central complex yard area. A-Yard was to the left, and C-Yard was to the right. Craft steered straight ahead on the walkway to B-Yard. She passed the package room and Receiving and Release to the right and came to a gate. She looked up to her left on the top corner of the building above at the yard gate tower booth. The officer recognized her, and the lock on the gate snapped, and the door opened. She waved at the tower officer, went through, and closed the gate. She turned right and walked past the medical complex and went into the PIA (Prison Industries Authority) corridor. She made a left at the inmate inspection (strip-out) tables and continued down a long corridor past the butcher shop and coffee mill room and arrived at the toolroom on the right. She unlocked the door went in and closed it. She stepped across an entry area and unlocked the solid toolroom door and went inside.

The toolroom was about fifteen feet deep and thirty feet long.

It had two long horizontal wire-plated windows with a counter in the center with a secured ported service window.

Inmate Draper, the inmate tool clerk, was standing outside of the toolroom at the counter talking to another inmate. Draper saw Craft enter and smiled and nodded to her. Craft smiled back at him and went to a small expanded metal cage with a short metal file drawer in it. She sat her lunch bag down and unlocked the cage and the file drawer. She opened the drawer and pulled out an inventory folder and relocked both the drawer and the cage. She opened the folder, and starting at the near end of the room, she began checking off the inventory and condition of the tools. Among the various electrical tools in the room were drills, sanders, shears, etc.

A plethora of hand tools—scissors, knives, hammers, cutting blades, screwdrivers, and chisels—were hung on a very large white board that covered the rear wall. A hook was attached to the board with a darkened outline (shadow) of the shape of the tool below the hook. When an inmate needed a tool, they would give the inmate tool clerk an inmate metal key tag (chit) with their number stamped on it, and the tool was removed and the chit was placed on the hook.

That was a quick way to scan the shadow board to check for missing tools. Either the tool was there or an inmate's chit was on the hook. There was a current copy of an inventory list hanging on the wall as a quick reference for the inmate clerk in charge of handing tools out to other inmates. It had happened that an inmate would "white out" the shadow of the tool and remove the hook from the board and take the tool. To prevent the always-working-mind of ingenious inmates from absconding with a tool, a master inventory list was kept in the locked metal container. That list was what busied Craft to start her shift.

Craft finished checking the tools and their working condition. Everything matched her master inventory list. She initialed the list and unlocked the cage and drawer and placed the list back into the drawer and locked it and locked the cage.

Inmate Draper finished talking with the other inmate. Craft caught Draper's eye and smiled. She went over to the toolroom door and let inmate Draper in. She closed and locked the door. She looked out onto the clothing fabrication area at the inmate workers and took a long look at the clothing supervisor's office at the far corner of the room. The supervisor was talking with a couple of inmates.

Craft felt it safe enough to move a couple of steps to the side near inmate Draper with her back to his back. The counter being four feet above the floor allowed two of their hands to clasp. Still back-to-back, inmate Draper, with his other hand from behind, reached around to the hip of Officer Craft and caressed it. Inmate Draper twisted a little more and moved his hand over her buttocks and in between her legs. Craft spread her legs apart and guided inmate Draper's hand to massage her crotch. Their other hands squeezed together tightly. Inmate Draper kept watch for any onlookers. A moment or two later, Draper saw an inmate get up and start to come in his direction. His hand stopped its work and froze in position. Craft sensed the change. The other inmate's intrusion was not to be as he turned and went the other way between the worktables.

Their activities returned with urgency. Craft eventually let out a sigh and slowly turned around and smiled at Draper and said, "Oh, David." She breathed his name softly.

They separated, and she slowly walked several feet away, and they faced each other.

Draper smiled and quietly asked, "I should be on 'S' time next month. Are you still taking your vacation weeks then?"

Craft nodded. "Of course, David, wouldn't miss it." He smiled. "I'm ready for you too, Danni."

Craft sighed. "I should make my rounds. I'll be back ASAP."

"Can't wait," he replied.

Danielle opened the door and stepped out and locked the door. She began a routine search of the clothing fabrication area for anything suspicious. She checked the shelves, tables, and inmate work spaces and the inmate restrooms. She went over to the clothing supervisor's office and peered in the office.

Shawna Grayson, the noncustody supervisor, waved Craft in. "Good morning, Danielle," Shawna said.

Craft replied, "Good morning, how's it going today?"

"Oh, you know, busy, busy."

"I know you've had a lot of work orders lately. Are you able to get them out on time?" Craft asked.

"Yeah." Shawna nodded. "The guys are doing really great.

They're really working hard."

"You had any problems with anyone?"

"No, not a bit of problems. The guys seem to work together much easier than I think women do. Just my observation."

"Maybe it's the catfighting you miss," Craft offered. "He, he, he," Shawna laughed. "Guess that might be it."

Craft shook her head. "Seems like the guys just want to take their minds off doing time."

Shawna lifted her brows and said, "I never thought about it that way, but it makes sense."

"Okay, guess I'll finish my rounds. I'll see you in a bit."

Craft left the office and continued her custodial functions. Her thoughts were split with her custody duties and her fantasy of spending time with David. He was getting ready to parole next month, and he would be on "S" time (not working) ten days before, so he could get his release process paperwork done and make living arrangements with his family. He was unique compared to the vast majority of the incarcerated. He chose to do a straight two-year sentence with no parole to hang over his head. Her plan was to make arrangements for her to spend her two weeks of vacation with her love, David. His two-year sentence for car theft and burglary would be behind him, and together they planned to make it work.

Craft went over to each of the trash cans and pulled the trash bag out of the can and looked into the bottom and turned it upside down to check the underside. She put the trash bag back in the can and used a long stick to probe the contents. Inmates have been known to secure notes and contraband in the trash. Often, in warm areas, there would be *pruno* (inmate-made alcohol) cooking in a plastic bag in the bottom of the trash can.

She made another security sweep of the worktables and headed back to the toolroom. As she walked by the service window of the toolroom, she smiled at inmate Draper. Several inmates waited outside at the service window. She went back inside the toolroom and slid open the service window. Inmate Draper retrieved the requested items for the inmates at the counter.

Craft sat at a small desk at the end of the room against the wall. She watched Draper hand out and receive tools from the inmates. He would also inspect and wipe down tools when needed.

Several hours went by and lunchtime arrived. The inmate workers filed out and one by one exited the door, and Craft searched each inmate and sent them down the corridor to the lunchroom. The officer at the lunchroom entrance handed each inmate a sack lunch from a cart as they went in.

Craft and Shawna would normally eat lunch together in Shawna's office. Occasionally, one or both would leave for lunch elsewhere. Today, they ate lunch in Shawna's office. When lunch was over, the inmates returned to work.

For the rest of the afternoon, Craft and inmate Draper went about their routine, Draper at the service window and Craft searching for contraband.

When the day was over, the inmates cleaned up their areas and checked out with Grayson. Inmate Draper was always the last inmate to leave. His final duty was to check his inventory before the other inmates left and Craft would compare the inventory with the master inventory.

Craft opened the exit door and the other inmates left.

Often Shawna and Danielle would leave together, but today, Shawna left with the inmate workers.

Danielle seized this opportunity. She locked the door, and she and Draper went back into the toolroom, and she locked the door. They quickly removed the necessary clothing to engage in a rare afternoon quickie. Sadly, they didn't have enough time to thoroughly enjoy the encounter. They quickly redressed, and Danielle went to the exit door and consumed a passionate kiss from inmate Draper, and then she sent him quickly out. She went back into the toolroom and scanned it for security needs. She picked up her lunch bag, locked the door, and waited for a minute to allow an inconspicuous time between inmate Draper leaving and her leaving. She checked her uniform appearance and inventoried her duty equipment. Satisfied, she left.

A few weeks passed and the two ships passed in the night on only one more occasion, before inmate Draper went on "S" time. Inmate Draper was not allowed to work while on "S" time and spent much of his remaining days talking on the phone to his friends and family in preparation for his return to society. He was very careful not to mention Danielle to anyone on the phone or mail, as phone calls were monitored and recorded and mail was read by staff at the institution.

Unfortunately, Draper did not take into account that his cellmate would have a slip of confidence. In a letter referring to inmate Draper, he implied that his girlfriend *Danni* was going to take him with her on vacation when he paroled and that he hadn't seen her since he went on "S" time.

Ordinarily, such a disclosure would escape the scrutiny of noncustody staff reading the outgoing mail, but his cellmate's revelation in his letter caught the eye of a savvy staff member.

The letter was given to the Investigative Services Unit (ISU) for their assessment.

Sergeant Cole reread the letter and checked incoming and outgoing mail for any similar references. She found none. However, her curiosity led her to go over the names of staff that might have contact with inmate Draper. She did make a possible connection between inmate Draper and Danielle Craft that she connected with the name Danni as spelled in the letter.

It took some convincing of the ISU Lieutenant Jones for Cole to follow up on the connection. The pieces seemed to fall together: Danielle was known by some as Danni, spelled the same way. Also, that she was scheduled for vacation coinciding with the release date of inmate Draper.

Sergeant Cole made some benign inquiries of some of her friends about Craft's vacation plans. Eventually, she discovered that Craft had rented a cabin in South Lake Tahoe for the first week of her vacation. Lieutenant Jones was lukewarm to Cole's proposal to follow inmate Draper or Officer Craft after Draper's release. One reason was that Draper was being released on a Wednesday and Craft's vacation was to start on the following Monday, but she did have weekends off on her job. So unless Craft called in sick, the two would have to meet after her shift. Cole reasoned that Craft would not chance picking up inmate Draper at the institution, but could meet him at the bus drop-off location. Otherwise, they could meet on Friday or the weekend. Lieutenant Jones felt that there were too many time frames to cover, and resources and overtime would tax the value of securing a possible violation of CDC policy. It was a stretch, Cole thought. Jones relented to a short time frame of three days' stakeout of Craft. He authorized Cole and Officer Ramirez to follow Craft after her work shift on Wednesday, Thursday, and Friday. Cole hoped, personally, that she was wrong about the whole situation.

On the morning inmate Draper was released, Officer Craft was working her normal shift. Inmate Draper was actually picked up by a male, possibly his brother. After Craft's shift, she went by a grocery store and went home. Cole didn't see her leave in her car. Cole waited for two hours and left. The next day, Cole followed Craft to a couple of stores in the mall, and then Craft went home and stayed. Cole left after two hours.

On Friday, both Cole and Ramirez followed Craft to her house and waited. Three hours later, a vehicle drove up to her house, and in no surprise, inmate Draper got out of the vehicle and got a suitcase out of the back seat. He began to roll it toward Craft's door. Ramirez was using a video camera to document the encounter. Cole and Ramirez got out of their car and walked toward Craft's house and watched from a distance. Draper knocked on the door, and Craft stepped out on to the porch and hugged and kissed Draper.

Ramirez was yet videoing the event as they approached the couple. Craft noticed the two walking up and released her hug on Draper.

Cole displayed her badge and ID. "Officer Craft, I'm Sergeant Cole, ISU, and this is Officer Ramirez. We want to talk to you and inmate Draper."

Craft was surprised but didn't seem concerned. "How can I help you?"

Draper backed away a step and held his hand up to show he had no weapon.

"We believe that you are in violation of CDC policy by engaging in a relationship with a felon without notifying your supervisor or the department."

Craft seemed flustered momentarily. She took several deep breaths.

She sighed and said, "Yes, Sergeant, I intend to have a relationship with Mr. Draper, a former felon, and I can notify the department of my contact with him. However, Mr. Draper is not on parole and he is a private citizen, and I don't believe it is mandatory to apprise the department of a relationship before it happens. Moreover, if contact with a *former* felon is required, I will do so. But I am not aware that it is necessary."

Cole was perplexed. She thought for a long moment. On the surface, it appeared that her statements were accurate. Cole took a breath.

"How long has this been going on?" Cole asked.

Craft smiled and replied. "You two have a good evening. Thank you for your concern."

Craft grabbed Draper's hand. He picked up his suitcase, and she led him into the house and closed the door.

Ramirez stopped the video camera.

"Well, Sarge, what do you think?" he asked.

Cole turned, and they started to walk back to the car. "I think I'll have to take this back to the lieutenant and let him sort it out."

"She didn't seem too concerned. She must have thought this through," he offered.

Cole nodded as she opened the car door. "Yeah, I guess it's true," she said.

Ramirez was curious about her statement. "What's true?"

Cole replied as she started to get in the car, "The heart wants what it wants."

THE HERSHEY HIGHWAY

Janet Nash got out of her car and walked across the parking lot toward the entrance building. She went through the front door and stepped up to the counter, took out her driver's license, and gave it to Officer Bailey. She wrote her name down on a visitor registration and who she was there to visit. Bailey checked the computer for the inmate's location and status. Janet knew the procedure by heart. She went over to a locker at the side of the room and opened the locker. She took a heavy clear plastic zip-up purse containing twenty dollars in quarters out of her regular purse and put her ID inside the clear purse. She put her regular purse in the locker. She closed the locker and took the key that was in the locker and put it in the clear purse. She walked over to the walk-through metal detector and put the clear purse on a tray next to the detector and walked through. The officer on the other side of the detector inspected the clear purse and handed it to Nash.

"Enjoy your visit," the officer said.

Janet nodded and headed for the exit door. The lock on the door snapped, and she pushed it open. She walked to the other side of the sally port and waited as the gate slid open. She continued through down a slope to the visiting room building.

She went through the door and headed directly to the bathroom. When she finished, she went down the hallway. An officer opened the visiting room door, and she went it. She found an empty table and sat down and waited.

In building 6, Officer Trejo hung up the phone and leaned down to the microphone and said, "Inmate Nash 122 upper, you have a visit."

Inmate Jerry Nash was waiting near the officer's podium where Officer Trejo sat. He immediately notified Trejo that he was there.

Trejo got up from his chair and walked over to the dorm exit door and let Nash out. Nash turned to the right and made his way to the yard exit door and pushed a button on the wall next to the door. He looked up at the camera on the wall to his left.

"Inmate Nash to visiting," he said.

The door popped open, and inmate Nash went in and closed the door behind him. He was in an expansive sally port controlled by an officer in a control room in the center of the complex. The officer pushed a button, and a large gate began to slide open. Inmate Nash knew to wait until the gate was completely open. He walked through and went over to an officer at a podium. He gave him his ID, and the officer placed it in a box with slots for IDs. The officer opened another door, and inmate Nash walked into the search room and up to a table. He began taking off his clothes and placed them on the table to enable a strip search. Officer Potts searched the clothing, while Officer Vasquez watched inmate Nash perform the *dance*. Inmate Nash opened his mouth and ran his finger around inside and stuck his tongue out.

He turned his head side to side so Vasquez could look into his ears, and then he lifted his head up to display his nostrils. He ran his hands vigorously through his hair to show there was nothing but hair. He extended his hands out in front and spread his fingers. He raised his arms up to show his armpits. He reached down and lifted his scrotum. He turned around and picked each foot up and wiggled his toes. Lastly, he did three deep knee bends, coughing on the last one, and then bent over and spread his butt cheeks apart.

Inmate Nash walked around the table and went through a metal detector.

Officer Potts finished searching his clothing and put them on a table behind him. Inmate Nash redressed and left the search room and into the visiting room.

It didn't take long for inmate Nash to gain sight of his wife. He walked briskly to her table. She stood up, and they embraced and kissed for a moment. A kiss too long was generally not within the visiting guidelines.

The visiting room was fairly large, perhaps one hundred feet by eighty feet. Various vending machines and a couple of microwaves lined the perimeter, and an officer's observation podium was placed in the center of one wall. Visitors have to bring money, only quarters, with them. Inmates were not allowed to handle any money or operate the vending machines. The vending pricing was broken down to the nearest quarter amount. Inmate and visitor contact was limited to a brief kiss or embrace upon meeting and then on leaving. Hands were to be visible above the table, and usually, continuous hand holding was limited. Cameras were liberally mounted on the ceiling. The officers at the podium monitored and recorded the visits. Depending on the number of visitors, the visits were initially limited to two hours. Children were allowed, but must be controlled. Food for infants was allowed, and diapers were limited to three. Visitors must not wear revealing clothing. Inmates were to wear only state-issued clothing: blue chambray shirts and blue jeans and no hats or handkerchiefs. Inmates were subject to a strip search on entering and exiting. Tables were lowered to help prevent improper interactions under the table. Violations of visiting rules could result in a loss or suspension of visiting privileges for either inmate or visitors or both. Visitors have been known to be disallowed visitation with one inmate, only to attempt a visit with a different inmate who was visiting at the same time the disallowed inmate was visiting another person. Historically, infractions of the visitation policies have created ongoing changes to prevent contraband from entering or leaving the institution. While introduction of drugs and weapons into the prison was a major concern, the passing of notes and letters presented a real threat to security. Visitors were often used as willing or unwilling mules to promote gang activity. A noted incident involved the use of drugs placed in an infant's rectum and the inmate removed the drugs while holding the infant. Other incidents are left to the imagination. Of course, it is well known by staff that inmates do make mistakes in juggling their visitors' scheduling. Occasionally, an inmate would find that two or more of his girlfriends or even a wife showed up at the same time. That obviously resulted in an uncomfortable or a violent confrontation.

Inmate Jerry Nash and his wife, Janet, were enjoying a pleasant visit. They decided to purchase some food from the vending machine.

Two burritos, two sodas, and two bags of chips were their choices. Janet heated the burritos in the microwave, and they went back to their table. Janet removed her lightweight jacket and placed it on the back of her chair. During the consumption of the food, Janet surreptitiously removed a cellophane ball from the loose seam in the jacket and put it in her bag of chips. They spoke for a while, and she repeated the act, putting another ball into her bag of chips.

After a few minutes, Janet took a chip from Jerry's bag of chips and laughed. Jerry reciprocated by taking her bag and moving it in front of him. He took a couple of chips and ate them and laughed. They continued their conversation for a couple of minutes, and Jerry took one of the balls out and stealthy palmed it and dropped it in his shirt pocket as he put a chip in his mouth. He performed the same maneuver a second time a minute later. They continued talking for a couple of minutes, and Jerry got up and headed for the restroom. He went into the restroom and took the two cellophane balls out of his shirt pocket and dropped his pants. He wet his fingers with water and secreted the balls into his anal cavity. He carefully adjusted them to a secure location. Satisfied, he pulled up his pants, washed his hands, and left the restroom.

He returned to the table and continued his visitation. A few minutes passed, and Janet once again collected another ball and put it in the bag of chips. Although she was adept at the magical retrieval and placement of the contraband, it was the one time Officer Rojas noticed the furtive gesture on the camera. He rewound the video and watched it again. After reviewing the act, he nudged his partner Officer Railey to watch a replay.

"Hey, Jessica, see if you catch anything here."

Railey watched, and she chuckled. "Wow, she's good at that. How'd you catch it?"

Rojas shook his head. "Just happened to be watching at the right time."

Rojas called Visiting Sergeant Murray on the phone.

"Hey, Sarge, come over to the podium, we got something going on."

Rojas listened and hung up.

They waited and saw Nash drop the contraband in his pocket.

Momentarily, Sergeant Murray walked up to the officer's podium. "What's up?" he asked.

Rojas had the video cued up and pushed play. Murray watched and nodded. "That was slick."

Rojas said, "We just watched Nash drop another one in his shirt pocket. I was gonna watch the tape from the beginning to see if anything else was happening."

Murray said, "Why don't you guys continue to cover visiting and I'll run through the video?"

Rojas shrugged and moved aside and said, "You're the sergeant." Murray settled in and rewound the tape and watched.

A few minutes went by, and Murray stopped the tape and said, "Hey, guys, watch this."

They watched the replay and saw the other two acts and then inmate Nash leave for the bathroom.

"Okay, Sarge, what's the plan?" Railey asked. "You want to gaff him up now or wait for him to go to the bathroom again?"

Murray thought for a moment.

"We don't know if she has anymore stashed, but I think we better scoop them up now, and hopefully she's still holding."

Murray dialed the number to the search room.

"Vasquez, visiting search."

"Hey, Vasquez, you busy?" Murray asked.

"Not at the moment."

"I may need one of you for backup in visiting."

"I'm there," Vasquez said as he hung up and went out the door to the visiting room.

Murray dialed another number.

"ISU, Officer Carter."

"Carter, Sergeant Murray in visiting. I'm gonna scoop a couple up for a likely drug bust. When you get a chance, you might want to pick up the pieces."

"This going down now?" Carter asked.

"Yep."

"You can't wait till we get there?" Carter asked.

"Nope, time is of the essence."

"Okay, be there in about five," Carter said and hung up.

Murray stood up and said, "You two circle, and when you get close, I'll take the direct route."

Rojas nodded, and Railey took out a pair of gloves from the pouch on her duty belt.

She and Rojas split up and casually walked around some tables and approached their target.

Rojas stood behind Nash, and Railey stood behind Mrs. Nash. Sergeant Murray came near their table and had another table of visitors move away to another table.

"Inmate Nash, stand up and turn away from me," Rojas ordered.

Nash started to reach into his shirt pocket, and Rojas grabbed his wrists, and Murray grabbed Nash's left arm and reached and grabbed Nash's shirt pocket with his other hand.

Railey started to assist in securing Nash but saw that he was under control. She got Mrs. Nash's attention. "Would you stand up, ma'am?" she asked.

Janet started to grab her jacket, and Railey put her hand on it and kept her from taking it. Janet stood up, and Railey waved her hand to the side. "Would you step over here, ma'am?"

Mrs. Nash complied, and Railey picked up the jacket off the back of the chair and escorted her away and sat her at an empty table.

Murray retrieved the ball of suspected contraband from Nash's shirt pocket, and Rojas placed cuffs on Nash. He walked Nash toward visiting search. Officer Vasquez met them halfway.

"You want me to take him?"

"Okay, he probably has it keistered," Rojas advised.

"We'll get it," Rojas affirmed as he led Nash back to the visiting search room.

Railey saw ISU staff enter visiting and waited for one of them to come to her. Railey nodded to her.

"This is Mrs. Nash."

"Hi, Ms. Nash, I'm Officer Fletcher. I've been advised that you may have some type of contraband in your control."

Railey intervened, holding up her jacket. "Fletcher, this may be what you are looking for."

Fletcher asked Nash, "Is this yours?" pointing to the jacket. Janet nodded.

Fletcher took the jacket and squeeze-searched it with her hands. She got to a bump in the garment and unfolded it. She retrieved a ball of cellophane from a seam in the jacket. She took out an evidence bag and placed the ball in the evidence bag and put it in her pocket. "This may be contraband, Ms. Nash. Do you have any other items that may be contraband?" Mrs. Nash shook her head.

"Okay, could you follow me, please?" Janet stood up.

Fletcher smiled, nodded to Railey, and said, "Good job." Railey nodded and said, "Thanks."

Fletcher gently guided Ms. Nash out of the visiting room. Officer Carter walked up to Sergeant Murray, who was searching the area around the table. "Find anything?"

"Nothing on the floor or chairs, but you might collect the food off the table as possible evidence."

"Okay, Sarge."

Murray said as he handed the ball he took off Nash, "It probably is a slam dunk with this and the video evidence, if the stuff comes back positive."

"Sounds good to me."

"Thanks for the assist, Carter."

"No, Sarge, thank you for making this easy."

Murray nodded. "Guess I'll go see what else Nash has up his ass." Murray smiled and nodded. "I saw two before he went into the bathroom."

"Okay. You want me to show them to you when I get them out?"

Murray smiled and shook his head. "That's a hard pass, Carter. Thanks anyway."

Carter smiled and left.

There was a line of inmates waiting to get into the inmate stripout area. Inside, Officer Carter was supervising Officers Vasquez and Potts' encouragement of Nash to disgorge any suspicious contents of his anal cavity.

"I already have one of your bindles, and we can place you on a three-day potty watch for any secretion that may present itself, if you've swallowed them, or you can retrieve them now and save yourself some discomfort, your choice. Either way, you are up the drug possession creek. Your wife will probably be charged with bringing them in also. I may have some sway with the DA on her behalf if you cooperate, but no guaranties. You and your wife's visiting privileges are kaput either way."

Inmate Nash thought for a little while.

"Okay, I'd appreciate anything you can do for my wife."

Carter was relieved at his compliance.

"Thanks, Nash, for making it easy on us."

"Can I do this in private?" he asked.

Carter shook his head. "Sadly, we can't take the chance that you might destroy evidence or swallow it."

Nash made a super stink face. "You fuckin' think I'd swallow them after I take them out?"

Carter replied, "Honestly, Nash, I've seen it done."

Potts said, "I don't need to watch."

Carter replied, "Actually, only one of you needs to be a witness."

Vasquez said, "I watch ass holes all day, so go for it."

With everyone watching, Nash bent over and, with some difficulty, retrieved the contraband.

Carter held out an opened evidence bag, and Nash dropped it in the bag. "You guys finished with him?"

"I don't know," Vasquez said as he looked at Nash. "You have any more to get out?"

Nash shook his head.

Vasquez nodded. "Yep, we're done."

Nash was allowed to wash his hands, and then he got dressed.

Carter placed Nash in restraints and walked him out of the search room.

Potts went over and opened the search door on the visiting side, and they began to reduce the waiting list for strip outs. After each participant passed the required activity, they were released back to their unit. The last two inmates to engage in the festivities were two cellmates: Jackson, an older inmate, and Harper, a first-termer.

Jackson was performing an unabashed free-for-all dance, gladly flinging his junk, and turned around, and after his knee bends, he spread his butt cheeks and bellowed out a large amount of gas.

Potts remarked, "What the hell was that?"

The youngster said, "The only thing he can hold in his ass is my dick."

Potts and Vasquez stifled their chuckles.

As Harper finished his dance, he showed his butt wares with a dark ring center mass.

Vasquez had to remark, "What is that?"

The old dude explained, "I'm breaking him in."

Laughter was not contained.

(Recognition given to Don Vasquez)

PLEASURE IS IN THE EYE OF THE BEHOLDER

Officer Ed Soares stepped up to the solid steel door and looked up at the camera on the wall above the corner of the door.

"South door," he announced.

Momentarily, the lock on the door snapped, and he pushed the unusually heavy door open. He was about to close it when he noticed Officer Troy McCall on the walkway coming toward the door.

McCall saw Soares holding the door.

"I'm coming, Ed," McCall said as he livened up his step a bit.

Soares stopped the door swing and waited for McCall to come in the sally port. McCall cleared the door and grabbed it and closed the door with the usual noticeable slam.

Soares called out, "North Gate."

The two continued through the sally port and stopped for a second or two, and the lock on the grill gate snapped, and McCall pushed the equally heavy gate open and went through into Center Corridor followed by Soares, who closed the gate somewhat gently. They noticed Center Corridor Officer Paul leaning on a short shelf hanging on the wall off to the right side.

"What's up, Paul?" Soares said, not expecting a reply.

"Hey, Ed," Paul responded.

McCall nodded to Paul.

They turned left and headed down the West Corridor, walking in between the two painted orange lines five feet apart. Inmates were to walk on either side of the lines of what some call the Hogg trough, as that was reserved for staff to walk or respond quickly to an alarm.

"So, Ed, d'you have a date Monday night?" McCall asked as they walked.

Soares shook his head. "You know, Troy, I never kiss and tell."

McCall laughed. "Since when?" After a few more steps, Troy said, "You know you're gonna blab to the other guys when they ask."

Ed chuckled. "They always twist my arm, so I'll tell."

"Yeah right, you old dog," Troy said. "You've been on the hunt since I've known you."

"She's out there somewhere," Ed stated. "I guess everyone can't be perfect like me."

McCall snickered. "We all have chinks in our armor from attacks on our heart. You gotta take a risk to get a reward sometimes. And I don't mean sex. People don't always show you who they are until they feel comfortable."

Ed glanced sideways at Troy and offered, "Actually, Brenda is growing on me. We even talked about our families last night."

"Last night? You got off at 2200, where'd you go that late?"

Ed sighed. "We met at Denny's in Lodi, and then we drove over to the lake and watched the water."

McCall smiled. "Reliving your 'submarine races' days, huh?" Soares twisted his lip in a sneer. "Yeah, except we mostly talked, like I said."

They arrived at their destination, F-Wing. The officer's station grill gate was open, and Officer Evelyn Painter sat at the desk.

Soares and McCall sat their lunch boxes on the floor. "Afternoon," Soares said.

"What's up, Eve?" McCall said. "Hey, guys," she replied.

Ed and Troy looked out on the tiers and saw two staff letting inmates into their cells and letting other inmates out for a shower.

They both turned and went back out of the unit door and made a left. They continued down the corridor and stopped at the window in RC Control. Officer Gallagher stood inside and saw Ed and Troy walk up. They each took several brass chits (key tags) off their duty belts and handed them to Gallagher.

Troy said, "F-Wing, number 2, and Ed is F-Wing, number 1."

Gallagher took their chits and went to various areas in the room, and swapped their chits for other chits on hooks on the wall. He kept the same names on the chits together in one hand and the other chits with the same names in his other hand. He came back and handed the chits to each Soares and McCall.

"Here you go. You guys be safe today and don't start any trouble."

Troy nudged Ed and said, "You hear what he said? He's talking to you."

Gallagher replied with a chuckle, "Talking to both you lops."

Ed chuffed. "You see, you're already starting something. That's why you're not number 1."

Ed lightly shoved Troy's shoulder.

They turned and headed back down the corridor.

They turned the corner at F-Wing and saw Officers Bandy and Quiroz standing at the desk. Soares looked at the name on the chits in his hand and handed them to their owner, Quiroz.

McCall handed the chits in his hand to Bandy. The quartet silently began giving and receiving duty equipment in the shiftchange ritual.

Ed took the cuffs, baton, OC spray, PAD alarm, and key group from Quiroz, and Troy took his equipment from Bandy.

When they finished the exchange, Bandy and Quiroz picked up their lunch containers.

Bandy said, "Thanks for the early relief, guys." Quiroz said, "Yeah, thanks."

"Anytime, brother," McCall replied.

They exchanged a combination of fist bumps between them, and Quiroz and Bandy left the unit.

Officer Painter was above the entry sally port navigating the buttons on the control panel.

Two inmates stepped inside the sally port, and Soares opened the inside grill gate, let them in the unit, and followed them in. One inmate walked in a few steps, turned, and looked up at Painter.

"Painter, 218 shower."

Painter nodded and wrote the number in a list. She waited for the inmate to get to cell 218, and she pressed the button for cell 218 and it slid open. The inmate stepped in, and she closed the door.

She saw the other inmate going to the far end of the unit. Soares went up the second set of stairs to a landing on the second tier and stood, watching the unit.

McCall came out of the officer's station, locked it, and stepped into the unit and stood by the gate.

Painter saw the inmate she was watching reach his cell, and he raised his hand. She knew his cell number and pushed the button, 126, and the door opened. The inmate stepped in, and she closed the door.

Soon several inmates returning from their work assignments began to filter in from the corridor. As they entered, each inmate would call out their cell number, and Painter would visually follow the inmate to their cell and open their door and leave it open.

The inmate would enter the cell and shortly come back out with boxers, a towel, and soap, ready for a shower. Their selection of one of the showers on each of the three tiers depended on their ethnicity or gang affiliation. Inmates in each housing unit decided the shower designation for first, second, or third tier.

Inmate workers didn't usually follow the shower location process.

After the inmate workers were all showered, there often was a slight lull in the unit that may last until count time at 1630 hours.

It came to pass that down the corridor near RC Control was an older housing unit, West Hall. Normally, the reading material allowed for inmates didn't include pornography. However, in the housing unit, an inmate they called the Paper Pimp, an older inmate, James Jefferson, had a collection of contraband consisting of explicit "girly" magazines. Jefferson basically could afford the top-dollar primo magazines. He would rent the magazines out to other inmates for items he didn't have access to. Inmate Nguyen borrowed one such top-of-the-line *reading* material. The rental period had expired, and inmate Jefferson was forced to go to Nguyen's cell to collect his property. Inmate Nguyen didn't want to give up the magazine so soon,

but his wishes fell on deaf ears, and the Paper Pimp did retrieve his property. When Jefferson got back to his cell, he inspected the magazine. He looked into the paper bag that contained the magazine and found that the pages were stuck together and moist with bodily fluids. Of course, that caused the Paper Pimp displeasure. However, it was time for institutional count and a confrontation was not possible at the moment.

Back in F-Wing, Soares and McCall walked out onto the unit floor. They separated, and McCall walked up the west-side stairway, and Soares walked up the east-side stairway. They went up to the third tier and went to the near end of the unit.

Soares announced loudly, "F-Wing, third tier east side. Standing count!"

McCall called out loudly also, "Third tier, west side. Standing count!"

During this count, inmates were required to stand up in their cell to assure the inmate counted was alive.

McCall and Soares each had a preprinted count slip with the tier and cell number of the cells in the unit. They each counted and documented the number of inmates in each cell.

They yelled out a similar announcement for each tier.

When they finished counting on the first tier, they returned to the officer's station and matched the inmate count with a unit count sheet. Soares dialed the number for Central Control.

Soares waited for an answer. Eventually Soares said, "Officer Soares with F-Wing count." There was a brief pause, and he continued. "First tier, eighty-two. Second tier, ninety. Third tier, eightyfour. Total count two fifty-six." There was another short pause.

Soares smiled and hung up the phone. He wrote the numbers on a count slip and signed it. He got up and went out to the corridor and clipped the count slip on a pressure clip on the side wall of the unit entrance.

The F-Wing crew relaxed for a few moments and exchanged some tidbits of conversation. Eventually, the announcement on the institutional radio blared out.

"Control to the Watch Commander and all radio units, count is clear, count is clear, at 1721 hours."

Another announcement immediately followed. "East Hall, West Hall, chow time."

West Hall staff opened the chow hall door and announced, "West Hall, chow time, chow time."

The control panel officer began opening doors on the third tier, and the procession of inmates filtered down the stairs to the front of the unit. They were directed into the dining area in the unit. Occasionally, an inmate would approach the officer's station and put a letter in the institutional mail drop box.

The Paper Pimp slowly walked to chow, waiting for the second-tier west side to be released. That tier contained inmate Nguyen's cell. Inmate Jefferson went into the chow hall and collected his food tray and sat down and began to eat. He saw Nguyen enter a minute later. Jefferson ate his food slowly, savoring his last meal in West Hall for a while. The dining hall approached capacity, and the flow of inmates was stopped, and the door was closed. Officer Vasquez leaned against the wall of the dining hall, watching the inmates. After a few minutes, it seemed that most of the inmates were finished eating. Officer Vasquez nodded through a window at the officer outside the exit door, and he opened the door.

"Okay, pick 'em up."

The inmates, in a somewhat orderly fashion, began to pick up their trays and dump the excess food in the trash can, stack their empty trays on a table, and exit the dining hall. Inmate Jefferson let several inmates pass him by so he could time his opportunity. As inmate Nguyen got near, Jefferson slammed his tray against the side of Nguyen's face and a couple more times on the back of his head. He hit Nguyen with his elbow and knocked him to the floor.

Officer Vasquez activated his PAD alarm and yelled out, "Get down!" as he maneuvered his way through the inmates. He got to

Jefferson just as he kicked Nguyen for a second time. Jefferson saw Vasquez coming with his baton drawn.

Jefferson stopped, turned around, and put his hands behind his back and said, "Cuff me up, Vasquez."

Vasquez was surprised and stopped behind Jefferson and put his baton away. He took out his cuffs and put them on Jefferson. Sergeant Hernandez came to the door and saw Nguyen on the floor. Some of the other inmates that had left the dining hall were on the floor of the unit. The other inmates that were left in the dining hall had cleared away from the incident. Officer Collier was standing over Nguyen, protecting him. Vasquez escorted Jefferson out of the dining hall and into the unit. Sergeant Hernandez came up to Jefferson and asked, "What was this about? Why did you tune him up in the chow hall?"

"The fucker juiced all over my best magazine."

Inmate Jefferson was taken to medical to get checked over and then placed in Ad Seg.

Jefferson was glad he waited to finish his dinner before getting locked up.

After the alarm was cleared, chow continued without any further incidents.

*****

F-Wing started its evening shower program and phone sign-up list. The inmates alternated taking showers on the west side one day and the east side on the other day. The inmates in the nonshowering side, who had a "red" privilege ID, were given an opportunity to schedule a phone call the next day.

In the unit was an inmate James Fields that some officers called a "he/she," a partial gender reassignment. Inmate Fields had augmented breasts, rather large.

He preferred to be called Kimmi instead of James.

During his tenure in F-Wing, he was single-celled or housed only with inmates of his perceived sexual persuasion. Also for his safety and the department's possible liability, he was directed to shower with a "like-minded" cellmate or alone and to wear a T-shirt while showering.

McCall was on the second tier covering the second tier shower where inmate Fields was showering, alone.

Several inmate workers were assigned to the unit to sweep and mop the tiers and pick up trash. One of Soares's favorite inmates was inmate Frazier. Frazier got along with all the staff and was a good worker. He and Soares bantered about on a regular basis.

Soares was sitting at the desk, watching Frazier dry mop the first-tier shower area. Inmate Fields finished his shower and went back to his cell and came back out dressed in acceptable clothing.

He came up to Soares. "Soares, I'm leaving for CMF tomorrow, and I'm tired of being celled with fuckin' homos. That's all you put in my cell. I want a real man for my last night."

McCall had come off the tier and joined Soares and Painter in the officer's station.

The devilish prankster in Soares looked at Painter and then at McCall. "What you guys think? Should we cut a bed move and get him a real man?"

Painter smiled and shrugged her shoulders, and McCall squinted in thought. "Well," McCall said, "if we did, who would we give him for the night?"

"Soares, you gotta get me a real man," Fields reiterated.

Soares smiled devilishly and looked over at the first-tier shower area. Frazier was yet mopping the area.

"Frazier," Soares called out. "You're needed over here."

Frazier leaned on his mop and said, "I'm almost done," and continued to mop.

"I've got a proposition for you," Soares said to Frazier.

Frazier shook his head, emptied the mop bucket into the drain, and pushed the mop and bucket over to the janitorial storage closet and rolled it into the closet.

He walked over to Soares. "What's up, boss?"

"I've got a deal for you," Soares said.

"Okay, what's the deal?"

"We just cut a 154 for a bed move for you," Soares said. "Why? Where am I going?" he asked.

"We're gonna move you in to 203 just for the night. Kimmi's last night is tonight, and she wants to have a going-away present."

"Fuck no, Soares. I ain't movin'," Frazier exclaimed.

Inmate Fields interrupted, "Soares, quit shittin' around, he ain't gonna move."

Soares said, "Yeah, I can talk him into it. I know you can make it worth his while."

"I'm not a homo. I'm not doin' it," Frazier said.

"How about it, Kimmi? You can make him cry, can't you?"

Fields exclaimed, "Soares, you're just fuckin' with me. You ain't doing shit." He turned and headed back to his cell.

Frazier said, "Soares, you ain't right."

"Okay, Frazier, but you coulda had the night of your life," Soares asserted.

Frazier shook his head and headed back to his cell. Soares persisted, "You can still change your mind." Soares's words fell on the floor of the tier.

Soares looked at McCall and Painter and said, "Try as you might, I guess you can't please everyone."

(Recognition given to Don Vasquez.)

SADLY: PRISON JUSTICE

It had been relatively quiet for several weeks, and Watch Commander Lieutenant Calvin Allen privately wondered how long the lull would last. He got up from his desk and went out his door past the Watch Sergeant's area. He went up to the gate at the end of the hall and unlocked it. He stepped out into the main corridor and closed the gate. He scanned both directions of the corridor. There was moderate inmate movement. There was yet unease in the calm he felt. Maybe that's what thirty years behind the walls had instilled in his persona. He looked at his watch and decided he had time before count to take a walk out to the administration building and see what the cafeteria had to offer. He went over to the exit gate and waited for the staff in the control room to snap the lock on the gate. As it did, he walked in. He met Officer Martin Salviejo in the sally port when he stepped in.

Allen left the gate open for Salviejo.

"Thanks, Lieu," Salviejo said as he passed by Allen.

Allen nodded. "No problem, son."

Salviejo smiled and went through the gate and closed it. He turned left and headed down East Corridor toward the housing units. He turned into E-Wing and saw Officer Lewis on the control panel above the sally port. Salviejo unlocked the officer's station gate and sat his lunch box on the floor. He sat down at the desk and turned behind him and took a clipboard off the wall behind him. He looked it over and put it back on the wall.

He called up to Lewis, "Faith, where did Jacob go?"

"He went to R&R to pick up an inmate," she replied.

Salviejo nodded.

Several inmates came in the unit and waited in the sally port. Salviejo saw the inmates and stood up and stepped out into the sally port and locked the officer's station gate. He opened the unit gate, went in, and pushed the gate halfway open. He took a few steps into the unit and stepped to the left of the gate. The inmates followed him in and headed up to their cells.

Salviejo watched the inmates funnel out into the unit.

Lewis was busy pressing buttons on the panel to open up cell doors. If she didn't remember where an inmate lived, she would wait for the inmate to get to their cell and the inmates would stand in front of it. Often she could tell from a distance what cell it was, and she would open it. Otherwise, the inmate would call out their cell number, and she would open it. If she was unsure, she would ask the inmate his name, and she would look behind her on the unit picture board and verify the name with the picture and with the cell.

Salviejo checked to make sure the inmates entering the unit actually lived there. If he didn't recognize them, he would check their IDs. Inmates would try to get into a different housing unit for various reasons. They might want to talk to another inmate or to drop off a "kite" (prison slang for a note or letter) that might contain instructions for bringing in contraband or for someone to make a hit on someone. It had happened that the messenger was the one that was making the hit right then. In any case, any inmate in an unauthorized area could be given a write-up, inmate counseling, 128, or a "rules violation" report (115) for being "out of bounds." One or more 115s could, depending on the circumstances, lead to loss of privilege (LOP) or placement in Administrative Segregation. Such disciplinary procedures might also lead to "loss of good time" and extend their time of incarceration or reduce their chances of getting released on early parole. On the other hand, a lifer wouldn't be concerned about parole and only risked temporary loss of privilege and placement in Ad Seg. The other possibility could result in being sent to a maximum-security level IV institution or given a DA referral for murder or for any other serious violation of law.

The number of inmates entering eventually dwindled to zero. Salviejo went back into the officer's station and sat down. Officer Lewis secured the control panel and came down the internal stairway and sat at the desk.

Officer Jacob Viles came into the unit with inmate Baylor, who was carrying a netted laundry bag. Viles unlocked the gate and directed Baylor into the unit.

"Baylor, wait there for a minute," Viles said as he went over to the desk and handed Lewis a piece of paper and an ID photo.

"Here's the 154 for this guy and a pic for our board."

Lewis looked at the 154, bed-move slip. She wrote his information in the unit roster, placing him in 123 lower, and put the 154 on a clipboard on the wall. She put the ID photo on the desk. The ID would be taken up stairs and put on the board behind the control panel.

Viles went back out in the unit.

Viles saw that Baylor wasn't wearing an orange jumpsuit. "They gave you shirts and pants in RC, Baylor?"

Baylor nodded. "Yes, sir."

Viles smiled. "Okay, let's get you some bedding, Baylor."

They walked over to a linen storage door, and Viles unlocked it.

Salviejo went across the sally port and unlocked a gate and went over to a locker and took out a medium-size paper bag containing a *fish kit* that consisted of soap, toilet paper, toothbrush, tooth powder, and a razor, all the things a new cellie would need to hold him until weekly supplies were handed out. He went out the gate and locked it.

He asked Lewis, "Which cell is he going in?"

"123 low."

He nodded and went over to cell 123 and unlocked the door. Inmate Reddick was sitting at a small metal table, writing. "Reddick, you have a new cellmate coming in, you need to step out for a minute."

"I hope he's not a fuckin' homo," Reddick stated as he stood up and went out of the cell.

Salviejo sat the fish kit down on the floor, put on some gloves, and went over to the lower bunk and checked over the mattress for rips and rolled and bent the mattress, searching for any contraband that might be secreted inside. He checked the solid bed support and bed springs for missing or loose springs. He checked the wall behind the bed above and under it for gouges and scrape marks.

Satisfied, he stepped out, and had Reddick step back in. Salviejo waited at the door for Viles and inmate Baylor.

Soon they came to the cell with Baylor carrying his laundry bag and sheets, pillow, pillowcase, blanket, and two towels.

Martin put the fish kit on top of the bedding, and Baylor started to step inside.

"Thank you, sir," Baylor said.

Salviejo had a half smile on his face and replied, "You're welcome, Baylor."

Viles slid the door closed, and he and Salviejo started to walk away. As they walked, Viles leaned against Salviejo and nudged him somewhat. "Don't feel special. He said, 'thank you' to me three times."

Salviejo smirked. "Wonder how long that will last."

*****

Watch Commander Allen almost made it to the cafeteria when the radio called him.

"Watch 1. Watch 2."

Allen stopped and keyed his radio. "Go for Watch 1."

"Can you 10-19, watch?"

"Watch 1 copies, in two," Allen replied, pivoted, and headed back to his office.

*****

Inmate Baylor put his stuff on the lower bunk. He held out his hand and said, "I'm Phil Baylor."

Reddick was sizing him up. "I'm Alan Reddick. You're not a homo, are you?"

Phil took a short breath. "No, sir."

Alan started to shake his hand but stopped and lowered his head and squinted. "What?"

"What?" Phil asked. "Did you call me, sir?"

Phil stammered a bit. "Sorry, I was told to be respectful."

"Who told you that?"

"My dad told me that people in prison want respect, so I want to show you respect."

Alan shook his head. "Dude, you show your respect in here by standing up for yourself and keeping your word. Calling other inmates 'sir' can send the wrong message, unless they've done something to earn that respect."

"Okay, thanks," Phil said.

"And, saying 'thank you' is okay but don't say that too much, unless the dude does something special."

Phil nodded and started unpacking and setting up his sleeping area.

Alan sat back down at the table and continued writing a letter. Phil finished putting his things away and sat on his bunk. He stared at the door and then at the walls. He sighed and lay back on his bed and looked up at his partial view of the ceiling. After a while he sat up on his bunk and looked over at Alan still writing. He saw that Alan had a TV but it wasn't on. He was afraid to ask if he could turn it on, so he just stared at the walls.

Alan finished his letter and put it in an envelope and put it on his bed. He looked over at the pictures on the corner wall.

"You have kids, Phil?"

Phil was slow to answer, "No, no children."

"I've got a boy and girl, but I doubt I'll ever get to spend any time with them outside of prison. I got a life sentence," Alan said.

Phil wrinkled his brows. "That's too bad."

"How much time did you get?" Alan asked.

Phil clinched his teeth slightly. "Six years."

"Six years...wish I only had six years."

Alan stood up and looked out through the small squares of metal-framed window overlooking the rear of another housing unit.

Phil did not want to ask or even know what Alan did to warrant a life sentence, lest he had to disclose his crime.

Whatever Alan did, it couldn't be good. Alan continued, "I killed a chomo."

"Chomo? What's that?" Phil asked.

Alan turned away from the window in growing duress. "You don't fucking know what a chomo is? It's a child molester. He molested my little girl."

Phil began a downward spiral. He felt the fear growing in his throat.

Alan calmed his tone somewhat and sat back down at the table. Alan asked the question that required an answer; Phil had practiced the response he was told to say. "What'd you do?"

Phil tried to hide his short breath. "Assault?" was his answer. Alan squinted. "Six years for fuckin' assault? Who'd you assault,

the governor?" Alan chuffed.

Phil added another part of his story. "I had a gun?"

Alan shrugged. "That makes a little more sense. What kind of gun d'ya use? You look like a nine-millimeter guy," Alan said with a touch of excitement.

Phil smiled a little, having given some credibility to his ruse. He decided to fortify his story with a little bravado in his response. "Yeah, you're right, a nine millimeter." He felt he was on a roll. "I pointed the gun at this guy and squeezed the trigger, and I forgot that I only loaded four bullets in the magazine and it hit on an empty chamber."

Phil seemed pleased with his response.

Alan half closed one eye and wrinkled his face in quandary.

He tried to imagine the scene Phil had described. He thought for a moment and took half a breath. Alan prepared to engage in his pursuit for clarity.

*****

The phone rang at the officer's station. Viles answered it.

"Viles, E-Wing."

"Viles, this is Lieutenant Allen."

"What's up, Lieu?"

"That inmate you picked up in RC, Baylor, where is he?"

Viles said, "I just housed him in his cell."

"What cell did you put him in?" Allen asked.

"He's in 123."

"You need to get him out, now. He was mis-celled. He was supposed to go into G-123. He's a 288."

Viles looked over at Salviejo and Lewis, and exclaimed, "Holy shit, guys, we gotta get Baylor out of that cell. He's a 288, and he's in the cell with Reddick. We got it, Lieu." Viles hung up the phone.

The trio scrambled out of the officer's station and sprinted out into the unit.

In the cell, Reddick, unknowingly, was within arm's reach of a PC 288, child molester, and was just starting to ask his next question when he heard the unit grill gate open with a bang against the bars and the rumbling of footsteps on the tier. Reddick went over to the window in his door and saw the throng heading his way. He wondered what was happening.

Viles unlocked the cell door, and Reddick backed away in surprise.

"Reddick, can you step out of the cell?" Salviejo urged.

Reddick stepped out, and Salviejo and Lewis escorted him away toward the far end of the unit.

Viles went into the cell. Inmate Baylor stood up and was taking deep breaths from anxiety.

"Are you okay, Baylor?" Viles asked.

"Yes, sir," he replied.

Viles continued, "You need to get your stuff, you are moving."

Baylor was relieved. He began to gather his things. As he started to remove the bedding, Viles stopped him.

"You can leave everything else, just take your personal stuff."

Baylor picked up his laundry bag and stepped out of the cell. Viles escorted him toward the sally port.

Salviejo and Lewis saw Baylor being escorted away.

"Okay, Reddick, you can go back to your cell now," Martin said.

Reddick was yet assimilating the event.

"What the fuck was that about?" he asked.

Lewis said, "The guy was put in the wrong cell, we had to move him."

"Why? What'd he do?" Reddick asked, as he got to his cell door.

"Can't tell you, but it was for your security," Lewis said.

Reddick stepped into the cell, and Martin slid the door closed.

As Reddick watched through the small window in the cell door, Lewis and Salviejo walked away. Reddick was yet perplexed.

Reddick sat contemplating what threat to his security Baylor could present.

Martin and Faith came back to the officer's station and took some deep breaths. Viles had Baylor wait beside the sally port, and went back to the desk and dialed the phone.

"Watch Commander, Allen," was the answer.

"Hey, Lieu, Viles. We got Baylor out of the cell and he's okay."

Allen sighed. "Thanks, Viles, good job. Still trying to find out who dropped the ball on this. That could have been a disaster."

"Yep, Lieu, it would have been bad."

"Did Reddick find out about Baylor's commitment?" Allen asked.

"We didn't say anything. Let me ask Baylor."

Viles called Baylor over to the talk to him through the bars of the officer's station.

He spoke quietly. "Baylor, did you tell Reddick or did he find out what you were in for?"

Baylor shook his head. "I didn't tell him. I told him I was in for assault with a gun."

Viles spoke into the phone. "No, Lieu, he didn't tell him."

"Well, I hope he doesn't figure it out. There's a new 154 being cut. Just hold him there," Allen directed.

"10-4, Lieu," Viles replied and hung up the phone. He turned to Salviejo and Lewis. "Watch Commander said 'good job,' guys."

"Yeah, that was a new one for me. Gotta write that down in my memoires," Lewis said.

Salviejo nodded. "That was a first for me too."

Viles added, "Yeah, I've had inmates housed in the wrong cell, but not like this. But now that it's over, I can say it was exciting." Salviejo and Lewis chuffed.

"But let's not do it again," Lewis added.

Viles asked aloud, flippantly, "So, honey, how was your first forty-five minutes of the day?"

They chuckled together. The unit business fell back to normal. Inmates filtered in returning from various activities, visiting, library, and some medical calls.

A half hour passed, and Officer Andre Caloca from F-Wing came into the unit.

"Hey, guys, I have a 154 for inmate Baylor," Caloca stated.

Viles was sitting at the desk. He smiled and stood up and walked into the unit and over to inmate Baylor, who was sitting at a table in the dayroom.

"Mr. Baylor, I'd like to introduce you to Officer Caloca. He wants the pleasure of escorting you to your new residence."

Caloca looked at Jacob skeptically. "I assume there is a reason for your weirdness."

Viles smiled and handed Caloca Baylor's picture ID.

"Mr. Baylor was, unfortunately, temporarily mis-housed, and the rest of the story is his to tell."

Caloca shrugged and asked Baylor, "You got all your stuff?"

"Yes, sir."

"Okay, let's roll," Caloca said and led Baylor out of the unit. Viles stopped Caloca at the gate and whispered in his ear, "FYI,

he's a 288."

Caloca nodded slowly. "Oh," he said and they left.

*****

Since Lieutenant Allen had been drawn away from his attempt to forage at the cafeteria by the Baylor incident, he felt he should try again. He went over to the door and peeked into the Watch Sergeant's office. "Pssst," he offered.

Watch Sergeant Wong looked up from his desk at Allen peeking in the door.

He smiled and chuckled. "What's up, Lieu?"

Allen whispered aloud, "Is it safe to leave my office?" Wong shook his head and looked away.

Allen made another journey out the gate into the corridor and then through the sally port to the administration cafeteria.

He perused the vending machines and surveyed the hot food offerings and ordered the special of the day, chicken and broccoli, to go. He picked out an orange juice container and took his purchases back to his office.

*****

The C-Facility institutional inmate count was started at the normal time of 1630 hours. All inmates were required to stand during this count process to assure they were present and alive.

Eventually, the Control Sergeant cleared the count and announced the tally.

"Control to the Watch Commander and all radio units, count is clear, count is clear at 1702 hours."

The feeding process began with the orderly release of one housing unit at a time. The corridor filled with eager searchers for sustenance in the dining halls. Officer Marina Abeyta was controlling Center

Corridor with Sergeant Jacob Glover. Watch Commander Allen was also observing from several yards away.

The feeding process was in full swing when an inmate approached Officer Abeyta, held out his wrists, and announced, "Hey, CO, Sarge, I just killed my cellie."

Abeyta was unsure if she heard correctly.

"Did you say you just killed your cellie?" she asked.

The inmate nodded.

Her brows lowered, and she asked, "Where'd it happen?"

"In my cell," he replied.

"What's your name?" she asked.

"Perry Spears," he replied.

Sergeant Glover joined the conversation.

"Where do you live?"

"G-Wing."

Abeyta said, "Spears, step over to the wall and put your hands on the wall."

Inmate Spears nodded, and Abeyta guided him over to the wall, and inmate Spears placed his hands on the wall. Sergeant Glover covered Abeyta while she searched Inmate Spears.

Lieutenant Allen saw the inmate being put on the wall, which signaled a high-risk search.

He quickly went over to Glover.

"What's going on? Do we need to stop the movement?" Allen asked.

Glover shrugged. "Probably not, Lieu. He came up to us and said he had just killed his cellie in his cell in G-Wing."

Allen cocked his head to one side. "He killed his cellie in their cell?"

"That's what he said."

Abeyta finished searching inmate Spears and placed him in handcuffs.

Allen asked Abeyta, "What's his name?"

"Spears from G-Wing," she replied.

Allen keyed up his radio.

"G-Wing, this is Watch 1. Stop the movement in your unit." Unit 2 Sergeant Alvarez heard the radio call. He was in the corridor near G-Wing and he went over to the unit. He stopped the inmate movement and called into the unit.

"G-Wing, hold up."

Officers Madrid and Duncan were in the unit and heard Alvarez tell them to stop the movement. Fortunately, there were only a few inmates to contain. They had the inmates sit at the tables on the first tier of the unit.

Alvarez keyed his radio. "Watch 1, this is Program 2 Sergeant Alvarez. The movement in G-Wing has been stopped."

Allen decided the situation might need a wider net cast. He keyed his radio again.

"Control, this is Watch 1. Stop all movement."

The inmate movement began to stop as radio units heard the call on the radio.

"Central Control to all radio units, stop all movement."

That announcement solidified the movement of inmates. The red lights in the corridor were turned on, signifying to staff and inmates there was an emergency and inmates were to get against the wall in the corridors.

"Okay, bring the inmate with us. We're going down to G-Wing to check this out," Allen directed.

Abeyta called out, "Escort."

Staff in the corridor echoed the announcement.

With the inmates against the walls, the contingent proceeded down the center of the corridor.

It was a long walk down the corridor to G-Wing. They entered the unit, and Sergeant Alvarez met them on the first tier.

Allen asked Spears, "What cell is yours?"

"123," Spears replied.

That number was familiar to Allen, and as he got closer, he realized why. They opened the cell door, and inmate Baylor was on the floor.

Sergeant Alvarez called on the radio, "Control, this is Sergeant Alvarez in G-Wing. I need medical and a gurney to G-123 ASAP. I have an inmate down."

"Control copies," was the response.

Allen slid over for a better view. Baylor had an electrical cord wrapped around his neck, and his hands were tied with a cord ripped from another appliance.

His body was lifeless. Officer Madrid went in the cell and checked for pulse. Officer Duncan helped Madrid remove the cords from Baylor and take him out of the cell, and Madrid began CPR.

Soon medical arrived, and they placed Baylor on a gurney and continued CPR. Allen watched as they rolled Baylor out of the unit and took him to the medical unit.

Allen took another look inside the cell and took a mental picture. He keyed his radio to summon ISU Sergeant Cervantes.

"Sergeant Cervantes, Watch 1." The radio call was answered. "Go for Cervantes."

"Your assistance is needed in G-Wing," Allen advised. "I copy, Watch 1, en route in three."

Allen looked at inmate Spears. Abeyta controlled him by holding him by the elbow.

"Spears, is it?"

Spears nodded. "Yes, Paul Spears."

"You know you don't have to say anything, right?"

"Yes, sir, I have the right to remain silent," Spears replied.

"I know I shouldn't ask you about this situation, but do you have anything to say?" Allen stated.

Spears was nonchalant in his answer. "I knocked the dude down and tied him up. Then I wrapped some wires around his neck and choked him until he was dead. He was a child raper."

"How do you know what you thought he did?" Allen asked.

Spears replied, "Someone dropped a kite under my door, and that's what it said."

"Do you still have the note?" Allen asked.

"It should be in the cell somewhere," Spears offered. Allen looked at Abeyta and Sergeant Glover.

"Okay, take him to medical and get him checked out and then take him to Ad Seg."

"You got it, Lieu," Glover said.

They walked Spears out of the unit and escorted him to medical. Allen took a deep sigh and keyed his radio.

"Control, this is Watch 1, resume normal movement."

The sergeant in control echoed the order. "Control to all radio units, resume normal movement."

Slowly, the feeding program continued.

Allen walked slowly back up the corridor to Center Corridor and again stood watching the inmate movement.

Watch Commander Calvin Allen stood and pondered if this was the end of a lull or the beginning of another. His thoughts turned to Baylor. "Is this just a part of what happens in prison, or is it just cruel prison justice?"

(Recognition given to Marina Abeyta and Jacob Glover)

18 INCHES OF FREEDOM

DVI Laundry Officer Marc Kline guided the thirty-foot van as it backed up to the loading dock. He held up his hand to signal it to stop. Darius Herring saw Kline in his mirror and applied the brakes. Kline held up both hands to show Darius about twelve inches between them. Darius eased off the brakes and smoothly bridged the distance until Kline clinched his fist. Darius applied the brakes, and Kline nodded in acceptance of the final separation from the dock, about six inches. Darius applied the air brakes and turned the engine off.

Kline reached down to the bottom of the van's roll-up door, took off the padlock, and pulled the strap on the door and raised it all the way up.

The van contained twelve four-foot-by-five-foot rolling bins of netted laundry bags.

Kline had two inmates slide a docking plate to securely bridge the separation between the dock and the van. Kline took his usual position, standing off to one side of the docking bay.

Laundry supervisor Brad Trainer had his inmate laundry workers—inmates Pratt, Nelson, and Harper—go in the van and roll out the bins of clean laundry. They would roll them to a sorting area at the far corner of the laundry room. The workers there would unload each bin, sorting the bags according to a label denoting the housing unit on each bag. When all the bins were rolled out of the van, one of the inmates would roll an empty bin up to the loading bay door of the van. One of the other inmates would roll a bin of dirty laundry bags next to the empty one. Officer Kline would carefully watch as one of the other inmates would join the other inmate in tossing the bags into the empty bin. When the bin was full and Kline was sure that no inmate was in the bin, an inmate would push the bin into the van and step out of the van.

This process was followed until the van was full. At that point, Kline would have two inmates remove the docking plate, and Kline would roll down the van door and secure it with a padlock.

Kline would signal Darius a thumbs-up, signifying that the van was loaded and secure. He would then unlatch the chain and pull it to roll down the bay door.

Occasionally, the van would be loaded with a few stacks of pallets being brought in or taken out of the institution.

Regardless of what was being transported, in those instances, Kline used a similar process to ensure that no inmate would be hiding in the van.

Darius drove the van directly over to the vehicle sally port to be inspected by the officers for inmates or contraband. They checked under the van inside the cab and the engine compartment. The Tower 3 officer could see anything on top of vehicles entering or exiting. Since the cargo door was secured by a lock, there was no need to check inside.

Darius was allowed to exit the grounds. His normal route took him along several freeways and then off the freeway for two miles on a well-traveled two-lane road to his destination.

He drove up to a vehicle sally port and was subjected to another search of the van. However, at NCWF (Northern California Women's Facility), this sally port only had a guard station and lacked an observation tower.

He drove over to the rear of the institution and backed up to the loading dock. Officer Stacey Woienski unlocked the cargo door and raised the door. Her female inmates busied themselves unloading the bins out of the van. Officer Woienski followed the same procedure as Officer Kline in unloading and loading the bins into the van. When the van was loaded, Darius followed the same route back to DVI.

*****

Back at DVI, at the end of the day, the laundry workers began to gather near a fenced-in holding area near the laundry exit door leading into the North Corridor.

Inmates Pratt, Harper, and Nelson finished lining up the rolling bin against the wall and headed over to the fenced-in area with the others. Inmate Nelson peeled off and went into the bathroom. Officer Kline went over to the washer and dryer appliances, fixed to the wall. Looking for any inmate that might be hiding, he checked inside each appliance, leaving the doors open. He walked along each rolling bin, looking into each one.

Inmate Nelson exited the bathroom and stood with the group of inmates. Kline walked over to the laundry supervisor's office and saw Trainer alone in the office.

"Brad, what's your inmate count?"

"Twenty-six," was Trainer's reply.

Kline nodded and went over to the holding area and opened the gate. He nodded to the group of inmates.

One by one the inmates stepped into the holding area, and Kline counted each inmate into the holding area. He counted to the number twenty-six and closed and locked the gate.

He continued to the staff laundry area and opened the door and scanned it for inmates. He went over to the tool cage and unlocked it. He unlocked a metal drawer and pulled out an inventory folder and carefully checked that all the tools were accounted for. Satisfied, he initialed a page in the folder and secured the folder back in the metal drawer. He came out of the tool cage and locked it. He exited the staff laundry area and locked that door.

Kline went past the inmate lunch area and back to the laundry office. "You have the worker list, Brad?"

Trainer walked over to a drawer and unlocked it. He pulled out a clipboard that contained the names, CDC numbers, and housing of inmates working that day. He also handed Kline the stack of inmate IDs from the drawer. Kline put the IDs in his pocket and went over and unlocked the gate of the fenced holding area. He stepped inside and locked the gate. The inmates parted to allow him to open up the exit door into the corridor. He stepped into the corridor and hung the clipboard on a hook on the wall at the side of the door.

He looked at the list of names on the clipboard and called out, "Johnson."

Inmate Johnson made his way out the door and stood facing Kline. Kline retrieved the stack of inmate IDs from his pocket and sorted through them until he came to Johnson's ID. He matched the ID with Johnson and handed it to him.

Johnson turned and faced away from Kline, and Kline searched Johnson for contraband. When he finished the search, he said, "Okay, Johnson, thanks."

Johnson turned and walked away.

Kline continued that procedure until the names, IDs, and inmates were exhausted. He took the clipboard off the wall and went back in and locked the door. He made a final security sweep of the laundry area. He started at the back dock, securing the bottom slide locks and roll-up door chains on the loading bay doors, and checked the side exit doors.

Kline went back to the office and handed Trainer the clipboard.

Trainer put it back into the drawer and locked it. Their day was done, and they left together.

*****

Inmate Pratt slowed his walk down the corridor to allow Harper and Nelson to catch up to him. They spoke quietly as they walked.

"Jessie, can your guy get the sheers?" Pratt asked Nelson. "Yeah, he just needs me to signal him," Nelson replied.

"I've got a place in the bathroom to temporarily stash it for maybe half an hour."

"Okay, so, Lance, it's up to us to find the right time for the forklift accident," Pratt said.

Harper stated, "It's gotta go without a hitch, Dale. Kline is pretty savvy."

Pratt nodded. "It may not be tomorrow or this week, but all we can do is try. I'm not doin' thirty-years inside."

The trio continued down the corridor. Harper and Nelson left Pratt as they arrived at their housing units, J-Wing and C-Wing.

Pratt entered H-Wing and stepped into the unit. As he cleared the sally port, he turned to look up above the sally port at Officer Ira Cisneros working the panel.

"Ms. Cisneros," he called out, "225 shower."

She looked down at Pratt and said, "Gotcha, Pratt."

Pratt scampered up to his cell, and the door opened. He took off his work clothes and gathered his shower gear and took happy steps toward the shower, imagining himself far away from this place.

*****

Officer Kline and Brad Trainer continued their daily routine for several days, and inmate Pratt and his cohorts waited patiently for just the right time to initiate their plan. A few opportunities did present themselves, especially when Officer Kline was off sick, but the timing to have the forklift and the sheers available didn't coincide.

This morning's activities in laundry were of the normal fare. Officer Kline was watching the loading of the soiled bins of laundry, but there was a slight change in the load. Kline announced that two stacks of pallets were to be loaded at the rear of the van. Inmate Nelson gave inmate Draper in the staff clothing room the "high" sign. Draper picked up a pair of sheers off a table and walked over to the door. He bent down and pushed the sheers partway under the door. Inmate Nelson cautiously walked over to the door and pulled the sheers out from under the door. He took them to the bathroom and placed the sheers behind a toilet paper holder. Inmate Pratt saw him go to the bathroom and waited until he came out.

He asked Kline, "Hey, Kline, can I make a pit stop?"

Kline nodded and said, "Okay."

Pratt went into the bathroom and retrieved the sheers and came back out but stood out of view, away from Officer Kline.

Inmate Harper was driving the forklift and picked up one of the stacks of pallets and slid them on the van and pushed them snug against the wall of the van. He picked up the second stack of pallets and backed up and headed for the empty space on the rear of the van but intentionally bumped the corner of the stack of pallets on a rolling bin. The stack twisted askew on the blades of the forklift. He continued to the van and intentionally approached the van with the twisted pallets.

Kline saw that the pallets were not going to fit in their position, and he held up his hands to stop Harper. He had him stop and raise the load. Harper raised the load and waited for Kline to push the pallets back to straighten them against the forklift.

As Kline stepped away, Pratt quickly leaped into the van into a clothing bin behind the other stack of pallets.

Kline finished straightening the load and had Harper put the stack onto the van in the empty space. Harper adjusted the pallets snug against the side of the wall of the van.

Kline rolled the van's cargo door down.

He had the docking plate removed and put a lock on the hasp. He walked to the driver's side of the van and gave Darius a thumbs-up. Darius saw the gesture in his mirror and started the van. He drove the van up to the vehicle sally port, and the gate slid open.

He drove the van in for routine inspection.

Inside the van, the hidden hopeful remained quiet, knowing that the van would be searched. He had made his way to the front clothing bin in anticipation of the cargo door being opened and an ensuing search of the van by the officers. He heard some bumping and doors closing, but the cargo door remained closed.

Pratt listened as the officers spoke to each other and to the driver. He held his breath. He heard the cab door close and the engine start. It wasn't until the van had made several turns that he exhaled.

Back in the DVI laundry facility, Harper parked the forklift and joined Nelson sorting out the clean laundry bags that the van had delivered. Kline continued his usual security routine.

Inside the van, Pratt tried to stand on the edges of the bins to reach the roof of the van, but the truck's movement made it difficult.

Pratt hopped into bins to get to the back of the van. He reached up and, quietly as possible, pulled two pallets off one of the stacks. He stood on the pallets and got the sheers out of his pocket and began to make short work of the lightweight aluminum ceiling of the van and cut a hole for his escape. Somewhere between the time that the van entered the freeway and arrived at the other institution, Pratt exited the hole he had cut in the van.

The conjecture is that Pratt waited until the van had stopped, and he poised on the roof, waiting for the first opportunity to climb off the van.

At NCWF, Darius, as usual, backed up to the loading dock, and Officer Woienski opened the cargo door.

One of her workers, driving a forklift, removed a stack of pallets from the van.

Woienski immediately saw the hole in the roof. She keyed up her radio. "Control, Woienski in laundry. I'm unloading the laundry van, and there is a hole in the roof of the van."

Control answered, "You say there is a hole in the roof of the van? Does it look like something fell on it?"

"Negative. It looks like it's been cut open. Send a supervisor or someone from the squad."

She crawled up on the pallets and measured the hole using the span of her two hands.

She keyed her radio and continued, "The hole is about eighteen inches wide. You should call DVI and advise them that we found a hole in the roof of the van. This might be an escape."

*****

Officer Kline was searching the inmate lunch tables when the radio crackled, "Officer Kline, land line the Watch, ASAP."

Kline responded, "10-4, Watch."

He started to walk to the office when Brad leaned out of the office, holding out the phone to Kline.

"It's the Watch Commander for you." Kline nodded. "Okay."

He took the phone from Brad. "Officer Kline," he said. "Kline, Lieutenant Shelton."

"Yes, Lieu."

"You need to count your inmates, right now. We might have an escape," Shelton ordered.

"Yes, sir," was Kline's response as he handed the phone back to Brad. "Brad, give me the inmate sign-in sheet and their IDs. We have to count them."

Kline shouted out, "Okay, everyone, drop what you're doing and step over to the count area."

The inmates slowly meandered toward the fence area. "Hurry up, everyone," he restated.

The inmates moved quicker. He went over to the staff laundry room and opened the door.

"Okay, I need you guys to come out for count."

The inmates in the staff laundry room stepped out. Kline searched each one and had them join the other inmates.

Kline went over to the fence and opened the gate. He had the inmates go in one by one for count.

He counted twenty-five. He saw the number of inmate signed in was twenty-six. Kline locked the gate and went to search the bathroom. There were no more inmates to count. He went back over to the fenced area and scanned the faces of the inmates. He pulled the IDs out of his pocket and started to match faces with the IDs. He thought for a second and said to himself, "Pratt, where's Pratt?"

He rescanned the faces and called out, "Pratt, where's Pratt?" Pratt did not respond.

Kline looked at the housing assignment for Pratt and went back to the office and dialed.

"H-Wing, Cisneros," was the answer.

"Cisneros, Kline in laundry. Is inmate Pratt in 225? Have you seen him?"

Cisneros said, "He hasn't come back from work yet. Did you send him home?"

"No, he's MIA. Can you check his cell?" he said.

Cisneros had put the phone down and was already moving. She went out and checked the corridor and then went back inside and ran up to cell 225 and looked in the window in the door. Pratt was not there, but she opened the door and looked under the bed to be sure. She ran back down to the office and picked up the phone.

"Kline, he's not here."

Kline exclaimed, "Fuck. Okay, thanks, Cisneros."

The institution recalled all the inmates for an emergency count. As expected, Pratt was missing. Escape procedures were implemented.

*****

Investigative Services Lieutenant Jan Moppins and Sergeant Ronald Greathouse were tasked with ferreting through all of Pratt's phone, mail, visits, and personal contacts for any clue as to where Pratt might go. They interviewed Pratt's cellmate and fellow workers and developed a list of possible contacts supported by phone calls and letters. The telling direction of travel came from tracking the addresses of visitors. Several visitors were from Stockton, but the name that helped pin down a likely location was the visitor from San Francisco. Using the driver's license information of that visitor, a search of prior addresses led to a San Carlos address. A three-day surveillance of that address found three individuals at that location that were known associates of Pratt. An unknown female showed up at the house and stopped her vehicle out front. One of the male associates of Pratt came out of the house with a small suitcase and a bag of what appeared to be groceries.

Moppins thought that was suspicious.

She keyed up her two-way radio and asked, "Hey, Ron, can you see the license plate on her car?"

In another vehicle down the street, Sergeant Greathouse replied, "Yes, I got it, Jan."

"Can you call Parnell at SWAT and get a name and address?"

"10-4," Ron said and called the SWAT commander on his phone.

Moppins watched the interaction between the male and the female in the car. The male seemed to take out his wallet and hand the female something, probably money.

The male turned and went back into the house. She sat for a moment, and Jan could see her on her phone. She talked for a minute and then started her car and started to drive off.

Jan decided to follow her.

She keyed the radio. "Ron, I'm gonna' follow the woman."

"Okay, call me and tell me where you wind up."

"Okay, Ron." She started the car and began to follow the driver.

Moppins followed her for about twenty minutes, and she pulled into a hotel. She parked and took the suitcase out of the car and went into a side door of the lobby.

Moppins parked her car and called Ron on her phone. "Hey, Ron, did you get a name on the license plate?"

"Yeah, and to no surprise, it comes back to Shelly Foster in Stockton, his last visitor," Ron said.

"Okay, I followed her to the Parkside Hotel on Cribbage. She took the suitcase inside and left the groceries. She'll probably come back out and get them." Moppins paused. "I'm going out on a limb and call Parnell. I think Pratt is inside."

"Okay, Lieutenant, I hope you're right."

Lieutenant Moppins made the call to SWAT Commander Parnell. It took some convincing, but he relented. He said his team would be there around 2100. That was two hours away. She hoped Shelly would still be there when they arrive, and even more so, she hoped Pratt would be there also.

After about fifteen minutes, Shelly, the driver, came back out to her car and retrieved the bag of groceries and went back inside.

Sergeant Greathouse drove up and parked beside Moppins. He got out of his car and got into Moppins's car.

At about 2115, Parnell called Moppins on the phone. "This is Moppins."

"Moppins, Parnell. We are assembled on the right corner of the parking lot."

"Okay, Parnell, it's your show. How do you want to handle it?"

"I've got IDs of Pratt and Foster. I'm going to go to the lobby and ask the clerk if they are registered there and go from there," Parnell said.

"Okay, I'll stand by," Moppins replied.

Moppins hung up the call. After a few minutes, Moppins saw Parnell go into the lobby. A couple of minutes later, he came back out and came up to Moppins's car and got in the back seat.

"Okay, it's a go. The clerk ID'd both pictures. They are in 322. I'll set up my team, and then I'll have you come in and bring your warrant and your PAL authorization. Then it's showtime."

Parnell left the car and went over to get his team. They scurried around and disappeared into two separate doors. Moppins and Ron got out of her vehicle and followed two of the SWAT members into one of the doors. They took the stairs up to the third floor and waited for Parnell to come down the hallway. He knocked on the door of room 322, and when the door opened, his team swarmed inside. After a few shouts and groans, Parnell called out to Moppins, "Moppins, come on in."

Moppins and Greathouse went in and saw Pratt and Foster sitting on the bed in restraints.

Moppins pulled out a paper from her vest.

"Dale Pratt, you are being taken into custody by authority of this fugitive warrant for escape from a California State prison."

Moppins and Greathouse followed the entourage to San Carlos Police Department and waited for the paperwork to be processed. They had the pleasure of escorting inmate Pratt back to prison.

*****

Back at the institution, the word spread about the recovery of their fugitive.

When Kline came to work, he heard the good news. He went into the Watch Office to get outside line access and dialed the phone number for NCWF and asked for Laundry Officer Woienski.

"Woienski, Laundry."

"Woienski, this is Officer Kline at DVI. We got Pratt."

Woienski smiled and said, "Well, I hope he enjoyed his eighteen inches of freedom."

(Recognition given to Stacey Woienski)

CAN'T WE ALL JUST GET ALONG?

Lieutenant Art Castellon sat in the conference room listening to the morning briefing. His Program Captain, Sara Saylor, and Associate Warden (AW), Neil Barker, joined him at his end of the table. Chief Deputy Warden Haller continued his summary of directives.

"I realize the last directive that was presented Monday is not popular among most of the staff. However, that was not our call. That rests with the director. We've adjusted the guidelines for the new Ad Seg yard integration policy to address the concerns of Mr. Barker's Program." Haller looked at AW Barker. "Is your program ready to implement the directive?"

Barker reluctantly nodded. "Yes, we have a plan of action." The chief deputy sighed. "Okay, let's get to work."

Most of the assemblage began to rise and leave. Castellon and Saylor were stayed by Barker raising his hand. They acknowledged his gesture and remained seated.

Barker waited for most of the attendees to leave before he began. "Art, I know it's going to be a 'no win' situation, being forced to integrate the different gangs on the Ad Seg exercise yard. I understand you've had a dry run for the last two days, with the white and Northern inmates. How'd that go?"

Castellon took a breath. "It went as well as expected. We put several low-risk whites and Northerns on the yard together, and the next day we put some Southerns and blacks out on the yard together. We didn't have any incidents, but there are no issues between those groups at this institution for their being together at the moment."

Captain Saylor interjected, "But, Neil, in addition to the Ad Seg yard gun position, we had three officers stationed around the fence line armed with forty-millimeter launchers at the ready. That may have been a deterrent this time, but that won't always be the case, especially when you put a hardcore gang member together with one from a different gang."

Castellon shook his head. "I still don't get the reasoning behind making rival gang inmates share an Administrative Segregation yard." Barker sighed and explained, "That was all discussed at the highest level, and the Prison Law Office (PLO) convinced the court to allow this experiment."

Barker leaned to one side in his chair. "The thought was that the gangs will never get along so long as they aren't given a chance to exercise together. So they said put them together, and that's what we are doing."

Castellon smiled. "It doesn't work in general population. What makes them think it will work in Ad Seg?"

Barker shrugged. "It probably won't last too long. There was a shooting on another institution's integrated Ad Seg yard yesterday, and the inmates are saying the officers set it up."

"We'll be videoing the yard releases to show what happens, and we know what's going to happen," Castellon said.

Barker nodded. "That helps the documentation, but it won't solve the problem."

Saylor added, "No, but they can't say we didn't try to comply." Barker stood up as did Saylor and Castellon.

"Okay, let's do this," Barker said as he led them out of the room. They left the conference room and walked through the Administration

Building. Castellon separated from them and went through the entrance building and headed toward C/D-Facility complex.

He went through the double doors into the foyer and stepped up to the desk. He showed his ID to Officer Tayson, who looked at the ID, touched it, and said, "Thanks, Lieu." Tayson pushed a button to unlock the C/D Yard entrance door.

Castellon nodded and went out the C/D-Yard door into the sally port and closed the door. He waited in the sally port while the exit gate slid open. He went through and angled left to C-Yard.

He stopped at the yard gate and looked up at the gun position on the corner of a building. The officer pushed a button to unlock the gate. Castellon pushed it open and went onto the yard and closed the gate behind him. He continued walking along a line of buildings and angled across the yard to Building 6, Administrative Segregation. Ad Seg Sergeant Lara Brennan was standing outside of cell 211, talking to the Southern shot caller, inmate Rivera.

"So, Sarge, you're gonna send us out to the yard with the fuckin' Norteños to see if we can get along?"

Brennan nodded. "Rivera, you know that this is not what the department wants. The lawyers are the ones that put this together. We would rather keep things the same."

"Then keep it the same," he said.

"Yeah, and Cortez said the same thing, but we've gotta try," she replied.

"Fuck it, no promises here," Rivera said. Brennan nodded. "I hear you."

As she turned and walked away, she said to herself, "That's what Cortez said."

She walked down the stairs and headed toward the officer's station on the unit floor.

The control booth officer opened and closed the doors in sequence in the sally port, which allowed Castellon entry. Sergeant Brennan was talking to Officers Ken Robie, Robert Orani, and Sam Buck as they sat at some tables near the officer's station. The group saw Art enter and waited for him to join them.

"Good morning, Lieu," Brennan said.

Art nodded and said, "Good morning, everybody."

The group responded with nods and some "good mornings."

"Just left the morning meeting, and sadly, the yard integration policy is still a go," Art stated. "We'll just have to do our best to control the likely incidents."

Lara sighed. "I just talked to Cortez and Rivera, and you know what they think about this. They know that they are going on the yard with only a T-shirt, boxers, and state slippers." She paused. "We were just going over our battle plan. We were waiting for Clark to arrive with the video camera."

"Don't let me get in your way," Art said as he stepped back and sat on the edge of a table top.

Lara turned to the group.

"Again, you all have your 40 mm launcher and your bags of extra 40 mm. I don't want to run out of rubber rounds. And each of you has two MK-46 pepper spray canisters and a gas mask."

Officer Buck smiled and patted his bag and held up a canister. "If this party lasts long enough for me to use all of this up, then,

we will have a problem."

Orani chimed in, "Sam, you know that these munitions don't always work the way we want them to."

Robie chuffed. "Come on, Walt, if we use all of ours up and Kloppy uses hers up, then the inmates would have to be wearing capes and have a big red 'S' on their chest."

Lara nodded. "Speaking of Klopstein, guess I should call and check on her."

Brennan went into the officer's station and dialed the phone.

The phone rang in the Ad Seg yard gun observation post above the Ad Seg yard.

"Ad Seg gun, Klopstein."

"Dana, Brennan."

"What's up, Sarge?" Dana said.

"Just checking to see if you had enough inventory."

"You kidding, Sarge. I have double the normal amount, pepper rounds, .38-caliber rubber balls, 40 mm CN rounds, rubber baton rounds, six CN canisters (tear gas expulsion), and two extra thirty-round mags for the Mini. I even have an extra 40 mm launcher in case my barrel melts down," Klopstein offered.

"Okay, we're going to try to balance out the yard release, but there is always going to be one more of one side than the other side. So at some point, things will get dicey. We'll try to handle it from the ground as much as possible, but you do what you need to do up there," Brennan advised.

"Copy that, Sarge."

"Okay, Dana, later." Lara hung up the phone and went back out to the tables.

While Brennan was talking to Klopstein, Officer Kevin Clark showed up with the video camera. Lara nodded to Clark.

"Clark, your battery fully charged?" she asked. "Yes, and I have an extra battery," he replied.

Lara looked at Clark and noticed he didn't have a gas mask. "Uh… Clark, hold on."

She went over to a cabinet and opened it up. She reached in and took out a gas mask and tossed it to Clark.

"You might need this."

Clark nodded. "Yeah, thanks, Sarge."

She took another gas mask out and held it out to the lieutenant. "Lieu?"

Art nodded and accepted the mask. "Yep, I'll take one."

Brennan said, "Okay, you guys go to the same places around the fence that you were yesterday." The detail stood up and grabbed their resources. They divided their directions, headed to their stations, and readied their equipment.

Brennan turned and walked over to her Ad Seg crew waiting at the exercise yard gate area. Lieutenant Castellon followed behind her. "My money is on Cortez attacking Rivera first," Ezell said to McDaniel.

Lara caught the conversation. "What's this about?"

"We are deciding which inmates to let out onto the yard first and last," Ezell replied.

Thomas Bobbitt added his opinion. "We know the yard is gonna go off. We're trying to put the most likely instigators out first so there will be fewer combatants."

Lara said, "You know how that's gonna play out if you change the rotation? They will say we set them up."

Castellon added his observation. "That's what they said about the yard incident at CSP Sac yesterday."

Lara nodded. "The LT is right. We don't want that can of worms here. Let's just release them normally, if that's possible. But we will alternate North and South to the yard. Don't want to put out more of one group than the other."

"Okay. You ready, Sarge?" McDaniel asked.

Lara nodded as she took a long breath. "Yep, let's do it."

Each officer pulled out the yard release list and split up to collect the participating inmates.

Lara and Art positioned themselves near the yard entrance sally port and the exercise yard. One by one the inmates were escorted out of their cells, searched, and placed in the sally port.

Klopstein remotely would slide open the gate so the inmates could enter along the fenced-in walkway to the gate that went into the exercise yard. The first Northern inmate entered into the yard. Inmate Hernandez claimed one end of the yard. The next inmate, a Southern, inmate Perez, went to the other end of the yard and stood.

Lieutenant Castellon positioned himself behind Clark, who was videoing the entire yard release.

Inmate Cortez, the ranking Northern in Ad Seg, was the next inmate out. The two-to-one Northern advantage was not seized upon. Inmate Rivera came to the end of the sally port, and Klopstein slid the gate open, and the balance was restored.

Ezell finished searching his Northern inmate, Medina, and Medina began his trek down the sally port along the side of the yard.

Ezell turned to go get another inmate and asked Lara, "How many you think it will take for things to blow?"

Brennan sighed. "I only plan to put ten out, five Northerns and five Southerns. Don't think we'll get that far though."

Ezell nodded. "Neither do I."

He went back into the unit, passing McDaniel escorting Southern inmate Juarez. McDaniel searched Juarez and waited for Medina to get onto the yard. When the yard gate slid closed, the sally port gate slid open. Medina walked through, and the gate slid closed. Bobbitt arrived with Harris for the Northern addition. Ezell waited inside the unit with inmate Turner until Bobbitt finished with Harris. Inmate Harris began his walk in the sally port to the yard,

and that signaled Ezell that he could walk his Southern to the sally port. Bobbitt started back inside and smiled at Brennan as he passed her. "I keep waiting for shots and an alarm, Sarge."

Brennan took a breath and offered, "I know what you mean, Herb."

McDaniel waited with the last Northern inmate, Meza, while Ezell processed inmate Turner into the sally port.

When inmate Harris stepped onto the yard and joined the Northerns, they seemed to get energized.

Robie was the closest to the Northerns, and he noticed the change in the atmosphere. The breach in his 40 mm launcher was still open, but he thought about closing it to enable it to fire the rubber baton rounds. The urge to make his weapon ready subsided.

The 40 mm baton rounds, by training, were to be shot in front of the inmates so that they would bounce up to the lower extremities. Of course, the design of the rounds did not bounce consistently and could hit higher on the target.

Inmate Turner's entrance onto the Southern side of the yard balanced the numbers and lowered the tension on the yard.

Meza, the Northern's last inmate, was in the pipeline to the yard, and Bobbitt had collected the last inmate, Torres, a Southern, and prepped him for the yard.

Klopstein saw Meza at the yard gate and pushed the button to open the gate.

As the gate slid open, inmate Cortez grunted, and the Northerns sprinted toward their adversaries. Cortez focused on Perez, and Meza was the closest to the Southern side and headed for Perez also.

The armed staff on the ground closed their breaches and yelled, "Get down!" almost simultaneously. Klopstein in the gun tower was already locked and loaded and was the first to fire the three rubber baton rounds at the feet of Cortez and Meza as they approached the Southern inmates. Officer Robie sent his rounds toward the feet of inmates Turner and Harris. The discharged rounds bounced off the ground and found the legs and stomach of the combatants. Officers Orani and Buck followed suit, delivering their rounds at the other fighters. Inmate Torres was stopped in the sally port by Bobbitt and turned around and locked in a holding cell, but it did not prevent him from encouraging his gang's assaults.

Meza and Cortez were two-on-one with Perez, and Robie opted for an authorized "direct fire" rubber round on the ribs of Cortez. The entire perimeter of the yard was alive with bouncing rubber baton rounds. The Southern side of the yard quickly attracted most of the combatants. Officer Buck pulled the activation pin on his MK-46 (a large pepper spray canister) and began spraying four of the combatants with a sweeping motion. The shouts of "Get down" from the staff were continuous. Klopstein grabbed a CN canister, pulled the pin, and tossed it to the middle of the engagement. The inmates sprayed by Buck were coughing and squinting but yet trying to fight. The baton rounds were still bouncing off targets.

The Ad Seg crew, Jack Ezell, Thomas Bobbitt, and Carolyn McDaniel, led by Sergeant Brennan, made their way to the yard gate entrance and joined in the shouts for inmates to get down.

Several officers from C-Yard had entered the unit and made their way to the yard gate and waited with the Ad Seg crew.

The inmates were slowing their mutual assaults, using feet, elbows, fists, and knees to do damage to their opponents.

Inmate Cortez was trying to strangle inmate Rivera with a T-shirt and was stopped by a delivery from Klopstein. Eventually, the inmates separated into two areas and obeyed orders to prone out (lay facedown) on the asphalt yard. Brennan signaled Klopstein to open the yard gate. It slid open, and the well-trained staff stood in a horizontal line (skirmish line), and two officers at a time approached one inmate and used premade zip-ties to secure the inmate and escort them off the yard. The armed officers on the perimeter kept watch for any inmate that might continue any assaultive action.

The last two inmates to be removed from the yard were a Northern, inmate Cortez, and a Southern, inmate Rivera.

As Rivera was being escorted out into the sally port, he passed by Lara.

"How'd this work out, Sarge?"

The department has a history of ill-advised changes in procedures and policies. Some continue, but many have been discarded. After years of bad blood, you can't force people to get along.

MERRY-USING XMAS

It was two thirty in the morning on Christmas Eve. A car slowed as it passed the prison entrance.

Carrie told the driver, "He said to go up to the pasture gate on the left."

The driver saw the lights of the car catch the reflection of the gate.

"I see it." She slowed to a stop. "You sure this is where you want to stop? There's nothing here."

Carrie nodded. "Yes, he said to follow the dirt road toward the other end of this field and wait where the road splits and keep going till I get to a building inside the fence."

The driver said, "Okay, if you're sure."

Carrie got out of the car, and it drove off. She walked across the road and went to the end of the gate. She slipped between the barbed wire fence into the pasture. She walked down the dirt road for several minutes and arrived at a convergence of four dirt roads and continued to what she surmised was her destination, a fence line and a building inside.

A short distance away, she saw the lights surrounding the Minimum Support Facility (MSF), where minimum-security inmates were housed. The inmates housed there were the inmates allowed to work outside the main institution with more lax supervision. These inmates were considered low-escape risk, as they were generally nonviolent offenders, often with less than a two-year sentence and a Classification Score of 18 or less.

Their work assignments were for general institution maintenance and operation, such as warehouse, vehicle maintenance, grounds maintenance, and dairy operations.

Carrie was waiting for some sort of signal, a whistle, for her to follow. She stood for several minutes and eventually heard a short whistle off to her left. She walked toward the sound and saw a figure near some sort of wooden bins. Inmate Jackson motioned for her to follow him. He led her to a small building that had a few boards pulled away from the backside of the building and said quietly, "Get in here and cover up with the blanket."

She did as he asked.

*****

Visiting at the minimum unit was brisk even for Christmas Eve. Officer Kyle Haase was performing the informal inmate count, matching the inmate visiting list, accounting for both inmates and visitors. He left the inside visiting room and locked the door. He went down the steps and went out to the outside visiting area and finished his count. He went back up the steps and sat in a chair, watching the area while waiting for Officer Mitch Valadao to finish his count of the inmates in the row house modular buildings.

The radio crackled. "Haase, Valadao."

"Go for Haase."

"My tentative count is good, coming back," Valadao said. "10–4, Valadao," Haase replied.

Officer Angel Freeman was systematically circling inside the minimum unit dorm, counting the inmates remaining in her unit. The inmates seemed to be more upbeat than usual. Perhaps the Christmas spirit was a factor. Regardless, she enjoyed the atmosphere. She continued her inmate count.

Dairy Supervisor Carmo was rolling a cart of some unused supplies up to the supply storage building. He unlocked the storage door and started to roll the cart into the unit, when he saw some movement under a moving blanket near the back wall. He pulled the blanket off to one side and was taken aback by the revelation, an older woman was lying under the blanket. He shook his head and asked, "What are you doing here?"

She leaned up to a seated position and put her finger vertical to her lips and said, "Shhh!"

Carmo lowered his brows and backed out of the unit and locked the door. He went over to his office and dialed the phone.

Minimum Units Sergeant Brennan sat at her desk waiting for the count results from her staff. The phone rang, and she answered it.

"Sergeant Brennan."

"Sarge, this is Carmo. I unlocked the storage building and found a woman hiding under a moving blanket."

Brennan wrinkled her brows and repeated, "You found a woman under a blanket?

"That's right, Sarge," Carmo replied. "Where is she now?" Brennan asked.

"I locked the door back and called you."

"Did she say what she was doing there?"

"No, she must have thought I was an inmate, and she just held her finger up to her lips for me to be quiet."

"Okay, Carmo, I'll meet you at the storage unit," Brennan replied and quickly pushed the button to hang up and dialed the watch commander.

"Lieutenant Walsh," was the response.

"LT, Sergeant Brennan. I may have an unauthorized female in the storage building in the dairy area. Just giving you a quick heads-up, I'm going over to check it out now."

"Okay, Sarge, I'll send you a couple of S&Es. Keep me posted."

"Copy that, LT," Brennan said and hung up.

She stood up and walked up to the entrance door and locked it. She turned and went out of the back door of the office and locked it behind her. She walked across the connecting walkway into the visiting area. She saw Officers Valadao and Haase at the end of the unit and went over to them.

"Mitch, Kyle, come with me," she urged as she exited the rear door with them following. They went down some steps, and Brennan offered her explanation as she walked. "Carmo said he found a woman in the storage shed and he locked her back in it."

*****

Inmates Lindsey and Parker had seen Dairy Supervisor Carmo leave the storage area. They went over to the rear of the storage building and pulled a few boards partially away from the rear and had Carrie exit the building. They ushered her over to the dairy supply area and had her put on an inmate blue shirt, blue pants, rubber boots, and a ball cap. They led her over to the large stack of milk crates and stacked them around her and on top of her.

*****

As Brennan, Haase, and Valadao walked toward the storage building, Haase asked, "Did Carmo say what she was doing in the storage unit?"

Brennan shook her head. "She didn't say anything."

"This is a first for me," Valadao said.

Brennan keyed her radio. "Freeman, Brennan."

Officer Freeman was at her desk in the minimum dorm filling out her count slip, when she heard the radio summon her. "Go for Freeman."

"When you finish your count, 10-20 the office and cover the office and visiting," Barrett ordered.

Freeman was a little curious at her request. "10-4, Sarge," she replied.

Freeman took her count slip and headed for the office.

Carmo was waiting at the storage unit when the trio approached it.

Carmo asked, "You want me to open it, Sarge?"

Barrett nodded. "Sure, go ahead."

Carmo unlocked the door and pulled it open.

Haase went in first as Valadao and Brennan looked on. Haase saw the blanket, but there was no one under it. Valadao noticed the corner of the building had some extra light coming through. He went around a fence connected to the unit and made his way to the rear of the unit. He noticed the side boards attached to the corner were loose.

He peeked in and called to Valadao, "Hey, Mitch, the boards are loose on the corner. She must have got out this way."

Brennan saw two S&E officers coming toward the area. She waved for them to come to her.

She addressed the group. "Okay, everyone, let's fan out. We're looking for an unauthorized female."

She pointed to the S&Es. "Can you two check the perimeter?" One of them nodded, and they split off toward the fence line. Brennan shrugged her shoulders and looked at Haase and Valadao.

"Okay, let's see if we can find her."

The trio separated and proceeded in search mode.

Valadao decided to check the milk plant. He checked various processing areas, looking around several vats, and pumps. He scanned the shipping area and saw that the milk crates were stacked unusually high. He moved some crates to make steps to climb onto the stack. As he got close to the top, he noticed the crates were misaligned. He saw a panel of wood under several crates. He removed the crates and pulled the wood panel to the side. That's when he saw the woman sitting in the hollowed-out center of the crates. Instinctively, he drew his OC Pepper spray and said, "Don't move, bitch."

The woman appeared to be terrified.

Valadao keyed his radio. "Brennan, Valadao. I found the female in the stack of milk crates."

Brennan answered, "Copy, Valadao, en route."

By the time Brennan arrived, Haase had removed the back side of the stack of crates to access the hiding place. Haase placed the woman in handcuffs and performed a cursory search of her inmate clothing, looking for possible weapons. Brennan walked up to her and shook her head.

"If I take the handcuffs off, will you do what you're told?"

"Yes, sir," she said.

Brennan nodded to Haase, and he took the cuffs off. "What's your name?"

"Carrie Grey," she replied.

Brennan nodded to Valadao and Haase. "Let's take her over to the dairy supervisor's office."

Brennan put her hand on Carrie's elbow and guided her down the walkway.

Brennan keyed her radio. "Officer Freeman, Brennan."

Freeman was sitting in the sergeant's office, heard the radio, and replied, "Go for Freeman, Sarge."

"Can you 10-20 Carmo's office?"

"10-4, en route."

As Brennan and Carrie walked to the office, a large number of inmates was watching the entourage.

"Do you know who brought you in here?" Brennan asked. Surprisingly, Carrie pointed to inmates Jackson and Lindsey, who were watching from a short distance. "Yes, those two let me in."

Brennan smiled and chuckled as she observed the reaction of Jackson and Lindsey having been "fingered."

Brennan led her inside the office.

"Take everything out of your pockets and put them on the desk," Brennan directed.

Carrie did as asked.

She pulled out a pack of cigarettes, a lighter, ninety-seven cents in change, a roach clip, and a pair of tiny thong underwear and placed them on the desk.

Haase handed Brennan Carrie's ID he had taken from her. Brennan asked, "Ms. Grey, you can take off the inmate clothing, hat, and boots."

Grey took off the apparel, and Valadao took each item and searched it. He placed them all in a pile on the floor.

Officer Freeman came through the door and took in her first view of the intruder. She was forty-plus years old, average build with a pale complexion, and had medium-length light-brown hair.

Brennan asked, "Officer Freeman, can you take Ms. Grey into the bathroom and search her thoroughly?"

Freeman's face wrinkled. She answered tentatively, "Okay, Sarge. Ms. Grey, could you step into the bathroom for me?"

She nodded and stepped toward the bathroom where Freeman was directing her to. As Grey went in, Freeman turned to Brennan and said softly, "If anything falls out, I'm not going to be happy."

Brennan smiled.

The unclothed body search results were negative for any contraband. Ms. Grey asked to use the facility. Freeman nodded and stepped out of the bathroom. She looked at Brennan and shook her head, signifying no contraband was found. Grey returned from the bathroom.

"Okay, let's all go to the sergeant's office."

Haase opened the door and stepped out with Grey following.

Valadao asked, "You want to take the inmate clothing she was wearing?"

Brennan thought for a second. "Yeah, we might need it as evidence."

Valadao nodded. He took a bag of trash out of a trash can and took out an extra trash bag from the bottom of the can and put the trash back in the can. He bundled the clothing and hat and put them into the spare trash bag. He picked up the bag and the boots and followed Brennan out the door.

Brennan, Freeman, and Ms. Grey settled in the sergeant's office, and Brennan gave Grey a bottle of water.

Brennan dialed the watch commander's number. "Lieutenant Walsh," was the answer.

"LT, this is Brennan. We found the female, and I'm getting ready to interview her, unless you want ISU to do it."

"Sarge, I don't think anyone on the squad is here right now, so find out what you can. If things change, I'll let you know. Make sure you read her rights to her."

"Okay, LT, I got you covered." Brennan hung up the phone. She reached into a drawer and pulled out a preprinted interrogation form.

She took out Ms. Grey's ID and began to enter some basic information on the form.

"Ms. Grey, I'm documenting our interview to protect your rights, okay?"

Grey nodded and said, "Okay."

She gave the ID to Freeman. "Look up her visiting information for me while I fill some of this out."

Freeman took the ID and busied her fingers on the computer. Brennan and Freeman were quietly working for several minutes. Brennan finally looked up from the form.

"Ms. Grey, I need to interview you so we can find out how you got here and what happened up until now. We want to try and prevent this from happening again. I don't know if any charges will be filed against you, but just in case, I need to read you your rights. Okay?"

She nodded.

"You have the right to remain silent. Anything you say can be used against you in a court of law. You have the right to have an attorney. If you cannot afford an attorney, one will be appointed to represent you before any questioning, if you wish. You can decide at any time to exercise these rights and not answer any questions or make any statements. Do you understand these rights I have explained to you?"

Grey answered, "Yes."

"Having these rights in mind, do you wish to talk to me now?" Grey nodded.

"Is that a yes?"

"Yes," Grey said.

"Okay, would you sign this document and the waiver?" Brennan slid the paper to her and gave her a pen.

Grey signed the paper, and Brennan pulled it back and signed the paper also.

"Officer Freeman, did you find her in the visitor's list."

"I see that she was not approved to visit inmate Jackson, but on her visiting questionnaire, she is listed as inmate Parker's fiancée and lives at the same address as his mother. Parker lives in the new dorm, 123 upper."

Brennan keyed her radio. "Haase, Brennan."

"Go for Haase."

"Go find inmate Parker in D-123 up and call me when you find him."

Haase replied, "10-4, Sarge."

"So, Ms. Grey, do you have children?"

"Yes, a nineteen-year-old and a seven-year-old."

"It's sad that you probably will miss Christmas with them." Grey dropped her head down.

"When did you get here?"

"I was dropped off on the road at two thirty this morning," she said.

"It's after one now. That's a long time to spend here. What have you been doing all this time?"

She looked down at the desk. "Parker wanted me to 'do' some inmates for Christmas so he can make us some money."

"How much money?" Brennan asked.

"He said $100 for a white inmate and $200 for a black inmate." Brennan wrinkled her face and asked, "Where's the money?"

"He said they would send the money to his mother."

Brennan refrained from asking how many suitors she serviced. The phone rang.

"Brennan," she said.

"Sarge, Haase, I have inmate Parker here."

"Ask him if his fiancée is Carrie Grey."

"Okay."

Brennan waited for the response.

"Sarge, Parker said she isn't his fiancée and doesn't even know her," Haase related.

"Really? Okay."

Brennan hung up the phone.

She looked at Grey and gave her the news.

"Ms. Grey, it comes as no surprise to us, correctional staff, that inmates are mostly users when it comes to women who write to them and come to visit them. It seems that inmate Parker denies you are his fiancée and even says he doesn't know you."

Ms. Grey was brought to tears. Brennan said, "I'm sorry, Ms. Grey."

*****

Ms. Grey was picked up by the county sheriff and taken to the county jail. She was eventually charged with trespassing and bringing contraband, marijuana, into a correctional facility.

(Recognition given to Angel Freeman)

SEARCH AND NON- SEIZURE—SHOTS FIRED

Working vacation relief suited Officer Troy McCall, having completed his shift rotations after graduating from the academy eighteen months earlier. His last rotation was spent in Ad Seg, covering staff serving in Desert Storm. His current assignment, J-Wing officer, had him working with some good cops, Gail Fish and Ed Barnes. He was on the tier covering chow returning from breakfast. He settled in to his routine in this his second week of a three-week assignment. He was getting acquainted with the routines of various inmates in the unit. One thing working in corrections made McCall aware of was that people are creatures of habit and inmates are especially receptive to consistency. Although the daily mundane activities can breed boredom and anxiety, there are simple things that inmates look forward to that helps them get through their plight; hamburger Thursdays, yard activities, work assignments, watching TV, receiving mail, visits, and making phone calls can help quell the loss of freedom. However, the dark side— prison gang violence, abusive staff, and changing regulations—often consumes hope or even a life. Surely, many of the "incarcerants" have done deplorable things, but McCall took away at least two things from his academy training—

respect and treat inmates as human beings. And he wasn't there to punish the inmates; their punishment is being separated from society.

That last of the inmates cleared the unit gate, and Officer Fish closed the inside grill gate. She followed the stragglers down the tier a ways and turned to look up at Officer Barnes operating the cell panel even with the second tier, above the sally port entrance.

"Ed, that should be it."

Barnes nodded and turned the power off on the panel. He stood, turned, and walked down the steps to the door of the officer's station. He unlocked the door, stepped into the officer's station, and locked the door back. He sat down at the desk and opened up the DAR logbook and documented the return of the inmates from breakfast.

Officers Fish and McCall circled through the three tiers of the unit, securing the cell doors, ensuring they were all closed and locked. When they finished, they headed back to the officer's station. Fish unlocked the grill gate, and McCall followed her into the officer's station. She sat on a tall chair at the end of the desk. McCall went over to the clipboards hanging on the bars that were set against the wired glass windows that looked out into the corridor. He selected the cell search log clipboard. He scanned the log and mentally selected a couple of cells.

McCall put the clipboard back and opened a drawer and retrieved a few cell search slips and put them in his pocket.

"Hey, guys, I'm going to search cells 206 and 125." Barnes nodded. "Okay, I'll keep an eye out for you."

McCall opened up a drawer and took out a small rubber mallet and turned and went out the grill gate into the housing unit.

Searching inmate cells is an ongoing daily process. Second and third watch is required to search three cells per watch. Inmates are masters at hiding contraband, weapons, drugs and drug paraphernalia, escape materials, and escape access. Inmates are limited to the amount and type of personal and state-issued property they may possess. Excess or unauthorized property can present a fire or health hazard. Inmates are sometimes keepers of small animals or rodents, even birds, as pets. They even create cages and mazes for them, but it is yet a health hazard.

McCall went up to the second tier and looked inside the window of cell 206. He saw inmate Harris lying on his bunk watching TV.

McCall knocked on the door. "Harris, I need you to step out for a cell search."

Harris looked up at McCall at his window and began to get up.

McCall slipped the mallet in his duty belt and grabbed his key group and selected a key and unlocked the door and slid it open. Harris was wearing boxers, a T-shirt, and slippers, which was acceptable attire to wear out of his cell on the tier in the housing unit. He stepped out, and McCall pointed to the ground, and Harris understood that he was to present himself for a search. He faced away from McCall stood still and stretched his arms out to his side. McCall searched Harris's scantily clothed body.

"Okay, Harris, have a seat in the dayroom."

Harris proceeded down the stairs to a table on the first tier and sat down.

McCall looked toward the officer's station and waved an "all clear" at Barnes. Barnes saw his wave and waved back.

McCall took a step into the cell and turned around and put his foot on the floor against the bottom of the door jam. He slid the door closed with his foot and inspected the inside of the cell door for scrapes, tape, or anything suspicious. His slid the door back to lock it open, and as he did so, he watched the upper locking mechanism. He reached and pulled the rubber mallet out of his belt and turned around and scanned the cell ceiling floor and walls for discoloring or damage. He went to the rear of the cell and tapped firmly on the metal window supports, listening and feeling for movement or change in sound. He pushed on each windowpane and tapped on the panes lightly with the mallet.

This "bar and window" check was a basic escape prevention procedure. McCall went over to the doorway and set the mallet in the doorway. He looked at the light bulb on the wall and removed a brown lunch bag covering the bulb that served as a lampshade—to McCall, a fire hazard. There was another brown paper sack in the corner by the cell door being use as a trash bag. McCall tore the bag used as a lampshade and spread it on the floor. He took the trash bag and poured it out on the paper on the floor. He didn't see anything suspicious in the refuse. He folded the trash up and put it back in the trash bag. He went over to the light switch and inspected it for tampering. He took the blanket and sheets off the top bunk one at a time and shook them and twisted each one. He folded each one and sat them on the lower bunk. He searched the pillow and case, twisting each and looking for tears, and sat them on the lower bunk. He inspected both sides of the top mattress for rips and rolled it top to bottom, feeling for any unusual content. He inspected the springs of the bed frame for missing pieces and checked the frame also.

He picked up the folded bedding and put it back on the top bunk. He searched the bottom bunk using the same process. A high-security cell search is extremely time-consuming, searching every scrap of paper, nook, and cranny. This was a standard cell search, looking for drugs, weapons, and escape tools or clothing.

McCall checked the contents of boxes and clothing irregularities. He noticed two extra rolls of toilet paper and two extra pairs of state-issued pants, but although he could have confiscated them, he didn't. He saw some personal pictures attached to the wrong side of the wall with tooth powder.

He carefully took them off the wall and placed them on the metal table. He inspected the working condition of the metal sink and toilet. He looked for missing metal and the secure seating of push-button operation of the toilet and sink. He took out a mirror, and shined his flashlight to inspect the underside of the toilet rim. There was no need to inspect a toilet seat as there is rarely a toilet seat on most of the toilets in prison.

He checked the electrical outlet for tampering and signs of arcing, usually from putting small pieces of metal in each plug to light a cigarette or to weld something by moving the pieces of metal close together, causing an arc effect.

Lastly, he went over to the TV, turned it off, and unplugged it. He lifted it up and rotated it, slowly inspecting it for alterations. Each screw head was sealed with a melted plastic coat put on by either the manufacturer or the property officer. This was to prevent the inmate from opening electrical appliances and hiding contraband inside. He checked to compare the inmate number that was inscribed on the back of the TV with Harris's number.

Inmates steal, loan, or pay debts with TVs, radios, and other appliances. Appliances cannot be traded, sold, or loaned. Having unauthorized possession of one other than the owner would result in confiscation and a "rules violation" report.

He put the TV back, plugged it in, and turned it back on. McCall stood up and checked his personal equipment and belt,

assuring he didn't leave anything in the cell. He stepped out of the cell, picked up the rubber mallet, and called down to Harris.

"Harris, come on back."

Barnes heard McCall call out to Harris and went back up the stairs to the control panel. He turned the power on the panel and pushed the button on cell 206 to release the pressure on cell 206 so McCall could manually close it. Barnes turned the power off and went back down the stairs to the officer's station.

Harris came back to his cell and went inside.

"Thanks, Harris," McCall said and slid the door closed.

McCall walked over to the stairway and went down to the first tier. He made his way to cell 125.

He looked into the cell, and as expected, he saw no inmates; Miranda and Tewksbury were at work. He looked down the tier at Barnes and waved another "all clear." Barnes waved back.

McCall began his search process just as before. He checked the door, bars and windows, walls, toilet, and sink. He came across a state-issued manual typewriter, a box of paper clips, a box of retractable pens, a box of copy paper, and a sleeve of carbon paper. He checked the typewriter to ensure all the key bars were there. They could all be removed and used as a weapon. He put a piece of paper in the typewriter and typed each key. All the characters operated properly. An inmate may be authorized to possess in their cell certain hobby tools and uncompleted works and may be authorized to possess state property, but there must be documentation in the form of what is called a chrono attached to or in the vicinity of the items. McCall saw no authorizing documents. He set all the items outside the cell on the floor and finished searching the cell. He sat down at the table in the cell and listed the items he was taking from the cell on the cell search log. He called out to Barnes to release the door pressure on cell 125. He waited for the noise of the release of the locking mechanism and closed the cell door.

He stacked the contraband items in his arms and carried them to the officer's station grill gate and placed them on the floor in the other side of the sally port near the staff bathroom.

He came over to the desk in the office and sat down.

"Where'd you get that stuff?" Fish asked.

"Cell 125."

"That's Miranda and Tewksbury's cell," she stated.

McCall nodded. "Yep, didn't see any chrono."

Fish partially nodded and shrugged her shoulders.

McCall took the search log clipboard hanging on the bars and punched some holes in his cell search paper, added it to the clipboard, and hung the clipboard back on the bars.

He logged his cell search and the removal of the items in the cell search logbook.

*****

Officer Manny Larkin was watching the inmates in the swimming pool area immediately below him in his Tower 5 position. He also had full view of the entire expanse of the main exercise yard and the venues: various weight piles, softball diamond, basketball courts, a running track, tennis courts, scattered metal tables with attached seats, and a two-hundred-foot-long handball court with a fifteen-foot back wall.

The swimming pool was an anomaly for a prison environment. Inmates with a red privilege card were allowed to be one of the fifty to sign up and swim in the medium-size pool. The pool officer monitored the inmates' in-and-out access on a one-out, one-in basis. The pool officer and Tower 5 kept watchful eyes to prevent drowning (intentional or accidental) and injurious horseplay. The word was that the swimming pool was on the "chopping block," which was good news for the pool officers and Tower 5 officers.

Rec Officers Julie Martinez, Aaron Bazan, and Keith Bennett were three of the six rec officers supervising the thousand inmates on this bright and sunny day. Towers 6, 7, 9, and 13 in the center of the yard complemented the observation detail.

Officer Martinez was holding down the handball court area, and Officers Bazan and Bennett were covering the softball field and basketball courts. Sergeant Allen was standing on the porch of the yard shack, looking out on the yard. He was trying to get the feel of the yard. Martinez and Bennett noticed that when the inmates were coming on the yard, they were waiting for their gang affiliates to assemble and walk together on the yard; that was never a good sign. So far, it seemed that the handball court was lacking the normal activity yet had a large number of Hispanic inmates on each end.

Officer Bennett scowled when she noticed the Hispanics stopped playing basketball and started to assemble. Groups of more than three inmates were cause for concern, but a larger gathering was not allowed unless they were participating in a sports activity.

She keyed up her radio. "Yard Sergeant, Hispanics gathering on the basketball court."

Sergeant Allen looked down the yard toward the basketball courts and turned and noticed that the play on the softball diamond had stopped and the inmates were looking toward the handball courts.

He keyed his radio. "Tower 13, put the yard down."

Officers Bryant and Catario in Tower 13 heard the call. Bryant was the closest to the PA microphone. She keyed the PA mic.

"Yard down! Everybody down! Yard down!" she announced loudly through the speakers attached to the bottom of the tower.

Some of the inmates on the other areas of the yard began to lie on the ground. However, the Northern and Southern Hispanics on the basketball and handball courts quickly formed various groups and began charging each other.

In Tower 13, Officer Catario slid open one of the windows and picked up a 37 mm launcher and scanned several groups as they began fighting.

Officer Bryant also grabbed a 37mm launcher and slid open another window to make her observations.

There were too many individual and group encounters for Catario and Bryant to follow. Bryant discharged three rounds of CN tear gas in succession along the handball courts. Catario followed suit, discharging several rounds of tear gas, extending his focused shots to the basketball courts.

Rec Officers Martinez, Bazan, and Bennett drew their batons and shouted, "Get down! Get down!" incessantly. They remained near the incidents but, as yet, didn't engage any particular combatants. Tower 5 Officer Larkin heard the "yard down" call and yelled down to the inmates in the swimming pool, "Everyone out of the pool!"

The pool officer shouted similar orders and locked the pool entrance gate.

Larkin was more than one hundred yards from the handball courts. He had no clear view of the combatants' specific acts.

The clouds of gas whiffed around, further obscuring his view. It seemed like an eternity, but in reality, perhaps a minute, when Larkin decided that the incident would not subside without some intervention. He glanced down at the swimming pool area and saw no emergency there. He had already picked up his Mini-14. He supported his stance on the dropdown window of the tower. He racked a round in the chamber and took careful aim at the upper portion of the wall of the handball courts. He fired once, waited a few seconds, and observed no change in the incident. He carefully fired two more rounds into the wall. Some inmates, hearing the report of the rifle, began to lie down.

The rec officers heard the shots and froze in place.

Catario and Bryant discharged two or three more tear gas cartridges into the fray from Tower 13.

Three more shots were heard, and several inmates, having felt the splintering residual from the shots on the wall, began to lie down. The rec officers on the far side of the yard maintained their positions, realizing their areas could be subject to eruption also. A few more staff was entering the yard. Sergeant Allen had moved up to the edge of the handball court and directed the responding staff to hold their position as he was not sure where the shots were being directed.

Catario and Bryant ceased their tear gas assault from Tower 13 and waited for the gas cloud to dissipate somewhat. Bryant had changed out her 37mm launcher for her Mini-14 and stood at the ready.

The shouts of "Get down" were sporadically heard as some inmates yet engaged in assaults.

Several more shots rang out, and eventually, only a couple of one-on-one assaults remained and were stopped by shouts and baton strikes by staff.

Sergeant Allen realized the shots were coming from Tower 5 and was about to key his radio when he heard his radio crackle.

"Yard Sergeant, this is Tower 5. I'm clear for you to approach."

Allen looked over at Tower 5 and replied, "10-4, Tower 5, we are going in."

Dozens of staff began to emerge onto the yard and began cuffing up some combatants and standing over other inmates.

Inmates Rios and Reed were lying on the basketball court and decided to attack their adversaries one more time. Together, they jumped up and ran over toward inmate Garza, who saw them coming. They stood punching and kicking each other, and inmate Rios began stabbing inmate Garza with a weapon. Officers Bazan and Bennett immediately ran over to stop the attack. Bennett struck inmate Rios with her baton on his right arm, which was wielding the weapon, and followed up with another strike to his ribs. Rios dropped the weapon. Officer Bazan used his baton as a two-handed horizontal strike to the chest of inmate Reed and knocked him to the ground. Inmate Garza tried to attack Rios but was stopped by a baton strike from Officer Bennett. Several other staff arrived and helped subdue the attackers.

The entire institution was placed on lockdown status for this incident. Since it was close to shift change, all staff were ordered to remain in their current assignment (held-over) until the yard was cleared and also until the inmate workers and school program inmates were returned to their assigned housing units. This facilitated an accounting for all the inmates for an emergency count. Often, incidents such as this could be used to disguise escapes or facilitate inmate hits in another part of the institution.

Much of the staff arriving for their shift would be diverted to escort duty or searching the yard for weapons or contraband. Officer Larkin realized that having fired his lethal weapon required him to remain in his post until he was relieved by another officer and his weapon and ammunition was secured and replaced by ISU. Also, since the incident involved a large number of inmates, his relief would also probably take a couple of hours. Larkin took inventory of his remaining unspent rounds, and he picked up any spent casings he could find. He yet kept watch of the yard to cover the staff and inmates should there be another surge in violence. He retrieved eleven spent casings and found that he had fired fifteen rounds. Four casings were yet accounted for. They possibly could have deflected out of the tower down to the area below. Although it was yet to be determined, he wasn't aware of any of his rounds causing any injuries; he didn't target any inmates, only the wall of the handball court.

*****

Officer McCall was standing at the grill gate in the unit, ensuring that the inmates returning from work or school, due to the riot on the yard, belonged in the unit. He recognized inmate Miranda returning from his work assignment, and as he passed, McCall spoke to him. "Miranda, I searched your cell and took some things out of it."

Miranda didn't seem concerned as he only nodded and kept walking. McCall was surprised that he didn't protest or ask what was taken. Eventually, the recall of all the inmates was completed, and the emergency count was started. After they had finished the J-Wing count, McCall was sitting at the desk in the officer's station chatting with Barnes and Fish.

The phone rang, and McCall answered it.

"J-Wing, McCall."

"McCall, Sergeant Pratt, just who I wanted to talk to."

"What can I do for you, Sarge?"

"Did you search cell 125 today?"

"Yes, sir, I did."

"What did you take out of the cell?"

"I found a state typewriter, some paper, paper clips, carbon paper, and some pens."

"Okay, you can give them back. They can have that stuff."

"There wasn't any chrono for them to have 'em."

"Apparently, they don't need a chrono."

McCall's brows drooped in confusion.

"Okay, but I don't understand why."

"What I understand is that Lieutenant Erickson was told to give the property back."

Still confused, McCall replied, "Okay, Sarge, you got it."

McCall hung up the phone. He showed his confused look to Fish and Barnes and said, "I guess Miranda and Tewksbury can have the stuff I took out of their cell."

Barnes nodded. "Yeah, that's par for the course."

"How's that?" McCall asked.

"It's not the first time," Fish replied.

McCall went across the sally port and unlocked the gate by the staff bathroom and picked up the contraband and took it down the tier to cell 125 and sat it on the floor next to the cell door.

He looked in the cell through the window in the door and saw Miranda and Tewksbury sitting and watching TV.

He knocked on the door, unlocked it, and slid it open. "Here's the stuff I took out of your cell earlier." Tewksbury got up and said, "Thanks, McCall."

They stepped out of the cell and carried the stack back into the cell. McCall waited and closed the door when they finished. He went back to the office and sat down at the desk. He opened up the DAR logbook and wrote in the time and the following,

Searched cell 125 assigned to inmates Miranda and Tewksbury and removed 1 state typewriter, 1 box of copy paper, 1 box of paper clips, 1 sleeve of carbon paper, 5 retractable ink pens. No chrono was found. Subsequently ordered to return the items by Sergeant Pratt under direction of Lieutenant Ericson. Officer T. McCall.

He closed the logbook and put it back on the desk. He wondered how the sergeant knew about the cell search, as neither Miranda nor Tewksbury had left their cell.

*****

Officer McCall returned to J-Wing after his two days off. He was refreshed and ready for his last week as a J-Wing officer. He sat his lunch box down in the office and stood looking out into the unit. Officers Barnes and Fish were seated at the desk talking.

"Good morning, Gail and Ed. How goes it?" McCall asked.

"Hey, Troy, how were your days off?" Fish asked.

"Restful," was his reply.

"You ready for chow?" Barnes asked.

"Have they called for us yet?" McCall asked.

"No, but you can wake them up, if you want," Barnes said.

McCall nodded and stepped out into the corridor and reached up on the edge of the wall and pushed a button and held it for about thirty seconds.

A piercing bell sounded in the unit. After about ten seconds, some of the inmates in the unit began to shout various obscenities to stop the bell. McCall was not persuaded. He continued for the duration.

The wake-up bell was necessary to ensure the inmates were ready for breakfast. McCall stepped onto the tier and announced loudly, "J-Wing, get ready for chow."

Eventually, the sergeant poked her head in the sally port and called out, "J-Wing, send 'em!"

Officer Barnes stood on the third tier at the end of the unit, leaning on the pipe rail, waiting.

McCall was on the control panel above the sally port. He pressed a sequence of buttons that opened the third-tier west-side cells. He called out, "Third tier west side, chow!"

Inmates began to come out of their cells and made their way down the stairs to exit the unit through the sally port where Officer Fish would look at each inmate's face and exposed skin for any sign of injury or unauthorized items bulging under their clothing.

When Barnes saw that the inmates had started going down the stairways, he walked from the backside of the tier, checking each cell for any remaining inmates and any suspicious appearance of the cell. If there was no inmate in the cell, Barnes would close the door. Occasionally, if an inmate was yet in the cell, he would be asked if he was going to chow and, if not, what the reason was for not going to eat. An inmate may choose not to go to chow for various reasons, but it would normally be documented. They might not want to leave the cell for fear of assault or were just not hungry or may be on a hunger strike.

The release process continued; McCall would open the cells,

and Barnes would check and close the doors, and Fish would observe the inmates leaving.

When all the inmates had left, McCall turned off the control panel and came down the stairs to the officer's station.

He opened up the DAR log and documented the chow release.

Later in the morning, McCall decided to search another couple of cells. He took down the cell search clipboard and selected two cells to search and wrote down the information. He started to put the clipboard back but noticed his previous cell search slips were missing. He put the clipboard back and opened up the DAR log and went back to the log date three days prior. To his surprise, the page of the day that contained the information about his cell search of Miranda and Tewksbury was missing.

McCall absorbed the curious circumstances and opened a drawer and retrieved some blank cell search slips. He went out into the unit and paused for a moment. He took out his personal notebook and wrote down his discovery of the missing DAR pages. He put his notebook back in his pocket and proceeded down the tier to search the cells.

*****

Some months later, McCall heard that Miranda and Tewksbury were quickly ferreted away to another prison in the middle of the night and an *associate warden* was implicated in inmate records manipulation and unauthorized dental procedures.

OF DESIRE AND NOT- SO-GENTLE TINA

The transport van rolled up and stopped in front of R&R, also known as Glass House among the staff at CMF (California Medical Facility). Officer Honrí France stepped out of the passenger side and closed the van door. He opened up the side door and motioned to inmate Gary Farris. "Farris, step on out."

France helped Farris out of the van and escorted him up a couple of steps and into the entrance and stopped at the desk.

R&R Officer Barry Gann watched them come in.

"Hey, France, good to see you."

"Back at you, Gann. Got a medical transfer from our IV yard to Program IV, B-Wing."

Gann understood the unsaid connotation—the inmate had been diagnosed with HIV.

California Medical Facility, its name often confused as being a public hospital by the uninformed public, is anything but an ordinary hospital. The exit sign on the freeway was changed to read Correctional Medical Facility instead of California Medical Facility, ostensibly, to avoid such public confusion. Although the institution is a licensed hospital and is classified as a level III, the security level of inmates confined here runs the gambit of level I (minimum security) to level IV (maximum security). Normally, a level III institution requires constant interior gun coverage. CMF, as many other "original institutions," was designed without constant gun coverage in the housing units. The inmate population of minimum to maximum security is rarely separated except in the Willis Unit, Ad Seg. The staff is accustomed to rubbing elbows with serial killers, rapists, mental patients, transgenders, and inmates with disabilities and life-threatening medical conditions. Staff, transferring from a regular level III or level IV, have a custody-level culture shock having to work in close proximity without knowing who is next to them.

France's partner, Officer Ray Mensik, came through the door and handed Gann a folder with the transfer paperwork.

Gann opened it, looked it over, and walked it into the R&R sergeant's office and handed it to Sergeant Trevon Jay and went back to the front desk. Jay opened the folder and studied the paperwork and seemed confused. He stood up and walked out of his office and went over to Gann. "Berry, we're missing a 123, 135, or 161. All I have is a 154 bed-move form."

Gann smiled. "Sarge, when we move an inmate from Solano to CMF, we only use a 154."

Jay shook his head, perplexed. "Really?" he asked. "Yep, Sarge, that's the procedure."

Jay stood and pondered for a moment. "Okay, Berry. You've been here in Glass House since dirt. You know what you're doing."

Sergeant Jay was on detached duty assignment from the Correctional Training Center, in Galt, while there was a lull in hiring new officers. He was an experienced sergeant instructor, but this was a first for him, not having a standard transfer form or Warden's Checkout form as required according to his training as an instructor.

Jay went back into his office and sat down and reviewed the file on Farris. It seemed that Farris was confined in IV-Yard at CSP Solano, the sister institution next door to CMF, and had a cellmate, Warren Blain, for six months and they became romantically involved. Somehow, Blain became infected with HIV and was transferred to CMF for treatment. Farris, according to his Central File, was devastated and summarily found a way to contract HIV, in order to be close to his lover here at CMF. In Jay's experience, these extreme solutions in situations of the heart are not unusual for the homosexual persuasion. It seemed that Farris was successful in his endeavor to contract HIV and was being assigned to the same unit inmate Blain was in. Most likely, Farris would make his way to reunite with Blain.

Gann processed inmate Farris, strip-searched him, and placed him in a holding cell; actually, it was a cage with bars.

Jay finished checking the paperwork and called Program IV office.

"Program four, Sergeant Carter," was the answer.

"Kerry, Sergeant Jay in R&R. I have a wonderful inmate for you to brighten up B-Wing. I have the 154, inmate Farris is waiting for a bus."

Carter chuckled. "TJ, you're so full of shit."

"You expecting me to change?" Jay asked. "Get your ass back to the academy."

"Shouldn't be much longer, but you'll miss me," he retorted. "Yeah, right." Carter paused. "You got an inmate for me?"

"Yep, and a story to go with him."

"How's that?" Carter asked.

Jay began, "Seems that he had a lover at Solano that caught HIV, and his lover was transferred here. Your inmate Farris apparently searched out a suitor to infect him so he could join his partner here."

"Wow, strange world we work in here," Carter exclaimed. She continued. "Okay, I'll send someone to pick him up."

"10-4. Waiting with bated breath," Jay replied.

"Bye," she said, shaking her head, and hung up.

Carter looked around her Program IV office and didn't see any of her officers.

She keyed her radio. "Program four S&E Porter, Sergeant Carter."

Officer Alfred Porter heard the summons and keyed his radio to respond. "Go for Porter, Sarge."

"What's your 20?"

Porter was walking down the corridor near the Watch Office. "Main corridor by the Watch Office," he replied.

"10-20 Glass House for a pickup," Carter directed. "10-4, en route," Porter replied.

He continued walking past the Watch Office and Central Control and arrived at his destination, R&R.

He pressed the button on the side of the entrance door. Shortly, he saw Officer Gann coming to the door. Gann opened the door and let Porter in.

"Good morning, Gann," Porter said.

Gann nodded his head. "Morning, Porter, you here for a pickup?"

"Yep, that's me."

"He's in holding. I'll get the paperwork for you."

Porter followed Gann in partway and stopped at the holding cell gate. Shortly, Gann returned with the paperwork and handed it to Porter. Porter opened the folder and saw his inmate, Farris, was bound for B-214. He read the part of the file about Farris's intentionally contracting HIV to get transferred. He took Farris's ID out and sat the folder down on a nearby table and turned to Farris and spoke to him through the cell bars.

"Are you Farris?" Porter asked, looking at the ID. Farris replied, "Yes, CO."

"What's your number?"

"AA89456."

Porter compared his response with the ID and put the ID back in the folder.

"I need you to strip out."

Farris began the ritual, removing his clothes and allowing Porter to visually inspect body parts that might conceal contraband and also to note any injuries.

Porter searched each piece of clothing and the footwear, and satisfied with his inspection, he told Farris to get dressed.

Gann unlocked the gate, and Porter had Farris step out. "Okay, Farris, you feel safe enough to walk out without someone attacking you, and do you have any enemies here that you are aware of?" Porter asked.

"No, CO, I'm okay."

"All right, keep your hands behind your back. Let's go."

Farris smiled and walked toward the exit as directed by Porter.

Gann followed them and unlocked the door. The two stepped out into the corridor, and they turned left.

Porter motioned down the corridor and said, "This way," and began walking with Farris a few steps ahead of him.

They continued past X-Corridor and Willis Unit and eventually arrived at B-Wing. They stepped into the sally port, and Porter unlocked the grill gate and had Farris step in, and they waited.

Officer Dina Richardson was on the tier and saw them at the gate. She came over to greet them.

"Okay, Alfred, what ya got?"

Porter handed her Farris's ID and the 154. "Here's your new charge."

She looked at the ID and then at Farris and asked, "So you're Farris?"

"Yes, CO."

"Okay, stand over here, and we'll get you set up." Farris stepped over to one side and waited.

Richardson called out to Officer Gilbert Muhammad, who was on the tier. "Hey, Gil, can you pull out some bedding for our new guy?"

Muhammad nodded and went over to a side storage door and opened it.

Richardson said, "Farris, go on over to the officer there, and he'll set you up."

Farris nodded and headed over to Officer Muhammad.

Richardson turned to Porter and said, "Okay, we got it from here."

Porter smiled and added, "Dina, just a heads-up. Farris's former cellmate and lover, inmate Blain, is in this unit."

Richardson asked, "Am I getting a problem here?"

Porter grinned. "Not unless Blain has hooked up with his cellie. Farris intentionally caught HIV to be close to Blain."

Richardson shook her head. "Oh, fuck, no. I don't know what Blain and his cellie have going on, but if Farris has gone this far to be with Blain, it's gonna be a shitstorm if Blain spurns Farris." She paused.

"You know as well as I do how protective and vicious these Cat Bs can get."

Porter nodded. "Yeah, I know, but I just happened to read the file, and fortunately, I caught it for you."

Richardson took a deep breath. "Okay, I'll have to break the news to Gil so we can be on the lookout."

Porter sighed. "Sorry, Dina. Catch you later," he said as he turned and left the unit.

Porter walked up the corridor to the Program IV office and went into the sergeant's office.

Sergeant Carter was sitting at her desk. Porter handed her the file for inmate Farris.

"Here's Farris's file."

Carter took the file and sat it on the desk and opened it. Porter continued, "You might find that file interesting."

Carter nodded. "Yeah? You mean the part about Farris catching HIV to be with his lover?"

Porter twisted his face. "You psychic now?"

She smiled and said, "No, Sergeant Jay in R&R gave me the short version."

She paused, and with a sigh, she waxed philosophically, "Oh, such lengths one goes for the heart's desire."

Porter raised his brows, shook his head, and asked, "Sarge, are you off your medication?"

Carter chuffed. "Thanks for noticing, Al." She took a breath. "Okay, now, back to state business. I need you and Frank to go up to Mary 3 and bring back one of their inmates. I think he's going to A-Wing."

Porter nodded. "Okay, where's Frank?"

"He took the 154 over to A-Wing. He should be back in a minute," Carter said.

Porter nodded, turned, and went out into the outer office. Porter keyed his radio and started to speak but saw Officer

Frank Booker come through the door.

"Frank, I was just going to call you," Porter said.

"Oh, yeah, what were you gonna call me?" Booker asked.

Porter shrugged. "It was gonna be something nice, but I've changed my mind." Porter smiled and continued, "Come on, Sarge wants us to pick up that inmate in Mary 3, the one on the 154 you gave A-Wing."

"Okay, General, your wish is my command," Booker said. Porter scowled at Booker. "What? No salute?"

Booker furrowed his brows and replied snidely, "I'll give you a salute."

Porter laughed, and he put his hand on Booker's back and said, "Let's go before I have to hurt you."

They left the program office and ambled their way up the corridor to Central Control. It was getting close to lunchtime, and several staff were making their way through the exit via the Central Control sally port. Inmate movement was sparse, and some inmates were lined up against a wall waiting to be called for their medical appointment.

Porter and Booker walked a ways further and came to a stairway to the second and third floors. They had just started to walk up the stairs when and alarm sounded that indicated there was an emergency on the second floor. Porter and Booker ran up the stairs and had just got to the first landing when two inmates tumbled down the stairs from the second floor. When the inmates settled after their fall, they began fighting and cussing each other. Booker forged ahead toward one of the inmates. Booker held his hands up in a "stop" and protection stance and moved toward the inmate. "Hey, stop, stop," he pleaded.

Porter recognized the inmate as a transsexual inmate, James Jackson, he knew by his a.k.a. and shouted, "Tina, stop, get down," and tried to separate the two by using his left hand and right forearm to push them apart. His effort failed as Jackson pushed Porter back. Officers Porter and Booker, neither being small of stature, both six feet tall, were certainly trained in physical defensive and control tactics. However, inmates don't always respond the same way that they do in training scenarios. Booker's inmate fell against the railing after being hit by Jackson, and his leg kicked out and tripped Booker, and Booker fell on top of him. Porter's combatant, Jackson, spun around, and Porter took the opportunity to grab him from behind. Porter grabbed him around the shoulders and waist and immediately realized that his arms and hands were grasping breasts. Jackson began spinning with Porter holding tightly and being flung around.

Jackson was cursing at Porter in a deep voice. "Get off me, you fuckin' bitch. Let me go."

Booker fortunately gained control of his inmate with the assistance of another responding officer. Porter was yet spinning with Tina, but slid his arm up around Jackson's neck and wrestled him first against the railing and then to the floor. Finally, he gained control, and another officer helped him hold Jackson down. Responding staff assisted Booker and Porter in placing the combatants in restrains and brought them down to the first floor and sat them against the wall in the corridor.

Porter looked over at Jackson. "Why didn't you stop when I told you?"

Tina responded in a faux female voice, "But, Mr. Porter, you put your arm around my neck and hurt me."

Porter shook his head in irritation. "Don't use that high-pitched voice with me, you're a man and that's the voice you were using when we were wrestling."

Porter and Booker relinquished custody of their inmates to the other officers and went back up the stairs to the third floor and continued their original mission. As they walked toward M-3 wing, Booker began to chuckle then laughed.

"I can't get the picture out of my mind—you holding on to Tina, getting flung around. That was funny."

Porter laughed also. "I can't lie, thinking back about spinning around holding on to his breast."

Porter shivered his shoulders, saying, "Oooo, yuck."

They were yet laughing when they arrived at the M-3 Unit door. Booker pressed the button near the door on the outside of the unit.

Officer Jerry Lockwood looked out the door window and unlocked the door.

"What's up, guys?" Lockwood asked.

Booker replied, "Alfred here is all jazzed after feeling up a he/ she inmate."

Lockwood chuffed. "Well, he's in the right unit for that. Am I supposed to keep him? He can cell up with Shitty Smitty."

Booker sighed. "No. Sarge would want him back."

Porter twisted his face and remarked, "Okay, talk like I'm not here." He continued, "You have someone for Program IV?"

Lockwood nodded. "Yep, I'll go get him," he said and walked away.

Porter and Booker decided to take a quick tour around the "fishbowl." Mary 3, as it was known, was somewhat unique; the cells were situated in the center of the unit away from the walls, with a walkway around the outside. Each cell had a large six-foot-long-bythree-foot-high two-inch-thick window on the outside to enable a full view of the cell. Inmates here had varied diagnoses of serious mental disorders. The infamous Shitty Smitty was known to smear feces all over his cell, the walls, windows, and all over himself.

Porter and Booker observed a couple of cells but found nothing worthy of note. When they got back to the officer's station, Lockwood was waiting with inmate Jerry Swain, wearing restraints as required in the unit.

"Here's your guy," Lockwood said. "He was under temporary observation, but was cleared for general population."

Lockwood continued, "We can transfer cuffs here, or you can take him outside and remove my cuffs and give them back."

Porter was wondering aloud, "Why did Sarge send two of us to pick up this guy?"

Booker shrugged his shoulders.

Porter asked inmate Swain, "Swain, you gonna give us any problems if we take you back with us without cuffs?"

"No, sir, you'll get no problems from me."

Porter thought for a moment. "I think we'll transfer our cuffs here and escort him back in restraints. I don't know his history."

Lockwood nodded. "Okay with me, it's your call."

Porter took his handcuffs off his duty belt and put them on the inmate and removed Lockwood's cuffs and handed them back to him.

Lockwood handed Booker two IDs for Swain and unlocked the door.

Porter, Booker, and Swain stepped out into the third-floor corridor.

This end of the institution was constructed with three separate floors with a stairway between them. There were a couple of stairways with chain link cages covering the access to contain a possible riot.

The trio walked to the end of the floor and then down two flights to the first-floor corridor. They took the long journey to the opposite end of the institution and arrived at A-Wing.

Officer Dianna Merritt was sitting at a table in the unit watching the inmates.

Booker called out to her, "Hey, Dianna, we have a delivery for you."

She turned to the voice and said, "Do you have a reservation?"

"He has premium membership," Porter said.

She smiled, stood up, and went over to the gate and let them in. Booker handed Swain's two IDs to Merritt. She looked at

Swain's restraints and asked, "What's with the cuffs?"

Porter replied, "Since he was in Mary 3, I left them on him. I don't know his history."

Merritt ticked her head to one side.

"Well, let's take 'em off and see if we're gonna have a rodeo." Porter removed the cuffs, and nothing happened.

Merritt shrugged. "Okay, Swain, let's get you situated."

She nodded to Porter and Booker. "Thanks, guys, I guess we're all good."

Porter nodded. "Okay, Dianna, we're only a phone call away." They turned and left the unit and walked back to the Program

IV office. They went over to a desk and sat down.

Sergeant Carter looked up and saw them sitting at the desk and got up and went over to them. Carter knew of their escapade with the two inmates. She looked at them and noticeably looked at the clock on the wall, showed a wide grin, and asked, "You guys take a long lunch break?"

Booker smiled and explained, "Well, you see, Sarge, Alfred here wanted some gentle affection from his main squeeze, Tina, but it wound up being not so gentle."

(Recognition given to Alfred Porter)

THE ZOO

Officers Holtz and Saulsberry joked as they walked along the rooftop walkway that skirted the top of Z-Dorm. They stopped at the center of the dorm, and Holtz unlocked the access door. They stepped inside and sat their lunch containers down off to the side of the gun-walk. Holtz closed and locked the door.

The floor of the dorm was only sixteen feet away at this, the lowest point of the gun-walk, but attached to the bottom of the gunwalk was a ten-foot-wide-by-ten-foot-long chain-link-type screen on both sides trimmed with razor wire. This fended off inmates below from stacking beds or lockers and climbing up to the gun-walk. The gun-walk angled upward to thirty feet above the dorm below. The three-foot-wide gun-walk hung from the roof near the center of the dorm and extended horizontally about seventy feet across the center length of the dorm. At each end of the gun-walk was an open-top wooden munitions box and a gun rack to hold two 40 mm launchers and two Mini-14s. The heavy-gauge expanded metal walkway allowed a view of inmate bunk beds below. The forty-inch-high heavy wire railing, trimmed with two-inch square metal tubing, enclosed the sides of the entire gun-walk.

Officers Braga and Wiggins saw their relief come in the door.

Braga was the closest to the door, so he walked down the slope to meet Holtz and Saulsberry.

"What's going on, Phil?" Holtz asked Braga as they fist-bumped.

Braga responded, "You tell me, you're the man."

They both smiled and chuckled.

Saulsberry countered Braga's remark, "Hey, you told me yesterday that I was the man."

Braga smiled and said, "Yeah, and you are more of a man than Randy."

Holtz took issue. "You say that now because you have a weapon. Give me that gun and then we'll see what kind of smack you have."

Braga lifted the Mini-14 off his chest and then off his shoulder and handed it port arms (pointing up) to Holtz. Holtz took control of the Mini-14 and removed the magazine and put it in his back pocket. He slowly partially pulled the slide back and saw no round in the chamber. He locked the bolt open and looked down the barrel, put his finger in the chamber, and clearly saw his finger; there were no obstructions in the barrel.

Braga chuckled. "You know, not everyone checks the weapon like that."

Holtz smiled and replied, "Not everyone is a range master."

He took the magazine out of his pocket, looked at the side of the magazine, and saw that it showed full. He inserted the magazine and slung the Mini on his shoulder and positioned it across his chest. Saulsberry wrinkled his nose and sneered at Holtz, "Fuckin' show-off."

Holtz smiled at Saulsberry and walked up the slope to the top of the gun-walk. Officer Wiggins saw Holtz coming up the ramp and high-fived him as he passed and walked down the slope to Saulsberry. "Okay, Wigg, let's do this." They high-fived, and Wiggins nodded. He took his Mini off his shoulder and handed it port arms to Saulsberry. Saulsberry slung the Mini and removed the magazine. He checked the magazine to see if it was full and inserted it back into the Mini.

"Okay, fellas, we got this." Saulsberry nodded and waited for the two to exit the dorm. The door closed, and Saulsberry walked up the slope to the top of the gun-walk. He stopped at the rightside end of the gun-walk and looked in the wooden munitions box and picked up an inventory logbook and opened it. He inspected the contents of the box and compared it with the inventory list. He looked down at the 40 mm launcher and decided that all was good.

He reached over and picked up the phone out of the metal box and dialed.

Sergeant Shelton was in the dorm office and answered the ringing. "Sergeant Shelton."

"Perry, Saulsberry, inventory is good on the Y side."

"Thanks, Ron, enjoy your night," Shelton said.

"I sure will," Saulsberry said and hung up the phone.

Holtz completed his inventory also and called it in. He scanned the inmates in the dorm and saw Saulsberry coming toward him and met him halfway.

"Well, Randy, another Friday night in Z-Dorm," Saulsberry stated.

"Yep, Ron, we got it handled." They fist-bumped and separated to each end of the gun-walk.

Holtz stood at his end of the gun-walk, looking out on Z-Dorm. This was the Zoo, famous or infamous, depending on one's viewpoint. For DVI, a level III institution, it was the only housing unit with gun coverage, and for good reason. The mere size of the dorm was intimidating even without the more than four hundred inmates on the Z-Dorm side and the more than two hundred inmates on the Y-Dorm side. With a length of about three hundred feet and a width of maybe one hundred and fifty feet, those dimensions were only overshadowed by its height of maybe sixty feet. In its day, it was called a field house, used for indoor activities, including boxing matches. One end, the short end, now called the Y-Dorm side, yet had wooden bleachers attached to the wall. The infamy could be that it was the largest dorm with the largest population under one roof. For those that patrol the hazardous, recently minted triple-bunk jungle, it was a matter of keeping your head on a swivel, being constantly aware, and getting used to your butt puckering. Some saw it as one of the "seven wonders."

Sergeant Shelton walked out of his office and angled over to the officer's podium and walked up the steps to the overlook, six feet above the floor of the dorm. Since the addition of triple bunks, to facilitate overcrowding, one had to stand up to see over the top bunks.

Normally, there were only three officers assigned to first watch in the dorm, but due to the addition of triple bunks and one hundred more inmates on the Z-Dorm side, two officers and a sergeant were added to the staffing package. Y-Dorm picked up one more officer due to the increase of fifty more inmates.

Officer Jamie Villanueva walked around the Cadillac beds on the south side of the dorm. They were called Cadillac because they were single beds and not double or triple bunked. Officer Charles Dangerfield was touring the center of the dorm flanked by Officer Mike Geist two rows over. Officer Regina Mount was posted at a makeshift two-step podium at the corner of the TV viewing area. Officers Ken Robie and Genevieve Picone were watching the dorm from the officer's podium when Sergeant Shelton joined them. Officer Picone was an extra officer hanging out in the Zoo for fun.

Villanueva skirted the perimeter of the dorm, walked past the TV area, and made a right at the twelve-foot fence separating Z-Dorm and Y-Dorm. He walked along the fence, which was a mere four feet from the rows of triple bunks. Dangerfield and Geist came to the fence that separated the dorm and the bathroom/shower area. Geist went down two more rows and turned back into the rows of bunks. Dangerfield looked up to the gun-walk, nodded to Holtz, and headed into the bathroom.

Holtz watched Dangerfield go into the bathroom, but due to the height of the gun-walk, he could only see partway into the shower area and could see Dangerfield from the hips on down. Any further into the shower area and Holtz would lose visual contact. Dangerfield was aware of the sight limitation and stayed out of sight for maybe ten seconds at a time.

Officer Saulsberry was scanning Y-Dorm and watching Officer Jim Twiford walking along the bleacher side of Y-Dorm. Officer Ed Rugnao was also watching Twiford from the four-foot officer's podium.

Sergeant Shelton looked up at the clock behind him.

He looked over at Picone. "It's almost 2300. Why don't you and Robie go help Regina shut down the TV areas for the night?"

"Okay, Sarge." She kicked Robie's foot and said, "Ken, I need backup."

Robie smiled and said, "Why? You're the badass."

Picone sneered and ticked her head in a "let's go" motion.

They both stood and went down the stairs and proceeded to the back of the dorm.

Officer Mount saw them approaching and stepped down from the podium. "Guess it's that time."

Picone replied, "Yeah, getting close."

Regina went through a gate and walked over and stood by the two large TVs that were placed back-to-back in the center of the area and waited. Officer Robie went past Regina and stood beside the other TV set and waited. The inmates knew TV viewing time was fleeting. They all had their own headphones that they had plugged into audio output receptacles along the bench seating. Many of the inmates started to unplug and leave. A few diehard viewers waited until the last minute to leave. Mount turned the power off to the TVs and went over to the podium. Picone was waiting for her.

"You want some company for a bit?" Picone asked. "Of course, I'd love it," Regina replied.

Robie said, "I know when I'm not wanted." Regina smiled. "Baby, you know I love ya."

Robie grinned. "That's just what I wanted to hear."

He slowly walked back toward the front of the dorm. He took the short route through the rows of triple bunks. He stopped a couple of times and talked pleasantries with a few inmates.

When Robie got back to the podium, Dangerfield and Villanueva were standing at the base of it talking to Sergeant Shelton. "Sarge, I did see a few strange bed moves, but that was second watch's call," Jamie related.

Robie asked, "What's up?"

"Danger was saying that some of the new intakes seemed to be rubbing some of the old-timers the wrong way, they seemed upset," Shelton replied.

Villanueva looked at Ken and added, "I thought maybe you and I might check out the OG's pulse."

Robie nodded. "Okay, I'm in."

Jamie and Ken turned and walked toward the forest of triple bunks. They eased down a row of bunks and stopped near a collection of old-time inmates. Inmate Ramirez and his bunkie, inmate Ariza, were sitting on their beds talking. Ramirez saw Ken and Jamie walk up.

Villanueva nodded to Ramirez. "Hey, Ramirez." Ramirez nodded. "Hey, Mr. V."

"What's happening, man? You guys doing okay?" Jamie asked.

Ramirez shrugged. "We're okay so far, just trying to check some of these youngsters."

"They not coming in line?" Robie asked.

Ariza shrugged. "They've been here a minute, and they think things gotta go their way right now."

Ramirez added, "They shoulda brought in one or two in at a time, not six like they did. They should have put them in different parts of the dorm, they're too close together."

Ariza said, "They're staying up too late talking, and the blue rags are getting twisted."

Villanueva asked, "If we move them, would that help?"

Ariza responded, "I don' know, it might, but those *vatos* don't listen much."

Ramirez added, "It's tough to school them in a dorm like this, too many dudes."

Robie conceded, "We are in total agreement there."

Villanueva took a breath. "We'll talk to the Sarge and see if we can make some moves."

Ramirez replied, "A'ight, CO." Robie said, "Okay, *con cuidado.*" Ramirez nodded.

Ken and Jamie turned and went back around the line of bunks and headed back to the podium and walked up the steps.

Officer Mount and Sergeant Shelton were holding down the podium. Dangerfield had gone over to the small podium by the TV area to keep Officer Picone company.

Villanueva and Robie chose their seats. Shelton swiveled in his chair and asked, "So…you two find out anything earthshaking?"

Robie's head dipped toward Villanueva. "I'll let Jamie give you the synopsis."

Villanueva smiled and sighed. "Seems just as we thought, the youngsters that were dropped in today are too wet behind the ears to take advice from the OGs."

Shelton swiveled to the front of the podium and looked out on the dorm. "Guess I'll see if I can make some bed moves to make things less shaky, what do you two suggest?"

Robie shrugged. "They thought they could be separated in the dorm, don't know who decided to bring them in as a block."

Shelton leaned back in his chair and took a breath. "I'll be in the office for a bit then. You guys don't talk about me while I'm gone."

Officer Mount chuffed. "Perry, why would you say that? You know we talk about you whether you're here or not."

Shelton stood up and replied, "But, I never hear the good things."

Robie said, "What good things, Perry?"

Shelton smiled, shook his head, and went down the steps.

Mount stood up and said, "Well, I'm gonna take another walkabout."

Robie stood and said, "I'll go with you, Regina. I don't feel safe being here alone with Jamie."

Villanueva sneered and said, "Ken, you best be afraid, you wimp."

The matching pair left the podium.

Holtz had slung his Mini-14 behind his back and was carrying the 40 mm launcher loaded with baton rounds. The density of the bunk bed rows made the discharge of baton rounds problematic for effectiveness. Although the rows of bunks were arranged vertical to the gun-walk, the height of the triple bunks left little target area the farther away from the gun-walk they were.

He watched Mount and Robie as they wove their way through the rows of beds. Picone and Dangerfield had made their rounds through the dorm and were on their last sections. Saulsberry watched

Dangerfield from his end of the gun-walk as he passed under him near the fence between Y and Z dorms. Picone had just passed the bathrooms when she heard some voices that didn't sound agreeable. She modified her course to follow the voices. As she neared the possible source, the audible disturbance ceased. She stood and looked up at Holtz on the gun-walk, who had also heard the unfriendly exchange. Dangerfield saw Picone standing between the bunks and walked over to her.

"You okay?" he asked.

She ticked her head in a "follow me" indication. Dangerfield followed Picone down the rows, and they turned left and came out of the mire. They stopped near the Cadillac beds.

"Thought I heard a problem starting, but it quit when I got close," Picone said.

Dangerfield said, "Yeah, it's a little off tonight."

Officer Geist was coming away from the TV area when he saw Picone and Dangerfield, and as he started toward them, he heard the sound of bed frames sliding on the cement floor back toward the bunks near the TV area. That caught the attention of Holtz on the gun-walk and Dangerfield and Picone on the floor.

The bunk beds slid again and a loud, "Fuck you, asshole" resounded across the dorm. That pronouncement grabbed the dorm for a split second of silence. A triple bunk tipped against another triple bunk, and scuffling and creaks of more bunks moving was heard. Holtz saw the first tower of bunks tip and saw three inmates bouncing against other bunks. He activated the emergency alarm and held his 40 mm launcher at the ready. Officers Mount and Robie were in the center of the dorm and sprinted toward the disturbance. As they got close, the bunks at the end of the row they were approaching were being turned across the aisle, and several inmates were fighting. Both Mount and Robie began to shout the standard "Stop, get down, get down" at the inmates. They both drew their batons.

Villanueva stood up at the podium and finally got a visual on the location of the shouts. He sprinted down the steps into the dorm. Sergeant Shelton heard the alarm and bolted out of his office,

taking a split second to lock the door.

Saulsberry saw the triple bunks moving on the Z-Dorm side and momentarily held his temptation to join the response. He scanned the Y-Dorm side and yelled down to Officer Twiford, "Twiford, I'm gonna check out the Zoo for a moment."

Twiford signaled with his hand "go."

He put his Mini-14 in the rack and picked up the 40 mm launcher and two baton cartridges and hurried over near Holtz.

Mount and Robie approached the fighting inmates and shouted words for them to stop. A triple bunk tilted and crashed against another triple bunk, and it buckled in two.

Robie and Mount looked up at Holtz on the gun-walk then looked at each other, and Robie said, "Let's back out of here."

Mount nodded, and they turned and took the quickest way out. Holtz leveled his aim of the 40 mm launcher and sent the projectiles toward several combatants. He reloaded and discharged another volley.

When Sergeant Shelton made his way around the podium, he peered through the spaces between the triple bunk beds and saw several fights in various areas.

He keyed his radio and said, "Z-Dorm staff, fall back to the main podium, fall back." He paused and said, "Break, Control, I have multiple fights in Z-Dorm, multiple fights in Z-Dorm."

*****

Control Sergeant Eddie Gonzalez had heard the alarm and was listening and looking out his window in Central Control. Center Corridor Officer Ernie Facio saw the blue light flashing at the Z-Dorm door and yelled over to Gonzalez, "Gonzo, it's in Z-Dorm." At that moment, he had heard Sergeant Shelton's radio transmissions. Gonzales went over to the microphone and announced, "There is a Code 3 in Z-Dorm, Code 3 in Z-Dorm. All available units respond."

In the 24-7 prison environment, of the three watches (work shifts), first watch (1w—10:00 p.m. to 6:00 a.m.) has the fewest staff available. Since the inmates are (should be) sleeping, there is no inmate movement. The bare-bones staff on duty left perhaps six to twelve officers to respond to emergencies. Even with the increase in assigned positions for overcrowding, tonight, DVI's response would be challenged to the max.

*****

RC Sergeant John Alves heard the Code 3 request and shook his head. RC was the farthest from Z-Dorm in the institution. Alves had been around since dirt, and he knew Z-Dorm and felt that the call for help was most likely dire. He stepped out of his office and saw S&E Officer Don Vasquez walking from West Hall. He called out to Vasquez, "Don, where's Turner?"

"Dennie is picking up mail," Vasquez replied. "Okay, you take off to the Code 3 in Z-Dorm."

Vasquez replied, "Got it," and sprinted down the corridor.

*****

Shelton took count of his Z-Dorm staff and didn't see Mount and Robie. He took a quick breath. "Jamie, where are Regina and Ken?" Perry pleaded.

"Ken saw Regina at the podium by the TV area, and he went to check on her," Villanueva replied.

When Robie got to Mount, she was trying to pull a semiconscious inmate away from under a toppled triple bunk. Robie lifted the edge of the bunk, and the inmate twisted his way from under the bunk with Mount's help. The inmate sat up and then returned to the fighting. Mount and Robie both shook their heads and turned and scampered back toward the podium.

Holtz leveled the 40 mm and discharged another baton round. He reloaded and reached into the metal box and picked up a CN tear gas canister and pulled the pin. He tossed it toward the rear of the dorm, and the gas cloud began to rise.

Holtz saw a triple bunk begin to tip, and it fell against another one, and they fell like dominos. Holtz saw some bunks being moved in the far corner of the dorm and started to unload the baton rounds and put in a triple gas cartridge, but he heard Saulsberry's 40 mm launcher report and saw the three gas canisters bouncing on the same target. Saulsberry had put his gas mask on, but Holtz preferred to hold his mud. As a range master, he was used to the effects of chemical agents.

Shelton called out to his cops to fall back to the podium area. The incident had transformed to a full-fledged riot. Shelton had his crew form a line from the podium to the wall to protect the entrance door behind them. The most important goal of any riot was to contain it and prevent it from spreading. They could not let the inmates breach the door and have the riot spill out into the corridor.

*****

OP Sergeant Sam Searcy had heard the Code 3 call and drove to the entrance building and parked his vehicle. He quickly exited the vehicle and rushed to the side of the entrance building and then to the side gate. He yelled up to the Tower 1 officer, "Tower 1, open the side gate."

Tower 1 Officer Marta Ortiz saw him coming and figured he was in a hurry and had already pressed the button to unlock the gate. Searcy pushed it open and slammed it closed. Ortiz pressed the button to slide open the sally port entrance gate, and Searcy squeezed through while it was opening. He scurried through the Administration Building to Central Control.

*****

The Z-Dorm crew watched the surreal event unfolding as a historic chronicle. Dozens of triple bunk beds were toppled and twisted, TVs and audio component were being tossed and smashed, and scores of inmates were engaging in the unprecedented destruction. For the moment, it didn't appear that the melee was interested in a desire to escape the dorm or engage with the staff. In any case, the contingent was prepared for assault with batons and OC pepper spray at the ready. On two occasions, an inmate appeared to want to direct their assault toward the staff. In both instances, they were struck with baton rounds fired from above under the watchful eye of Holtz.

On the other end of the gun-walk, Saulsberry had the need to send several baton rounds to quite a few scuffles near the fence in Y-Dorm. Officers Twiford and Rugnao stood ready to defend their exit access, but fortunately, there were no attempts to approach the door.

Outside the Z-Dorm entrance door, S&E Officers Ron Clark and Dana Klopstein looked through a small view port into the dorm. They used their batons to bang on the door to get the attention of the staff inside. Shelton heard the banging and knew that responding staff was most likely the source. He rushed over to the door and scanned behind him to see if it was safe to open up. He saw no inmates nearby and quickly unlocked the door.

Officer Clark was the first to enter with Officer Klopstein behind him. Shelton was about to close the door when he saw Officer Vasquez coming down the corridor. He waited for Vasquez and let him in also. Shelton closed the door and locked it.

The recent arrivals fell into the line of staff and drew their batons.

Clark exclaimed aloud, "Holy shit, this is crazy."

Vasquez shook his head in amazement and asked Shelton, "Is Y-Dorm okay?"

Shelton looked up at the gun-walk and shook his head. "Damn, I'm not sure, but they probably need some help." Vasquez said, "Let me out and I'll go see."

Shelton nodded and ran back to the door and opened it. Vasquez ran out and Shelton locked the door back.

Vasquez made a left and ran down the corridor to the Y-Dorm door and banged on the door.

Twiford heard the banging and turned and went to the door and unlocked it. He let Vasquez in and locked the door.

Officer Lowery arrived at the Z-Dorm door and looked in. He saw several staff lined up defending the exit. He decided to continue to Y-Dorm. Twiford heard his rapping on the door and let him in. Lowery joined this crew as they watched the incident continue.

*****

Sergeant Gonzalez anxiously waited in Central Control for any update on the incident. Watch Commander Gene Jones and Watch Sergeant Walter Lomax had come out of the Watch Office into the corridor and stood at the Control Room window; they also awaited more information. It had been fifteen minutes since the alarm sounded; that is an eternity for an incident.

Sergeant Gonzalez keyed his radio. "Any unit in Z-Dorm, status report."

Sergeant Shelton responded, "This is Shelton. The inmates are not letting up."

Lomax turned to Lieutenant Jones. "Gene, I'm not doing any good here, I gotta go help."

Jones nodded and waved him on.

Lomax stepped over to the control room window. "Gonzo, give me a baton and some OC."

Officer Linus Oliver was sitting at the desk behind Gonzales and heard the request. He sprung up and went to the back room and grabbed a baton and an OC canister with a holster. He spun around and rushed to the window and gave the baton and OC to Lomax. Lomax scooped the items up and ran down the corridor to Z-Dorm, putting on the OC holster as he ran.

Oliver looked at Gonzalez and said, "Gonzo, the gun has got to be low on munitions, how 'bout I run some up?"

Gonzalez looked at Watch Commander Jones, and Jones nodded his approval.

Oliver went into the armory in the back room and began filling a canvas bag with as many 40 mm cartridges and handheld CN canisters as would fit. He also picked up a 40 mm launcher. Gonzalez saw the launcher and started to tell Oliver not to take it, but he said nothing. Oliver loaded a 40 mm baton cartridge in the launcher and slammed it closed and slung it on his shoulder. Gonzalez reached up and took a key group off the wall and gave it to Oliver.

Gonzalez pushed a button to release the lock on the grill door, and Oliver opened it and stepped into the stairway that led to the roof access. Gonzalez pressed another button that unlocked the roof door. Oliver hurried out and slammed the door closed.

He ran up a slope and turned right toward the Z-Dorm roofline. Protocol dictates that the ammo and weapon are to be transported separately so they couldn't be used if the transport officer were ambushed. However, this was an extraordinary situation.

*****

The situation in the Zoo was becoming hazardous. The inmate conflict was gradually getting closer to the skirmish line formed by the Z-Dorm defenders. Villanueva and Klopstein saw an inmate get knocked down and an attacker had an object in his hand and was using a slashing motion hitting the other inmate. Klopstein and Villanueva ran over to the fighters, and Villanueva sprayed the attacker, and Klopstein struck him on the elbow. The attacker ceased his attack and moved backward. A TV bounced off the top of a triple bunk and landed on Villanueva's shoulder and caromed onto Klopstein's lower leg. The two eased back to the defensive line.

Saulsberry had discharged six more baton rounds at targets in Y-Dorm and thrown two CN tear gas canisters.

Holtz's munitions resources were critically low. Saulsberry found his combatants were down to only two, and one more baton round made their decision to separate.

The sudden appearance of Officer Oliver on the gun-walk startled Saulsberry, and he almost struck him with his 40 mm launcher. Saulsberry shook his head and noticed Oliver was refilling the metal munitions box. Oliver put one last canister in the box and proceeded toward Holtz's end of the gun-walk.

Holtz quickly acknowledged Oliver, but reacquired another target. He sent another flight of triple tear gas canisters into the edge of the dorm. Oliver saw a pair of combatants and unslung his 40 mm launcher and took aim. He directed his baton rounds in a corrective direction, and the inmates stopped their assaultive activity.

Officer Villanueva heard Sergeant Lomax banging on the dorm door and let him into the unit.

Lomax assessed the clusters of violence and took a deep breath. "Jamie, where do you need me?" Lomax asked.

Villanueva replied, "Just join in wherever you want, Walt." The Z-Dorm fray had some short periods of slowed activity.

Just as it appeared the inmates were tiring, another eruption seemed to reinvigorate their resolve for violence.

At some point, Sergeant Searcy made his way from outside the institution and had in tow Officer Melvin Colvin from minimum dorms. They were a welcome addition to the protecting force.

Unknown to these bravados, at this point, forty-plus minutes had elapsed since the beginning of the incident. Slowly, the contingent quelled some of the fires with OC spray, baton strikes, and numerous 40 mm rounds discharged from above.

It became apparent to Holtz that his less-lethal munitions were having less and less of the desired effect on the diehard combatants.

Holtz set the 40 mm launcher in the holding rack and unslung his Mini-14 from behind his back and held it at a forty-five-degree angle above the gun-walk and slammed the charging handle back, and it responded forward with a louder metal clank. Some inmates might have heard the familiar racking of a round into the rifle.

He took careful aim at the empty top of a triple bunk bed.

He squeezed the trigger. The bullet deflected off the metal bunk and away from any harmful result. The noise was unmistakable, and it resulted in its intended effect—most all of the inmates took cover and ceased their assaults. Staff was surprised, but pleasantly, and some instinctively ducked. The staff, in a controlled manner, instructed the inmates to lie down and stay put.

Holtz held sway with the eyes of the inmates and continued his grip on the intimidating weapon.

*****

Three days later, Sergeant T-Mac pulled into the parking lot and parked the bus at the far end of the lot. The COSIT (Cadet On-Site Institutional Training) was an integral part of acclimating the new officers to the workings of the prison regiment. Rubbing elbows with inmates and shadowing staff allowed the cadets to see firsthand how the job is done.

T-Mac stood and turned to the forty cadets seated on the bus. "Welcome to DVI. Check all of your equipment and uniforms.

Everything you take in is what you bring out. Ensure you have your IDs, and hats are optional."

Academy Sergeants Andre Morton and Cheryl Parr stood and gathered their belonging and stepped off the bus. The cadets disembarked in an orderly manner. T-Mac secured the bus and followed the line of cadets through the parking lot, and they gathered at the left side of the entrance building. T-Mac took out a list of the cadets and handed it to Officer Michael Johnson. Tower 1 officer opened the side gate of the sally port, and Johnson compared and checked off the names on the cadet list with each ID presented by each cadet. Morton and Parr showed their IDs, and T-Mac and Johnson fistbumped as Johnson checked his ID.

T-Mac led the entourage through the Administration Building and held them in the patio area.

"When we get inside, walk between the orange lines. If there is an alarm, staff will be responding down the center of the corridor, so stay out of the way. I will walk you as a group down the West Corridor, and I'll drop you off, most likely in pairs, in housing units or work areas to work with staff. If you find the staff is too busy or you get bored, step out and find me or one of the other sergeants or use your discretion to find something interesting to do. Just keep busy and learn. If you're paired up, don't lose your partner."

T-Mac led them a few yards forward up to the large heavy solid metal South Door entrance to the institution. T-Mac divided the cadets into two groups: A-Squad and B-Squad.

"Okay, A-Squad first. When you go into the sally port, wait for this door to close and the North Gate to open, go through, close the gate, and stand along the walls of the corridor."

T-Mac called out toward the camera and speaker above the door, "South Door."

Momentarily, the lock on the door snapped. Sergeants Morton and Parr went in with the first group, and T-Mac closed the door.

A moment later, the door lock snapped, and the door opened, and T-Mac waited until the leaving staff had exited and then he waved the next group inside.

"Okay, B-Squad."

They compacted in the sally port, and T-Mac closed the door with an intentional thud he meant for intimidation.

He yelled out, "North Gate."

The gate opened, and the remaining cadets flowed into the corridor. T-Mac led the group down the corridor and dropped cadets off to work in housing units as planned. When he ran out of cadets, Parr and Morton joined him as he walked back up the corridor to Center Corridor and turned down the North Corridor toward the Zoo. As it so happened, the doors to Z-Dorm were opened for the first time since the now-infamous incident.

T-Mac having spent many shifts in Z-Dorm, the nostalgia welled in his chest. He went down the three long steps into the dorm, and he took a long breath. The dorm had not been put back in order. It had remained as it was since the eruption.

Almost half of the back part of the dorm was a pile of completely twisted and toppled bunk beds. There wasn't any appliance that wasn't broken, and mattresses and overturned lockers were everywhere.

He walked over to the two-step podium near the TV area and noticed blood on the lower step and the floor. In his mind, the imagined chaos of that night deeply furrowed his brow. He long had the opinion that the triple bunk arrangement with an extra locker was a problematic solution to overcrowding. The number of inmates, notwithstanding the lack of visual security, was of primary concern. He looked up at the gun-walk and recalled the many hours pacing the walkway with the permeating heat and encompassing smells of humanity. The bright incandescent lighting that was dimmed somewhat during late hours at night, yet denied the inmates sufficiently darkened eyelids. His memories of walking this dorm had lingered since he promoted out, but this vision of reality left an indelible smear of anxiety on his future recollections of the Zoo.

BLOOD ON THE TIER

Officer Jenny McCray followed three inmates on the second tier of the 180-degree housing unit. Each inmate stopped and stood in front of their door as Booth-Gunner "Pepper" Wilson carefully watched his officer. He opened each door individually to let each inmate into their cell. When they were inside, Wilson would press a button and close their door. McCray would step over to the door and push and pull on the door handle to ensure it was locked.

After the second inmate was secured, inmate Burrows, the last inmate, waited for his door to slide open, and he stepped inside, and his cellmate handed him an inmate-made slashing weapon. He bolted out the door and sprinted over to Officer McCray. She saw him coming and grabbed at her baton. Wilson saw the inmate running and grabbed his Mini-14 from its hanging position across his chest and stepped over to an opened window and leveled his aim. Inmate Burrows readied his weapon as he slammed into Officer McCray, and they both fell against railing of the tier. Officer Wilson racked a round into his weapon and looked for a clear shot at the inmate, as yet he had none. With several quick movements of his hand, inmate Burrows found his target: the face and neck of Officer McCray. A split second later, a shot rang out. Blood spilled onto the tier.

EPILOGUE

This second offering of *Prison Journals* brings a somewhat darker side of the prison environment. As an author, I find that my depictions of events can be both edgy and light. It is my intent to show the varied characteristics of those who choose this profession. It's a challenge to select events of interest for you the reader, as I can only guess what you would like to experience. Hopefully, my next HOGGS deliverance will portray a grittier aspect of the correctional world. I realize that to you who work in the domain of daily danger that I have yet to delve into the truly dark side of the job. Some of those stories need addressing with sensitivity for the families of the victims. At this juncture, I will offer my personal mantra of corrections: If you can imagine it, it probably has happened or will happen.

Be safe.

ABOUT THE AUTHOR

Terol McCullar actively pursued his twenty-six-year career as a California correctional officer and sergeant instructor known as T-Mac. Having lived through the 1950s and 1960s and his passion for the law and teaching has helped mold his intrinsic belief in self-efficacy. His latent passion as an author has flourished into three published works: both *HOGGS I* and *II* and a novel, *SICQ.* He looks forward to writing sequels of his offerings and developing into whatever comes next.

The author yet acknowledges the undying support of his wife Tricia, daughters Angela and Marnie, and a growing list of great friends.